JOURNEY TO RALLEM

MARIA A LEVATO

JOURNEY TO RALLEM

To all my bookish fiends, demented queens,
and everyone with kinky dreams.

JOURNEY TO RALLEM

This book contains dark themes and content that may be disturbing and/or inappropriate to some readers. This includes, but is not limited to the following:

- War
- Sex
- Death
- Grief
- etc.

JOSIE

_____

C haos. It bursts into my life and takes hold of my throat with its vice-like grip. Those few moments of perfect serenity when the hues of the sky dance become tainted by the chokehold it has on me. My friends and I are several miles from Loft, the kingdom of my birth, heading towards the wilderness that lies between my homeland and Pastels. Rallem is its name. We're going there to figure out how to bring dead people back to life. I lost two men, both of whom I am in love with. We were, what many call, a non-traditional coupling. They were both bisexual and loved each other long before I came along. They made room in their hearts for me, though. The three of us loved each other so much. Naturally, I want them back.

Trying to get a feel for our immediate surroundings, I look around to see trees, bushes, and shrubs in front of us, and a faint view of the palace in Loft from across an enormous field behind us. It's all a blur of an endless, beautiful contradiction, from the contrast of the illustrious colors to the tug-of-war between the light and dark. A harmonious contrast, yes, that's what the world is. I'll never understand it in full, but I know it'll be worth spending my life trying to comprehend. I could die in contentment with that. Given my current state, I don't think there's much else left for me, anyway. I miss them and the grief is tearing me limb from limb. It's been months since I last had a proper night's rest. My appetite is non-existent. Even while I'm surrounded by those I love; it feels empty and alone. I can't recognize myself without them by my side. I will forever be incomplete. As I glance up at the sky again, I cannot help but wonder if I will ever find harmony like that.

"It's getting late. We must settle in for the night. Now." Malachi says. He speaks with such authority in his tone, as always. His voice tears me from my thoughts, although I know that is the furthest thing from his intention. After all, it is Malachi. The half-demon who changed my life. The man who is my brother in every way but blood. He's the King of Tendu, an island of highly active volcanoes where those who harness fire magic from runes thrive. Malachi is also my greatest rival, best friend's husband, father of my nephew, and the one my adoptive daughter, Lilly, calls her uncle. I don't know if I'd have survived the grief this long without him. He's the one who gave me this broken family that I love with every broken piece of my soul. I know that. Yet, at this moment, the depth of his voice and powerful nature of his speech are just too much for me. It's an immediate sensory overload that makes me want to disassociate from everything.

Sensing my spike in anxiety, Jameson, who stands beside me, pats my back. He's a good friend of mine. I met him a while after I met Malachi. They're cousins. Jameson, unlike his cousin, is a half-angel, though. He's the Crowned Prince of Oceanica, an island of water magic users, and the wealthiest nation in the known world. It has serene beaches, a few trade docks, and a market unlike any other. His touch is gentle. It's so soothing that the gesture that draws my attention away from the anxiety.

Pastel, who lingers a few feet away, also picks up on it and follows up to draw my attention from Malachi. "Yes, we should. Tomorrow is going to be the first of many long days. It's about three thousand miles of rugged, unmapped terrain to get to Rallem."

Three thousand miles. For most in this group, we could travel that distance in a mere twelve hours if we flew. It's unfortunate that we don't know where we are going, and Pastel, though not without his strengths, can't fly like most of us can. He's entirely human and doesn't have any natural magic. His power comes from his sword. I haven't seen it myself yet, but I trust my instincts enough to know that sword is not something one buys from the nearest blacksmith.

I smile at him. He and Jameson aren't comparable to the ones I seek to resurrect, but they bring me a certain solace in the absence of my heart's genuine desire. I appreciate that. It's just that I don't think solace is what I need. I don't want to be comfortable with my suffering. I want to be happy in the most disgusting, unreasonable, insane, unjustifiable, socially unacceptable way. Is that so wrong? I want love like what I had. Love that overrides traditions and obliterates obstacles. I want it obsessive, possessive, and tinged with an underlying toxicity that makes it impossible to look away. To me, love doesn't have to be normal, or even healthy. I'd rather it feel like fire and lightning than the gentle flow of a river.

As Malachi ordered, we set up our camp for the night. We each attend to our duties. We knew each other so well. Pastel is the "newbie" around here. Jameson, of course, made fun of him a bit for it. It's petty, yet I giggle a little as Jameson tosses out a teasing comment. "I thought it was obvious Johanna would gather for us. Don't you know she's tribal? She's the best natural survivalist here."

Pastel doesn't seem to mind. He takes Jameson's antics in stride. "No, I didn't. That's awesome. I haven't had the pleasure of visiting all the territories in the alliance yet, but I look forward to getting to know all of everyone's cultures better."

Jameson continues to poke fun at Pastel, eager to get a reaction from him. To those of us who know Jameson, we know it's also semi-serious. He has always been on the judgmental side, at least with other men. Though, it's himself that he always judges the harshest. He can be insecure. I've always thought the behavior is his way of trying to hold others to the same standard he's held to. He feels like he must be perfect. If he has to, why shouldn't those around him?

I listen in on them while setting up barriers around our campsite without looking their way. The mild amusement I get from hearing them is shameful, but I don't care. It's cheering me up. Besides, I need to set up barriers here. My spiritual power is useful when preventing attacks so the members of our group can sleep without worry.

A few minutes later, Malachi gets irritated with Jameson bickering with Pastel. "Shut up and come with me."

He grabs Jameson by his blonde hair and drags him off to go hunt.

By the time they return, Johanna finishes gathering some plants, herbs, and fruits. It is the most productive thing she could do since none of us had a clue what is and isn't poisonous aside from her. That left Lilly to pitch our tents while Pastel worked on mapping out the route he took to get to us in the first place, which isn't great given that he is working off the memory of a trip he took but once, then trying to reverse the whole thing.

Soon, they finish their respective jobs, and everyone sits around the fire while I prepare our meal with the ingredients Johanna gathered. Everyone always loved my cooking. I'm able to make a stew over the fire that Malachi set with a snap of his finger. Benefits of having a fire user in the group, I suppose. This left some fruits for breakfast the next morning too. We all sit and eat together. During dinner, I take notice that Malachi and Johanna seem irritated and short with one another. They wouldn't even make eye contact and every word one uttered, the other rolled their eyes at. They must be in some type of disagreement, though I don't have the faintest idea why. It probably isn't my business to ask. She's my best friend; he's my brother. Getting involved in their marital spats would be a recipe for disaster.

Everyone else notices their moods as well. I can tell by the discomfort in their expressions. We all try to ignore it and make the dinner pleasant. For some time, that works out well. We have some laughs, and the tension lightens. It's nice to see everyone in good spirits. If anyone deserves a glimpse of happiness, it's these people. We have all been through so much. I want them to know only the brightest smiles. They want the same for me, too. That's what family does, right?

"Ah!" I can't help the screech that rips from me. Something is wrong. I'm being dragged into the spirit realm by an unknown force. Its grip on my soul yanks at me, causing screams of agony to tear from my throat as I struggle to pull back. What the hell is this and why is it so strong? I'm the strongest priestess in the Realm of the Living, yet I know I cannot win this tug of war. It will consume me if I don't do something, but this presence is so paralyzing that all my efforts are useless. In the heat of this crisis, I can't think straight either. My thoughts get jumbled like... like something I can't think of because what the hell is this? My attempts to ask the others for help get scattered and muffled by the force of the agony. I can't get anything coherent to come from my mouth as I writhe in pain.

I try, but I can't do anything besides cry as I feel myself losing my anchor in this world. My options being limited, I gamble, putting more of my spiritual power into conveying information to my friends than I do pulling against this unknown attacker from the other side. A weak sound squeezes from my rasping, moisture-less throat. "S-strength..."

Lilly and Jameson both take one of my hands. Mine and Lilly's spiritual power are a diluted version of his angelic power, so we can transfer power between the three of us in an emergency. Both of them fuse their powers with my own. I feel the warmth of the glowing runes that cover Jameson's body. He channels his water magic through them. They're beautiful, but that they're activated right now shows he's unable to separate his runic magic from his bloodline powers. This is the only way he can get me the angelic energy. Much to my dismay, he has not yet mastered his angelic power, and I can't purify it while I'm fighting for my life. I doubt that it's enough for me to overcome this attack, but I have to try. With all my might, I pull back again and again, but the grip of this enemy trying to pull me in is still too powerful. Exhausting myself more with each pull, my attempts grow weaker by the second. All seems lost. My hope begins to die and prepare myself to join my beloveds in the Spirit Realm. I know it's over as my senses fade away and I feel myself losing what a miniscule bit of an anchor remained.

A flash of light... Not from the mortal side, but from the Spirit Realm. It's bright beyond belief, but it reaffirms my consciousness a bit. It takes a few seconds to realize what it is. When I do, I realize it's two spirit orbs hindering my attacker. They take form as they help me loosen the grip a little. "We gotcha, lovely. Just relax and give us a minute."

All the fear drains from me when I recognize that firm, comforting voice. It was Kai. My Kai, protecting me even from beyond the grave. And just as it should be, Cal was with him, too, yanking at my attacker. "Damn, this guy has a real grip on you, Josie. As tempted as I am to let him drag you down here to be with us, I have to say, it's not time for that yet. No worries, though, Kai and I will fix it. Just trust us."

They must have sensed my partial presence in the spirit realm and came to find me. My voice comes out shaky with relief. "You two haven't changed at all."

I'm not sure whether to be overjoyed to see them, terrified of the attacker, or sad that I know we'll be apart again if they get me back to the Realm of the Living. The rush of emotions is too much to bear.

"We're going to shake this guy in three..." It was Kai. His voice was gruff and masculine, but I could hear the passion in it even when others failed to.

"Sure am! Two..." That one was Cal. He sounds so youthful and sweet, like a mischievous kitten looking for trouble.

"One..." I cry, knowing this is goodbye once more.

A quick tick, a crash, and a bang later, and I'm free. There's no sign of the anonymous assailant or my loves. I don't know what happened. It was too quick to say, but at least I'm free now. I want to thank them, even if they can't hear me anymore, but the words that pour from my mouth end up limited. "I love you both."

Grounding myself back in the Living Realm with as a firm grip as possible, I try to maintain my composure, but tears stream down my cheeks. This means more than I know. We need to make sense of this. I need to make sense of this. Whatever just happened, whatever lost soul just tried to pull me into the Spirit Realm, it was dangerous.

My friends gather around, asking what happened. I wish I knew that just as much as they do. What if that force hurts Kai and Cal's souls for helping me? Or it tries to pull me in again. And if it got free somehow? Panic overwhelms me, and I hyperventilate. It's like my lungs are shrinking and my heart is pumping overtime. I'd mistake it for a heart attack if I didn't know any better. I stand up and break down all at once. Then, turn to Jameson and Lilly. "An unseen threat is on the rise. While we travel, you will both train. Expect it to be intense. Whatever that was, it is too strong for us to beat right now. We need you both to reach your full potential."

I continue crying, pacing, and panting. I can't stop. With wide eyes, the two of them nod. Their expressions teeter between concern and shock. Then Johanna lost it on me just as I needed her to be my best friend and help to ground me. What's more? It was in a way I had never expected. Not from my best friend on this planet, but more important is that I would never expect it from the fearsome warrior I've always known. Her words laced with a cowardice that made her unrecognizable to me. "What the hell, Josie? You cannot be this oblivious to the way your actions affect others. Has your grief blinded you to such a severe extent?"

Malachi stopped her there, placing himself between us. He gritted out his words, the frustration with her temper palpable. "Johanna, don't do this."

"No," she met his gaze, "I will do this. She needs to hear it before we all end up dead on account of her not being able to let go of them." Her attention snaps back to me. "Josie, you have to know you trying to resurrect them is weakening the divide between realms. Even thoughts of it would do so, at least when those thoughts come from a priestess as strong as you. We all miss them. You are not alone in your pain. Kai and Cal were our friends, not just your lovers. We understand your suffering to some extent. That doesn't mean that we can allow you to do this with no consideration for the consequences. Everyone here knows this, but they all refuse to betray you. Whether that is out of fear or loyalty, I am not sure anymore. I beg you, let this go before you do something you cannot take back, and before someone here dies."

I look around at the faces of those closest to me. It is easy to see that they all have reservations about what I'm trying to do. Overwhelmed by my own thoughts, as well as Johanna's words, I walk away, needing to clear my head. Malachi stopped me just as he did Johanna. "You can't wander by yourself. Who knows when this attacker from the spirit realm will come for you again?"

Pastel, understanding what I was feeling, offered to come with me. Jameson and Malachi tagged along as well, just to be on the safe side. We walked for a while. It took nearly thirty minutes for me to calm myself enough to have a reasonable conversation. When I finally do, I'm curious about what doubts everyone holds. I ask Malachi first, since it was his wife who snapped at me. He didn't seem to mind explaining it to me. Although he chose his words with more caution than normal. It is plain to see that he's walking on eggshells. He must be worried that he'll upset me more. "It's concerning, but I'm confident that I want to do this. You're my sister. I want to help ease your pain. When Cal died, I was not there."

I remember, he refrained from taking part in the war via combat, thinking of and prioritizing Tendu's best interest, as any king should. His kingdom has to come first, always. I don't blame him for what happened, but I also understand what he's getting at. I would feel the same way if I were in his shoes; there is no doubt about that. He and I shield each other from the pain. It's what we've always done, ever since the day I met him. Regardless, this causes the rift between Johanna and him. He hyper-focused on protecting me because he wasn't there to help me when he thought he should have been. To her, it must feel like he's choosing me over his kingdom and his family.

"What about you, Jameson? Do you have any thoughts to add?" I look up into those sickeningly blue eyes of his as I await his reply.

"If I did, I'm not sure it would be worth much. You are a centerpiece, and I am a mere ornament hung on some obscure wall. As an angel, half-blooded or otherwise, I've a duty to protect the light. If having Kai and Cal back preserves the blinding light that is your smile, it's not a matter of what I think. My duty is to deliver them to you. It is a duty I shall bear with pride, for I know I'm not worthy enough to have it, let alone enough to reject it."

My eyes go wide as he speaks. His words both touching my heart and flooding my soul. "I see. Thank you, then, Jameson. Your support..." I pause, choosing my words carefully, so as not to lead him on. "Your support is reassuring, deeply so. I will remember Oceanica's loyalty in my time of need."

Malachi choked on his water as he laughs at my awkward, diplomatic response, knowing that there's far more to the interaction than Jameson and I would say aloud. "Wow. You two are something else. Oceanica's loyalty, huh? Yes, because Oceanica's Crowned Prince is loyal to you solely out of political obligation," His eyes turn to Jameson. "is that how it is, little cousin?"

Jameson glares at him, but Malachi just gives a knowing smirk in return. Pastel speaks up before the two spiral into a death match. "I, for one, have to say Johanna has a point. What she was saying makes sense. I will lend you my support, Josella, but keep in mind that I limit it to a point. The moment it becomes a choice between your goals and my kingdom's welfare, know that I won't hesitate to lodge my sword in your back."

The tension between Malachi and Jameson a few seconds prior is now directed at Pastel. From my right, I feel the demonic energy in the atmosphere triple as the heat from Malachi's hellfire consumes the nearby plants. "Did you just threaten my sister?"

His voice is flatly menacing and his already crimson eyes shine in contrast to his dark skin. It's easy to forget how terrifying Malachi's demonic side can be. Most of the time, he's reserved and controlled, but never when the safety of someone he loves is at risk.

The situation to my left isn't but marginally better. Jameson's elegant beauty is quick to turn petrifying when that blue in his eyes turns to an icy white light and storms rage around him as the water answers his call. His pale skin and fluffy, blonde hair no longer soften the regality of his presence when his anger gets provoked. "Mortal, I have half-a-mind to kill you for so much as *thinking* we would let you harm her."

His voice echoes as if it's coming from the heavens. The forest is being destroyed by the force of these two. I have to stop them. I raise my spiritual power. Its auric glow appears in a shimmery purple. I promptly use it to knock both of the hotheads on their asses. "My apologies, Pastel. They should know better than to speak that way to our ally." I force a smile. "Let us hope it does not come to that. For now, though, thank you for lending me your support whilst you can do so in good conscience."

Pastel musters a nod but can't form a vocalized response. The terror in his quivering lip and evasive eyes is proof that he couldn't follow through on his threat if he tried. This is the thing with him that bothers me. He cares and supports me, but in the end, his loyalties get restricted because he doesn't want to make real promises. I'm a diplomat too, at least in some ways. Yet, with those I care for, there's no room for diplomacy. I'm with them, right or wrong, for better or worse. I deserve that in return, and he and Johanna are both denying me the loyalty I give so freely to them. Jameson might not be like my beloveds were, but at least he's there in the thick of it. Malachi, too. Although, Malachi's loyalty is different. It's not fueled by romantic longing, but by an uncomplicated brotherly love. Sheer romantic love fuels Jameson's. Even if I'd never admit it aloud, even if I pretend to be oblivious; I know how he feels.

Regardless, the sole person who did not think this was worth trying at all was Johanna. Before I could be sure, there is one more person I need to speak with still. Lilly is the one who is most affected by this decision, almost as much as I am. I owe it to her to listen and understand if she feels this is the right course of action. After our walk, once I calmed down a bit, we return to the campsite, where I speak to her about it. I ask, "Do you feel like this is too risky? Is this preventing you from grieving or moving on with your life? Am I being selfish?"

She chuckles as if she thought my questions to be outlandish. "You know, I have ever seen you do anything selfish? Not once since the day you found me half-dead on the shores of Oceanica. I will admit that this is the first time, but you have earned the right to be selfish at least once. After all, it was you who gave up the most for this alliance, for this peace that our people now enjoy. Of course, it's preventing me from grieving or moving on. It is preventing you from doing so as well. Why would I want to move on if I don't have to, Mom? I want them back too. You are doing this for you, but I am doing it for me as well. I loved them. You three are my parents, regardless of the lack of blood ties. That is nothing less than a fact."

Shocked by her words, as well as her insight, I know then that we have to do this. It is the right thing to do. It is as right as leaving my parents' home to pursue Malachi's dream of uniting the islands against injustice was. With that decision, we settle into our tents for the night. Much to my loathing, I'm still unable to let go of Johanna's harsh words. Mere days ago, she supported me in this venture. I wonder what changed her mind. It is probable, I guess, that she supported it in theory more than she did in actuality. Once we began, it forced her to leave her child behind in Tendu under the care of a nanny. She would have realized that she and Malachi would have to put their lives at risk by coming with me. The difference is this time it wasn't so we could make a better world for the next generation. It was for me, just for me. Best friend or otherwise, I kind of get where she stands when I break it down. I might feel the same way if I were in her shoes. I think most people would.

She must have reevaluated her position; she had every reason to do so. Johanna should know that I would appreciate her support if she were to give it. I would never ask her to act contrary to her instincts, though. She should do what she thinks is best for her family, kingdom, and the islands.

My thoughts make it hard for me to find rest. Lilly, with whom I'm sharing a tent, did not seem to share that problem. So as not to wake her, I leave the tent until I'm closer to sleeping. As I sit on a log, I drudge through my mind as I attempt to reconcile with everything that is happening. It is peaceful this far from the kingdom, but it's not quite peaceful enough. I need to be in a void. I want to go realm walking. It's risky, given the attack from earlier. Still, I crave the nothingness bad enough to assume that risk.

With the snap of a twig, I realize that I'm not alone. It's Malachi. He's awake as well. Perhaps it's for the better. If he's up, I won't be able to do something reckless like go realm walking. In a few of those measured strides of his, he approaches. At first, he seems to be in complete control, just as always. He sat beside me before letting that image give way to the truth. An exasperated sigh pours from him. It must have come from a place that is deep, for I have never heard such a sound from him before. "Josie, she shouldn't be here, should she?"

I shake my head. "This will be far more perilous than our previous exploits. For the sake of Rallem's interest in our alliance, one of you should stay. But given our true objectives for this trip, and the untold danger they pose, it would be best if she returned to Tendu. She can care for your kingdom, the alliance, and your son whilst we pursue this."

"So, it will be. I forget sometimes. My wife is no longer the warrior I wed, but a queen and a mother. Though I love her no less, I can't deny that I miss the enthusiastic, hotheaded woman. She was one that would take on the world for what she believed to be right."

I chuckle. "Malachi, she will always be an enthusiastic hothead. She doesn't believe in this. Johanna believes in your family and will protect it in the best way she knows how. It's why she snapped at me. I am asking her husband to risk his life for my family, instead of staying safe for his own. Her anger is more than justified."

"As usual, you are wise beyond your years, and even mine. Point taken. I will send her home in the morning."

I nod, then we continue to sit. It's a silence filled with nothing and everything all at once. It varies between peaceful and tormenting every few minutes. I would relax, then fidget, then relax again, then have the overwhelming urge to scream into the debt of this night. Yet, it is where we remain until dawn. I'm sure Malachi noticed my restlessness throughout the night, but for whatever reason, he opted to remain silent about the matter.

***

When the others wake, they see our exhaustion. We should have expected as much since we put little effort into hiding it. We have to continue our arduous journey today, but before that, Malachi and Johanna take some time to speak, and he urges her to return to Tendu.

"Ugh! Malachi, dammit! What are you even thinking? We should *both* be returning to Tendu, idiot. Josie is dragging us into this, and it's wrong. Listen, Josella is my best friend, and I love her just as much as you do, but we cannot get caught up in this shit. We have to go."

"Johanna, I will not abandon my sister because there is cowardice in your heart. Josie is the most powerful woman known to our world. I'm a half-demon, woman. We have my cousin, a half-angel. Pastel, who may not be like us, but isn't weak either. And there's Lilly too."

Johanna hisses. "Lilly is a goddesses-damned child, Malachi."

He rolls his eyes. "Yet that *child* could beat you on her worst day. If you will not do as your husband has asked you, then you will do as your king is ordering you. Take that lovely ass of yours back to our kingdom and hold down the fort while I help my sister."

They bicker for several more minutes before Johanna relents. She made both him and I promise to be careful, as she wishes for us to return from this voyage intact. We did, then she left. With that, we are down to five. We move with haste, as we leave the camp and continue to-wards Rallem. Pastel informs us it will be many days be-fore we arrive. I suspected as much, given the distance he noted yesterday. With what has happened thus far, the group's suspicions that this task would not be a sim-ple one confirmed themselves already.

On this first day of our journey, we travel one hun-dred and seven miles, which we know thanks to Pastel's detailed tracking. We are moving twice as fast as or-dinary humans can, but since most of us could move much faster, it feels like a slow journey. I have to keep reminding myself that I have to keep pace with the slow-est person in the group, being as though he is the one with some semblance of an idea of where we are going. At dusk, we set our camp near a stream. It is disorienting, setting up camp in a forest that seems infinite. For the first time all day, I regret Johanna's absence. Her experience with the wilderness would have been most comforting. Even in times of war, I had never had to experience such rural conditions as these for any prolonged period. Neither had the rest of us.

After making camp, I decide to take some time to train Lilly and Jameson before we relax. Lilly's power is nearly identical to mine in type, but Jameson's isn't. Angelic power, like Jameson's, is a parent of spiritual power, like mine or Lilly's, which is a derivative power. As such, he should be stronger than me, but his lack of training makes him less so. I suspect that his mixed bloodline is making it more difficult for him to master. After all, most people's need to master power is limited to but one power type. Those from mixed lineages, like he and Malachi, have to master both runic and bloodline abilities. I can't blame him for feeling inferior to Malachi, since the half-demon mastered both powers with ease. I just wish he'd remember that Malachi is not the norm, but the exception. It's perfectly understandable that Jameson leans into his runic magic more than his angelic power. Half-angel though he may be, his upbringing was as a human, surrounded by humans. Therefore, he had more examples of how to use humanly accessible magic. It's not his fault that his angelic relatives have never made themselves known to him.

I'll work with Jameson and Lilly for about an hour, starting with fifteen minutes of meditation. Then, have them do five of basic stretching and ten of physical strength training. For the last thirty minutes, we focus on ability training using a unique method. Because of Lilly's past, I thought it best for her mental health if the training method I use differs totally from the hell she experienced back in Mallishrine, Island of Priests and Priestesses. Thus, I developed a more empathetic approach that focuses on the shape of one's manifested energy. For Jameson, I wanted to start small, teaching him how to separate out his angelic and runic powers. I coach him. "Okay, what I want you to do is, without summoning water from your runes, just make a small sphere of tangible angelic energy."

Within a minute, he creates a sphere about the circumference of a copper coin. "Good." I offer the praise alongside further instruction, "Now, spend the rest of the training session trying to grow it."

He gives a strained smile. I can see how difficult this is for him to maintain. I'm glad I started here. "Yes, um... I'll try, Josie. Sorry for making you coddle me."

I give him a look that may have been more sympathetic than I intended. "I don't see it that way. You're strong, Jameson. Next to Malachi and me, you're the strongest of us. This just isn't your area of expertise, and I respect your willingness to learn and get better."

He looks down at his sphere, trying to cover the light blush on his cheeks. I can't tell if the compliment flustered him or made him feel bad. Either way, the look on his face is... "kind of adorable." I gasp. "Oh! I'm so sorry. My intent was for that to remain a thought."

Bolting across our makeshift training site, I run towards Lilly before he could respond. I shouldn't have said that. So much for not leading him on. For her ability training, we work on a new idea. She ran it by me while we were in the traveling phase of our day. The training goes well. I can't wait to see the move when it's perfected. Although, I hope I never will because it's kind of terrifying. Soon, our time is up, and we settle in for the night.

CHAPTER

TWO

JOSIE

The next day, we travel and soon find ourselves in an area with heavy fog. It was about fifty miles into our one hundred seven-mile stint for the day. We act with caution upon seeing it swirling around us, giving the distinct aura of death. Pastel may have made the journey once before, but that isn't enough to make it again without error. It's possible that we've gone off course, or that the weather is more varied in this area than we know. I find something about this fog is off-putting, though. I doubt it's that simple. It's thick beyond what is natural and feels like when Linola appeared to me before we left Loft, as a spirit. It holds ominous, mystical properties, but they're so abstract that none of us can discern what they are. The intensity of it is so bad that we can't even see well enough to detect where our next steps will land us.

"Be careful and stay close together," Jameson barks, as if he meant to order us. "I don't know what it is about this fog, but it's ominous enough to set my every instinct on edge."

I trust that. As a half-angel, he senses evil better than most. Malachi scoffs in, making a show of irritation at Jameson's tone. "Are you sure you aren't sensing my demonic energy, *little cousin*?"

Jameson sighs. "I would recognize your demonic energy, idiot. This is darker, and more dominant, as if I were face to face with the devil."

Then, another voice enters the conversation, one only I seem to hear. It is soft and casual, not at all aggressive. With that said, the underlying sarcasm in it didn't escape my notice. Something about it still chilled my bones, even if I couldn't detect hostility. It's just as before. It paralyzes me. This is undoubtedly the force that tried to pull me into the spirit realm before. "He compares me to Myrkr, that fool."

I cross my arms, praying the action conceals the trembling in my hands. I speak to the voice, unable to see any physical form to it. "Tell me. Who are you? What do you want with me?"

A dark chuckle before the words, "What a bold little woman my niece has become?"

He moved out from the poisonous aura which had surrounded him. When I look around, there isn't much shock when I learn he and I are alone in this space. His words capture my attention the most, though. *His niece?* I was his niece. Those troublesome words echo, whether in my mind or in this hollow space around us. I can't tell. The others, I could see and hear them, but they were not here. The mist is an effect, a parlor trick of sorts. It's meant to distract them so he can speak to me alone. He's isolated me with such ease, taking advantage of my mind, my connection to the Spirit Realm. He's exploiting my power and using it against me. This threat is not one I can afford to underestimate. I wonder what sort of monster he is. The man before me towers over us all. His build is bulky, and his face has a generic attractiveness with a frightening twist. What bothers me most about him, though, is his eyes. I've never seen such cold, calculating, and soulless eyes before. His essence is pure evil. Not darkness; evil. Darkness feels cloudy, like a person lost themselves in it. He isn't a lost soul at all. I'd even wager that he knows exactly who and what he is. He's content with the evil he plays with in the same way as a teenage boy in possession of a pack of matches. Who is this man? What does he want with us? So many questions flood my mind the exact moment he calls me 'niece.' I cannot be this man's niece. If he's my uncle, why does he intimidate me so much? As he continues to speak, I hope more answers will reveal themselves.

"Do you mean to tell me you cannot recognize your own flesh and blood? Have my sisters' descendants become that weak? How many in your family hold power, girl?"

I look away, feeling ashamed by the answer without knowing why he can provoke such a foreign feeling in me. "As far as I know, I'm the only Spade to inherit it since the great priestess Linola. You mean to tell me you're my uncle?"

"Well, several times great uncle to be exact, that wench Linola was my sister. It is she who sealed me into the spirit realm, thus ending the Great War I started. My name is Rath."

I couldn't believe what I was hearing. In my head, I know I should conceal my distress, but I can't force myself to do so. Any attempt at bravado could only agitate him further. "That's how it happened, huh? Why did you start the war, and how are you here if she sealed you?"

"I'll save story time for later, but for now, you should know this much: I know what you seek and how to get it. Free me completely and I will show you."

I quirk my eyebrow. He's bold to assume I'd do that. "And why do you think we should trust you?"

Laughing in the most condescending tone, he responds. "Simple girl, you have no other choice. If you are to succeed, you need me."

I bat the idea around in my mind for a minute. It's true. Our understanding was limited to but the vaguest of ideas of how to resurrect Kai and Cal, and we hadn't the slightest clue what we actually needed to find. We couldn't do this alone. With a sigh, I answer. "So be it.

Release your illusion and let my friends see us. I will speak to them about this matter and *if* they agree; I will cross the divide and free you."

"No. Free me now. Explain it to them later."

I contemplate it but relent to him. "Fine, I'm coming, but at least give me something. Tell me something real. Give me a reason to believe our interests align."

"Lying to you would be purposeless, Josella. I'm not on your side; I am on the side of what I view as right. Before Linola sealed me, I was a protector, her protector. She got herself caught up between Rettferd and Myrkr. I saw her soul tearing between the two of them. No human other than I had the strength to fight them. So, I went to war with both heaven and hell. I knew my sister didn't agree with me, but never in a thousand years did I suspect she would betray me. She gave her life to maintain the seal on my soul. Now time has passed, and the magic has weakened enough for it to break, if given the right push. In time for me to protect you from the fate of angels and demons, the way I wanted to do for her. If I restore the lives of those you are in love with, you won't find yourself dragged into the wretched future I foresee."

I nod. "I see. You think yourself the good guy?"

"No, Josella, I know I'm not a good person, but that doesn't change the fact that I'm right."

I thought about his words and decide that I believe, at the very least, he thought himself to be honest. "I'll free you, but you won't have my trust until you've earned it. We will meet you in the Realm of the Living with nothing but suspicion. Right now, you can't sense it because you are little more than a projection here, but I am prepared to kill if you make a false move."

"Trust me, I can sense the hostility in you, but I am a man of my word. I will show you how to bring them back."

I descend into the spirit realm, still maintaining the mental connection between us. From what I gather, he is a living soul, albeit a sealed one. This should be easy enough to do. When I cross realms, I find myself surrounded by a familiar energy. "Lady Josella!" Kimble, a fox spirit who once served as my familiar, leaps into my arms. "What are you doing here?"

I giggle, momentarily forgetting my purpose in coming here. "Hey, Kimble. How are you? It's been a while, huh? How are those pups of yours doing?"

"They're great, milady. Thank you for asking. I doubt you're just here to check in, though."

"No, you're right. I have a purpose in coming here today." The reality of my mission settles back in. "Do you have any clue where I might find a deranged priest sealed here? He is apparently my uncle, and I have need of him."

Kimble thinks a moment. "You mean the one Lady Linola sealed? I do, but I must warn you, milady, he is not a good man."

"Kimble, I need you to take me to him."

"As you wish then, milady." Her high pitch, playful tone fails at masking her apprehension as she guides me. Her tail wags as she moves forward in a light trot. "Follow me."

She leads me through the streets of the spirit realm. Contrary to popular belief, the realm of the dead is a rather lively place. Those who dwell here aren't really dead. Rather, they've just moved into a new state of living. Life, afterlife, is a better life. That's why I know my goal of resurrecting Kai and Cal is selfish. They live in peace here, among those souls which are no longer tormented by the hills and valleys of their last life. I can't speak to where they are now, but I certainly scan every face in the crowded market as I follow Kimble. I'm sure they can feel my presence, just as they did before. Why aren't they coming to me?

I try to distract myself from the million reasons that cross through my mind. I keep my pace as I follow Kimble, idly consuming the scenery. The rich sound of laughter fills the air as some children bob and weave their way through the streets, playing a game of tag. The smell of candied strawberries catches my attention as a light breeze wafts the scent in my direction. They smell delectable. I'd stop to get some, but now isn't the time. I'll have to make a mental note to grab some next time I'm here for leisure.

We continue to wander down the road of laid stones lined with colorful signs and bright lights until we reach the edge of the populated area. Kimble looks up at me, a hint of sadness in her kind, round eyes. "This is as far as I may take you, milady. Keep straight beyond here until the stone path turns to dirt, and the city is no longer in your sights."

I nod. "Thank you, Kimble. This means a lot to me." I lean down and kiss the top of her head, giving her a few pets before I continue, "I must be going then. I wish you and your young all the best."

With that, we part ways as I continue my journey alone. I've never been this far into the spirit realm before. It makes me nervous. The environment beyond the city is different. Harsher. Colder. It feels the way many imagine death does. I almost pity Rath for being sealed somewhere out here. It's not a suitable environment for a soul, let alone a living person.

After some time, I find... something? It looks like the end of the world, in a literal sense. In one unnaturally straight line, everything just ends. The ground, the sky, everything. It makes no sense: the world *is* round; every world is round. This is certainly one way to deter people from wandering in this direction, though. It's clear I must do from here. I step forward, just as I expected; I find ground beneath my feet. Being right leaves me with a burst of confidence that I can beat Linola. After all this time, she has no real power left, just petty tricks.

"Don't hold your breath on that," Rath comments, letting me know he could hear my thoughts. Which is worrying since I had pitied him briefly. He continues with a warning. "Some remnant of Linola is still here, protecting that seal. Weak and tired as that part may be, it would be wise not to underestimate my little sister. I made that mistake once. Look at where I ended up."

Just as he speaks those soul-crushing words that remind me just how insane this really is, I see it. That small light that transforms into my ancestor, the great priestess, Linola Spade. I take a deep breath. "I can do this."

"You are a diluted girl." Rath's haughty nature makes my jaw tick as he speaks. I stand face-to-face with the last remnant of Linola's soul. Rath is in chains behind her. Her power, though weakened by the centuries, is still great. I can see that now. Of course, rather than being helpful, or just grateful because I'm trying to free him, he decides that antagonistic is the way to go. I should have expected this from him. Some uncle... Even though we just met, I can tell he is scum, albeit useful scum already.

I struggle against Linola, searching for a way to overcome her, but her attacks are fierce. My being her descendant did little to convince her to hold back. Energy bomb from below, light spear from behind, attack after attack, I give my all to deflect them. She has me on the ropes. My body can't hold up. My breathing is erratic. These people... these monsters... This power... It cannot be what I descend from. Overwhelmed, I pant, longing for the air to reach my lungs. I'm on my hands and knees as Linola stands before me. Her stature is petite and slim, yet she looks like a beast right now. She glares down at me with ire. "You, who could have been the greatest of us, have fallen. My brother will not be leaving here today. Forfeit, and leave this place alive, lest you die by my hand."

I tremble. There isn't even a sliver of hesitation in her eyes. But... what was that? There was something there. If you look past the ferocity and strength, there is something more. Even in the less restrictive form of a soul, her energy isn't limitless. I can see the exhaustion marring her face as dark bags and weary eyes. Attacking at this level for a prolonged period is taking its toll on her. Unable to defeat her as she is, I wonder, what if I can make her defeat herself? I have to force her to use what little energy remains. I gather myself, resolved to make one last ditch effort at this. *For them, I must. For them, I will.* The words play on repeat in mind until they form a chant that offers me the willpower I need to follow through on my insane plan.

I grab her wrists, my grip firm. I pour spiritual power out into our surroundings, creating a spirit bomb that will annihilate us both if given the opportunity to explode. "What, no!" She sounds panicked, presumably realizing what my strategy is. She has no choice. She can either stop the bomb and trust me not to allow Rath to bring destruction, or I can die here, destroying the last piece of her soul along with me and leaving him unguarded. Defeat clouds her expression as she neutralizes the energy, leaving herself unable to fight any longer. I stand, speaking in a firm, yet solemn tone. "Rest now, Linola. Enjoy your afterlife. I promise, I can handle things from now on."

She fades, becoming just another soul. I watch for a few moments as she drifts towards the city. Her work is done. She'll know peace at last. I stand, my legs trembling as I approach Rath. I reach out and touch him, trying to get a sense of just how alive he is before I try to break the chains that seal him. Turns out, he is fully and completely solid. He's a fully living person, even after centuries. This wasn't like what I was trying to do with Kai and Cal. I didn't have to resurrect him at all. I didn't need to create a new body from that which had decayed or force a soul back into said body. He was whole, complete. All I had to do here was unbind him. He's a priest. He can walk with the dead just as I can. I suppose it's natural that being here wouldn't have killed him.

I take a moment to contemplate what I'm about to do, wanting to feel sure about my decision prior to it. Then I answer his previous comment. "You are correct, if I'm to be frank. I'm diluted. My friends and I are all okay with that. People like us must do these things. We must go as far as possible, save as many lives as possible. I sacrifice myself time and time again to restore some semblance of normality to the world, both at-large and in a personal sense. We do this even if it has long since been irredeemable, even if it means losing ourselves. Do you not understand that? What is so wrong with giving the same effort as I give to others to myself, just this one time?"

"I know that, far better than you think, my dear niece." His tone becomes near affectionate in that moment, giving me a glimpse of a real person. I never stopped before to wonder what horrors he must have suffered to cultivate such a jaded view of life. "For what seems like an eternity, I have wondered if there is another way for those like us. With a good heart comes pain that would jade even the purest soul. Child, there is nothing wrong with what you seek to do."

I take a deep breath before placing my hand on the chains that bind him and whispering. "Rath, with the blood of she who chained you, I claim the authority over these bonds and, by extension, of that which they bind. By my word, freedom graces you."

As I expected, the singular ingredient required to break the seal was me. It had to be a priestess of our blood to free him, since blood was why he fought, and blood was how he got trapped. It's straightforward for such a powerful sealing spell. The chains fade, disappearing into the blackness of the spirit realm as if they never existed. The lone shred of evidence of the metallic spiritual power is the scattered, glowing sparkles of energy that could easily be mistaken for soul orbs at a distance. "I'm not sure if this is a mistake. It probably is. I don't trust you at all, but I believe you are the key to getting Kai and Cal back. I hope you will be true to your word. If not because you gave it, then maybe because I am your blood, no matter how distant that relation may be. We are family and I have to believe that means some-thing."

He stands strong, as if he had suffered nothing by be-ing bound here for centuries. "I will, Josella. That is the only thing I can promise you, though. I want those boys alive just as much as you do. I'm not willing to explain why just yet, but my goals, though different from yours, require them to be the ones at your side."

He takes a long moment, then offers a teasing smirk. "You aren't even close to being as pathetic as I had imag-ined, just so you know."

I couldn't help but to giggle a bit. This jerk. His com-ment almost reminds me of the sense of kinship I knew when Malachi, Johanna, and I were on the boat together that first night after leaving Pallentine. I've never felt that around someone who's related to me before. It's new, but most welcome. I shouldn't get too close to him, though, so I remind myself who he is and what he's done. A process I'll need to repeat whenever I think that perhaps he's something more. He's left no room for con-fusion in his words. We aren't on the same side.

Together, we travel back to the mortal realm. Time passes slower in the spirit realm, so it had been a frac-tion of time that my friends could not find me. About thirty minutes in living time, I'd say. The relieved faces of my friends greet my presence. I'm tired, but I try to stay on-guard. I'm unsure of what Rath would do now that he had attained his freedom. Without question, the others raise their guard when they see me do so. They didn't need the details to figure out that he would be a threat if he made himself one. Rath laughs. "Settle down, children." He looks at me. "Seriously? I just told you that our interests align right now."

Malachi looks at him with suspicion burning behind his flaming red eyes. "Who are you and what exactly are your interests?"

Rath sighs. "I suppose they are the same as they have always been, little demon. Since the time of the great war when I stood face to face and fought hand to hand with those who spawned you and your cousin, I've wished for nothing more than to protect my bloodline from those like you two. Those who become involved with your kind always get consumed with sadness and despair. If not for you, Josie wouldn't even have been in this situation. You ruined her life, and I intend to restore what you have taken from her."

His words are vague by intent. We have no way of knowing how he plans to 'protect' me. I intervene, not liking the way he's speaking to Malachi. "You will not say such things, not to my friends."

"Very well, if that's what you wish. I will continue to think said thoughts, though. As you cannot dictate my thoughts, will you be more at peace being unsure of what I am thinking? Or was I correct in my belief that you would rather hear it spoken? At least you can respond, right?"

I groan, "Whatever, speak freely. It's an uncomfortable topic, but I suppose it's also one that is better to be open about."

Rath's point is valid, so I let it go. His perspective, though skewed, is not invalid. Lilly tugs at my sleeve. "We do not have time for this. Let us move so we can make some progress on our journey before sundown."

I nod. "Yes, we can train a bit on the road, too."

Along with the group, I walk, keeping a close eye on Rath as we travel. It is an unstable and harsh alliance. One of paramount importance to both sides, though. We all try to find comfort in that. Lilly and Jameson are both making impressive progress in their training. Something that the team finds quite reassuring, since none of us are certain that we wouldn't have to fight Rath, eventually. This development even put Rath at ease as well. He acknowledges we all be at full strength if we are to succeed. There is still one part of the plan that he struggles with, though. The door that we need opened to resurrect must get forced open from two places at the same time. One is in Rallem. That is easy enough, since we are heading there, anyway. The other is in Alacrium, about another three-thousand miles northwest of Rallem. It presents a challenge. We would need one with spiritual power on the same level as his and mine to be there, but for reasons that are obvious, I want to keep Rath close. His leaving my side was not an option, given the distrust between us. Lilly is the only other who could supplement.

I bring up the idea and Rath replies, "I see no issue with that. Her current skill should be enough to serve our purposes, but given her age, she would need protection. The Alacrians would not allow a foreigner into the mountain kingdom, anyway. At least, not without justification. The queen, Alexandria, is a demon queen. The best chance of entry is if Malachi goes with Lilly on her arrival."

The connotation of his words implies the belief that Malachi and I would shut down the idea of splitting up. It would send one of our strongest three-thousand miles away from where he could help us. The thought occurs to us, but I think he's underestimating Jameson. Jameson may not have fully mastered angelic power, but his mastery of runic magic is unquestionable.

If we weren't already missing a half of our numbers with Kai and Cal dead and Johanna back in Tendu, this wouldn't even be a thought. We see why Rath thought sending Lilly and Malachi now would be for the best, though. It would give the other two the time they need to get to Alacrium and meet with the demon queen. Even for a half-demon like Malachi, it is likely the Alacrian people wouldn't take kindly to the visit, but he certainly had better odds than anyone else.

Pastel lays out an idea of his own. It's a compromise, of sorts. He mentions that if we continue to travel together, we will reach the town of Jubilee, which marks the midpoint between Loft and Rallem, in about twelve days. He had come across it on the way to the islands. It's the sole identifiable landmark between Rallem and our homeland. While he was there, he learned a bit about the landscape. There's a river in Jubilee leading all the way to the base of the Alacrian Mountains. It would likely be safer to travel along a river since Jameson wouldn't be there to create water if they couldn't access some naturally. Plus, Malachi and Lilly wouldn't have to leave right away. Within that time, we hoped to grow more comfortable with Rath's presence. Perhaps he would prove trustworthy if we got to know him more.

Rath liked the idea, too. That put me at ease some. Knowing that our comfort level with him being around was at least a factor in my uncle's thinking feels nice. He will do his part to establish trust and ensure that everyone felt safe with him around. Jameson didn't like it one bit, though. While he didn't openly object, I could see that he wanted to draw a line. I'm not sure if I should be happy that he's giving this the thought it deserves or pissed that somewhere in his mind he doesn't trust my decision. It's Jameson though. I assume the discontent stems from his insecurities. Did he think he couldn't protect me without Malachi around? He knows I don't need him or Malachi to shield me from Rath, right? I appreciate his concern, but I'm not so helpless. If it comes to a fight, he can be damn sure that I'll hold my own. Besides, Rath's actions in the past proved misguided more than they did evil, from what I knew of the story. Granted, that wasn't much. There are a few generations separating us, but he is still my uncle. I have to give him the benefit of the doubt here. Surely Jameson knew that.

By traveling later than we planned, we complete the stint we had hoped to for the day. We set up camp again and crash right away after we eat. To my surprise, I got a decent rest. The back and forth between realms must have tired me more than I realized.

***

We continue to chat and try to get to know Rath better today. Mostly, he seems reasonable, but also something relative to harmless. I'm inclined to believe he isn't all that bad. We are a bloodline of priests and priestesses. His spiritual power would have abandoned him if he had broken the basic tenants of using it. Rath even told Malachi and Jameson a bit about their ancestry. He knows their ancestors on a personal level, apparently. Much to our mutual astonishment, their original ancestors are the Brothers, Rettferd and Myrkr. Although they had gone by many names throughout the centuries, Michael and Lucifer are the most common in the modern age. Rath knew them before all of that though, back when they were just two brothers learning about humanity. According to Rath, the queen of Alacrium is also one of Myrkr's descendants. His daughter, who is from his distinguished full-blooded demon line. Beings like demons and angels have such long lives that I guess centuries account for a mere two generations of them. Like Malachi's family, most of his lines were mixed with humans or angels. Jameson was from Rettferd's main line, even though he was not pure blood. It seems Rettferd isn't as obsessive about keeping his main bloodline pure. The coolest part is learning about runic magic. It has many more historical connections to bloodline than I thought. Lilly seems to be interested in doing more research on those connections in the future.

Jameson soon starts asking more about Rettferd. The moment his thought had come out, though, we hear a joyous, gentle laughter nearby. We all look around, trying to determine where the sound came from. Rath chuckles. "Relax, kids. I figured he would be somewhere nearby. He would have felt my presence enter back into this world. You will not find him until he wants you to, though. Whaddya say, Rett? Wanna come out and introduce yourself to the little ones?"

"Rett?" Jameson inquired. He's as baffled by Rath's friendly nickname for Rettferd as the rest of us are. The tone he said it in seemed joking, but not in his typical condescending sense of humor. It sounds like he likes Rettferd, yet he thinks angels and demons are dangerous. This guy sure is an enigma. Rettferd appears, as in manifesting, from thin air, rather than walking over like most beings would. Why are ancient immortals so weird? I don't even understand how it was possible to just poof like that, let alone how he did it so casually. "Very well, Ra. Here I am. I was curious about what you all are up to. I've been listening long enough now that I have a grasp on the general idea, though."

Rettferd looks around until his eyes fall on me. He stares with an intensity that makes me unable to move, think, or even feel. Then, his eyes widened for a moment before his face fell into a softness that defines the word angelic in my mind. "Young Josella, you are the blood of her blood. I see it in your beauty, your purity, and your stubborn nature. I loved her, you know? She was the moon, the sun, and every single star in the sky."

Jameson goes on the offensive, exposing a type of aggression I had never seen manifest in him before. "It is best I say now that your love for the great priestess will not be reigniting with Josie." He shoves between us, his power levels becoming palpable. "Keep away from her." He grits out the words, making no attempt to mask his anger at Rettferd's word. I enjoy seeing this side of him. Rather than his typical manner, which lacked in confidence, this is fierce. It's sexy, seeing him get fired up like this for me. His voice echoes with a ferocity that left little room for any response besides immediate and total obedience. "Family or not, I will kill you over this woman."

Malachi's expression becomes one of amusement as he watches Jameson threaten Rettferd in such a bold way. He is enjoying seeing his little cousin act like the man he had imagined would one day emerge from the boy. Rath nods, reluctant to admit that he agrees with Jameson's words. "I hate to say it, old friend, but he's right. You remember how the last war began, do you not?"

Rettferd rolls his eyes at the threats. "Remember? That's not something one forgets, Ra. Best that I don't get you going all murder-y again. I am sorry, Josie, but you're spoken for anyway, several times over, from what I hear. Much like Linola, you have an abundance of love. I'm surprised Myrkr's boy isn't head over heels for you as well." He gestures towards Malachi. "It seems he carries a deep love for you, not in a romantic sense, though. Heh, Myrkr himself, would show an interest in seeing the two of you together. If you run into him, tell him I would like to speak to him. If there is nothing else, though, I'll be on my way now."

"*Tch-*" Rath replies, "Best get going then, Rett. We'll talk again soon."

In an instant, Rettferd had disappeared in just as strange a way as he came. Jameson, irritated, asks, "Why all that drama if he wasn't saying anything important?"

"Didn't he though?" Rath replies, "Rettferd is a puzzling man. You might try to read between the lines. He told us several things of key importance. First, he said my niece's fate has ties to those beyond the ones she already loves, meaning she could indeed love someone who is not Kai or Cal. He also implied that Myrkr would appear on our journey. Somehow, the baby demons' feelings about Josie reflect Myrkr and Linola, Rettferd seemed to think so anyway. Myrkr was an angel long before he was a demon; I suppose it is possible..."

"Suppose what's possible?" Malachi speaks up.

"You know how they say history repeats itself? With angels, this is especially true. When something plagues one of them, it will reflect in their bloodline until they figure it out. Meaning it's possible. That's why Myrkr has so many bloodlines, I think. It's because he's in distress, trying to use his descendants to figure something out. Then, the full-blooded line would act as his control in the experiment. It must be why he protected it by making them his heirs. The thing I can't figure out is why Rett thought we needed to know that. I get the impression that those two have a larger game in the works here too, but then again, don't we all?"

Malachi nods. I'm sure he heard just as well as I did. Rath's words were ominous, but he seemed to ignore it. "I see. I will have to think about this some."

Three

JAMESON

"Myrkr... The first demon, an angel who descended. What could it be that he is trying to figure out through our lives? I'm most curious about what he's thinking."

Malachi and I walked a few paces behind the group as we contemplated the details of the encounter with Rettferd. Is he asking a question or are his thoughts just leaking from his mouth because they overflow from his mind? I find myself perplexed by the concept. Could Myrkr be more fearful or confused than we are?

"What if the demon is more than demonic? Could he have cared about Linola, somehow, even in a twisted and tainted way? And what about Rettferd..." I flinch as I vocalize the thought. If that's true, does that mean

I'm competing with Malachi for Josie's heart? A sense of dread sends a chill to my bones. It's difficult enough to see her love Kai and Cal so fiercely, but if it were Malachi... that would break me. He's always been better than me at everything; a genius through and through. I love my cousin, but I also hate him. I hate the way I'm compared to him every day of my life. During my educational years, it was always a question of why I wasn't more like him. Family or otherwise, we are born to be rivals, to balance each other. He was fire; I was water. He was a demon; I was an angel. He was the darkness; I was the light. We should have been equal and opposing forces. However, it turns out he's stronger, and better at being 'good,' and more likable. Many even consider him to be better looking. Even in my kingdom, he's beloved more than I. I can accept losing Josie to them, but not to him. That is one thing I could never allow. "If that is true of someone great like you, Malachi, what if I am just the result of Rettferd trying to sort out his own feelings? What if I am a pawn too? At least you're a well-positioned pawn that poses a threat. I would be nothing more than a poorly placed pawn, ready to be taken with no return capture."

His eyes shine with more pity than I can swallow. He puts an arm around my shoulder in a brotherly hug. I'd never tell him this, but I hate this too. He treats me like some child he knows will never live up to the expectations placed upon him. Doesn't he know I know I'm a disappointment to everyone in my life? His pity serves no purpose besides making it hurt more. That would be so selfish to say, though. My cousin doesn't deserve that. He's so much better than me. Josie deserves better than me too, better than Malachi even. She deserves Kai and Cal. The only thing good enough for that woman is one hundred percent of her heart's deepest desires. I let the feel of anguish fuel my resolve even as it lashes and thrashes about, trying to my alter will so I can love her out loud. "You are no such thing." Malachi speaks with such warmth. "We are all more than just a reflection of our ancestors, no matter their magics and powers, we are born with wills and strength all our own."

Malachi examines the situation out loud, isolating the elements. "Myrkr and Rettferd are brothers of equal stature. Rettferd fell in love with Linola, we know that. What if Myrkr felt Rettferd had diminished his stature by falling for her? That would have increased the 'distance' between them. Meaning, my view of you, Jameson, being someone who needs to look up to me or follow my lead could be a reflection, right?"

I nod before he continues. "What I can't understand is Josie? If he did not like Linola and felt she undermined Rettferd's status, why do I love her as if she is my blood? Wait..." Malachi's face flushed, turning his copper skin nearly as pale as my own. "As if she is my blood. Myrkr did not dislike Linola at all. He was the one who granted her the power of a priestess, I think. He loved her, but he never could learn in which way. Was the love romantic or familial? He never got the chance because he was more concerned with protecting her, hence the power. What if he is using the reflection to work that out? Through me, he'd be playing out the dynamic as a sibling one to, I guess, see if it resonates with him?"

The wider implications of that still me and him both. I blurt out words, almost defensively. "Protect Linola from who? Not me. Or, not Rettferd, I mean." I look at Josie, who is a few feet ahead of us, laughing about something with Pastel. A flare of jealousy rises in me, but I soften the second she turns, and my eyes meet hers. The things I would do for her... If I am an angel, she is the goddess I serve. And no, I don't particularly care how blasphemous that thought is.

Malachi laughs, snapping me back to the conversation. "Distracted, little cousin?"

I could punch him for that remark, but I just scoff. "You're proving my point, even though that wasn't my goal here. I would never hurt her. I have to believe Rettferd would not have hurt Linola."

Malachi shakes his head. "I don't believe that you would. In fact, I don't even believe that Rettferd would. I think this has more to do with external threats coming from beyond. What was their inner circle? Perhaps it's simply that their presence in her life brought with it dangers from those who opposed them."

Unsure of how to respond, I huff. Then I jog a bit to catch up to Josie and pull her aside. It was best if I separate from Malachi before I try to kill him and end up dying myself by his hand. It is understandable that he would wish to sort through this and my being on edge wasn't helping him do that. In the meantime, I want to be at her side while I can. Though wild and uncharted, this is the most eye-catching of places. I know, if only by the way she looks at the world around, that I had no interest in looking for myself, though. Watching her watch the beauty is perfect.

She catches me staring and offers that empty smile. The friendly one she gives so we don't notice that she's falling apart at the seams. It's not as effective as she thinks. We all see how much pain she is in. "Look at the forest, silly. Not at me. You see me every day, but this may well be our only chance to see this lovely landscape."

I oblige, but only because she wants me to. It's clear how these wilds flourish. There are flowers of every color. The wildlife roams free and with peace, undisturbed by humanity. It is serene. The sound of the gentle winds blowing eases my troubled mind. It reminds me a lot of the way I loved to sit on the shorelines of Oceanica whenever reality threatened my sanity at home. It brings our time there to my mind. The first time I met Josie. That way she has about her that made her so quick to challenge my misconceptions and push me to be a better man and a better prince, the way she supported me through my internal path. The way Rettferd said it is so obscenely accurate: the moon, the sun, and every single star in the sky. That's exactly what she is to me. What a fitting way to describe the love I feel for the woman beside me. I always will, even after we get them back and she continues on about loving them the way I love her. For as much love as I have for the others, the way she dominates my mind and heart will forever be unparalleled. I am glad to have her here, at my side, if only for a short time. It also brings me peace of mind to know that whatever happens next, we will have had these small moments beforehand where the world was just me and her. I want to collect as many of them as I can before they come back, and I have to let her go be happy in the arms of another.

That night, I sit alone, filling everyone's canteens with the magic of my water runes before I train with Josie. It takes but a few brief moments, then we get straight to work with a sparring match. It's hard to acknowledge one's own weakness. I believed that even though I'm not great, my friends are the strongest this world offers. Yet, I find my belief shattered a few days into this trip. The truth stares us right in the face. Angels, demons, Rath; we stood not a chance against any of them who may become a threat to us, or to our kingdoms. As we are now, it's hopeless. Another thing is clear as well, though. If they are stronger than us now, it implies our powers may all be capable of growing much stronger. We are their descendants, after all. We have need for nothing but the will to find our true strength. The power left to us by our ancestors, whose poor decisions have led us into danger once again, will become our weapon against them. I fear I'm repeating their mistakes by loving her. To avoid the same outcome they had, I need to get stronger.

I push back the attack Josie launched at me. "Impressive," she starts. "Not bad for someone running on willpower alone." She doesn't even look mildly close to tired. "You're getting much better, Jameson. Good job."

I admit, it's better than I did a few days ago, but why is being on the defensive the best I can? She's been one hell of a teacher. I hate myself for not performing better. At least if I could do more, she'd be able to see just how profound her impact on me was.

Interrupting my personal thoughts as I walk towards my tent to criticize myself more, Rath questions me. "You seem to have much on your mind, angelic child. You should know, whatever you are feeling towards my niece, you'd be wise to keep it to yourself. Your kind are a plague in this world. Love, coming from something like you, can do nothing but hurt her. Got it?"

"If only it were that simple," I reply. "If only I had the strength to look away. I know it's pathetic, okay? I know I'm not good enough, not strong enough, not worthy of even a second of her time. Trust me, I tell myself that every day. I loathe myself for loving her when I know I don't deserve to. Enough so that I spend half my time punishing myself for it mentally. Every. Single. Day. You are not telling me anything I haven't told myself already. So, don't worry. I agree with you in that matter. Kai and Cal are what's best for her. Regardless of that, I cannot leave her side unless she tells me she tells me she doesn't want me there. I think you should know that I give zero fucks how weak I am. If you so much as harm a hair on Josella's head, I will cling to you and release so much power that we both explode and die. Do not test me, *Priest.*"

"It's hard for me to imagine that. At the very least, it sounds like I may derive some entertainment from watching you kill yourself while failing to kill me. You fail at everything, don't you, Jameson? What makes you think that would be any different? You've become accustomed to believing that with will, there's comes a way, but it's not true. There will never come a day that you can ever scratch me, nor one where you will be competent enough to protect my niece from anything. I'm sure you'd do your best, though, kid. All the while, I'd be laughing at you. It'd be like a kitten attempting to kill a bear. Your bravado is meaningless, and your threats are empty. I'd call your mind empty too, but I don't suspect that's true. It is rather full of manure, it seems." He pauses for a moment, contemplating his next words. His tone changes completely as he asks a baffling question. "Tell me, how do you suppose the heart of an angel may react to the mind and world of a human?"

"Hm?" I ask, "What is this? That'd be like throwing dirt on a white tunic. Purity becomes tainted when surrounded by filth."

Rath smirks. "Interesting. Maybe there is something under all that crap, kid. Always keep in mind, though, she will never have so far to fall as you do, Angel. The heavens have always remained beyond human reach, even when that human is a priestess. Thus, she will reach hell much quicker."

His words shake me in a way that I hadn't thought possible. My eyes go wide for a moment, shocked by the revelation. Then, I just want to cry. My poor Josie, she won't be able to take much more before she breaks, will she? I glance over at her and realize just how ridiculous that sounds. It's Josie. She is unbreakable. It's impossible, right? Anyone else, maybe. Not her, though. I know because when I look at her; I don't see a human or a priestess. As I've said, she *is* a goddess, my goddess. I look back at Rath. "That'll never happen. I don't know what happened all those many years ago and I may never know that, but I know Josie. If there is one thing you'll learn about her, it'll be that Lady Josella Spade is, in fact, unbreakable."

"I agree," Malachi adds, having listened to our conversation. "That she is." He waves her over. "She is unbreakable because she has us and we will never let her break. Myrkr knows that. He knows we won't let her break. That scum is counting on it, I'm sure of it now. He is counting on the fact that we're all so worried about her that none of us will leave her side. As long as I'm with her, we stand no chance. From here on out, she and I need to remain separate. I have more trust for you right now, Rath, than I do him. If he catches us both, it will be a catastrophe. Lilly and I should leave the group immediately. We need to get to Alacrium."

Scared of what separating means, I look at Josie. Even if my mind could make this decision, my heart knows it isn't mine to make. She's the one most at risk if the group separates, given her role in whatever mess is between our ancestors. I see the reluctance on her face as she speaks. "But Malachi, if you're what's making him interested, would you and Lilly even be okay by yourselves?"

In the annoying way he seems to be prone to, Rettferd reappears. Once again, his presence startled us all. "There is no need for concern, little Linola. I will travel with that group."

Curious, I ask, pressing for further information. "Why though?"

He sighs. "Skeptical, are you? It is simple. My primary orders are to protect you, young ones. At all costs. It seems the Master wants you all alive. It is unlikely that we can change your minds while you're still under the protections of free will. Meaning that this is the one option we have that will see our own goals fulfilled. As a warning though, I have secondary orders as well, Rath. I am to monitor you and my brothers' movements and ensure that neither of you does anything stupid. If it means I have to kill you, then I'll do it. I am not a fan of taking life, though it is a necessary part of the job, so I ask that you refrain from making me do so."

They exchange intense looks of conflicting friendship and hatred. I couldn't tell if Rath seemed more irritated because he was being threatened, or if it was something more. Had his grand scheme taken a blow because of Rettferd's presence? Assuming Rettferd is trustworthy, his presence would balance things out. If Rath goes off the deep end, my preference is to have Rettferd on our side. Even from a distance, he and Malachi could get to us pretty quick. I could not trust Rettferd yet either though, even if it would be convenient if I could. The way he presented that information bothers me. It sounds like he's opposed the orders he received to protect us, but following them, anyway. There is too much that we remain unaware of. I will have to trust Malachi's judgement. I know he wouldn't have even proposed this if he felt like it would put Lilly in any more unnecessary danger. He loves her, as we all do. Her life is too precious to him. Also, he wouldn't risk exposing Josie to further grief.

"Fine, Malachi." Josie speaks. "You had better make sure that you both return to us alive, though. Otherwise, I will come down to the spirit realm and destroy you a second time."

He gave an amused scoff. "Of course, Josie. We will see you again soon, I promise."

Trusting him, I let them leave. I have reservations, but I suppose it does not matter much now. It was the only way. I look at Josie. I can see that she felt the absence of him and Lilly almost immediately, as she did Johanna's. It was the fear that she would lose everyone chasing after those whom she had already lost. She is clinging to feelings of loneliness and grief because they motivated her to continue. It must seem like our family was coming undone. As it is, she may not be wrong. This journey would once again change our lives forever; I knew none of us would ever be the same after it. There was nothing I felt confident of besides the fact that my feelings for her wouldn't change. As for everyone else, I can't be sure.

I stay with her, saying nothing. Being there for her in how she seems to need me to be right now. If all I can do to ease her suffering is sit beside her until she falls asleep, that's exactly what I will do. I'm consistent in that, at least. For her, nothing can stop me. Her side is where I will always be. I hope we will not lose that if we are successful in our mission to bring Kai and Cal back. She doesn't have to love me back, not the way I love her, but we are good friends. I had been there for her through so much after their deaths. She probably doesn't realize how much I want to continue being there for her. I doubt she had any clue how I feel about her, but even if she did, I don't know that she can those feelings while Kai and Cal still consume so much of her heart. I'll never ask her for that. Just this. Just the opportunity to be someone she leans on.

Regardless, it was not the time to think about such things. I grab her hand. She basks in the temporary comfort I'm able to provide. She leans on me as she rests, exhausted by the thoughts plaguing her beautiful mind. I chuckle softly, seeing how cute she is when she's asleep.

I whisper to her. "It will be okay, Josie. We will figure it all out. Whatever happens, I'm here."

Just like that, she relaxes fully. Whatever happens, huh? I should choose my words more carefully. Even while she's asleep and not listening, I shouldn't make promises. There's no way someone like me is strong enough to keep them. On a mission like this, I could well die trying to deliver them back to her. If that happens, I may not be here. I couldn't just refuse her, though. She needed to hear that promise. Unrealistic as it may be, I think I did the right thing. I'll just have to force reality to let me keep my word. I can no more break it than I could refuse to give it. Her whims are law to me and I've a responsibility to uphold that law no matter the cost. Without a doubt, I will do exactly that.

***

We continue our journey this morning, with Pastel leading us. "We're nine days from the halfway point I mentioned before, guys."

Meanwhile, Malachi, Lilly, and Rettferd are on their way to Alacrium. Rettferd led their way since he had been there before. Malachi knew more danger was on the horizon. Just before he left, I saw it in his eyes. It's soul crushing to see him afraid. I spent my whole life thinking he was the strongest and now someone I see as a giant is being dwarfed by something much larger and more dangerous. I may as well be an insect trying to walk among these giants. There was fear of coming face-to-face with a reflection of ourselves. I feel it just as he did. It's a version of ourselves that our ancestors reflect, carried by them, even. After all, Myrkr's intentions are perhaps even more dangerous than Rath's.

If our ancestors have been manipulating things from behind the scenes, I have to wonder what it all means. Is the entire purpose of them derailing Josie's mission to bring her men back to settle this petty dispute they had over her ancestor? It cannot be. No sane being of any kind would do this. Subjecting their own bloodlines to this ridiculous situation? For what? To decide who a woman that has been dead for centuries should have loved. Besides that, Linola had a mind of her own, did she not? Who did she actually love? I wished she were here to tell us herself, but she's not and Josie is. I know her answer. Kai and Cal are the men she loves more than any other. They were perfect for her. There is no debating that fact.

JOSIE

Family: it is a strange concept. One that implies those born of the same blood have an unassailable bond. This assumption fueled by nothing but a shared a common ancestry. It's why those such as us are born with inheritance and the right to live rich lives, while others get condemned to a life of suffering. It is the belief that those of the same blood must be the same person, share similar ways, and have the same beliefs. I've never quite understood the purpose of it all. Then again, I suppose if it were not for my family, I wouldn't have had the right to question the way things are. 'Tis quite the contradiction. If I am to be honest, though, my very existence is a contradiction. That thought petrifies me but reassures me as well. If you look at it close enough, then contradiction is but balance by a different name. If I am to say that though, it implies that my identity is Rath by a different name, or Linola, or my mother and father. Could it be true that my identity is not my own? If it were, how would that make me feel? Is it such a terrible thing that I could be like those who came before me?

"Jameson, guys..." I take a deep breath, "I would like to spend some time with Rath, alone. When we get to Jubilee, in about a week, I would appreciate it if you two let him and I get to know each other while you two get some rest?"

Pastel, understanding why I made this request, agrees to it. Although, he did so with an obvious discomfort. Jameson understands, too, but he doesn't agree. He must feel uneasy about splitting ourselves up any further, even if it would be for a short time. He worries that if Rath does plan to betray us, that this would do little aside from giving him an opportunity to do so. His point of view makes some sense. I argue that the best way to know for certain if Rath's offer holds some truth is to give him the opportunity to betray us. Then watch and see if he does. I assure Jameson, "Not to worry, the town is small, according to Pastel. He and I are both rather high powered. Our combined strength would obliterate the town within seconds, so you'd know." I try to keep my tone light and teasing, to comfort him.

His head turns down a bit as he tries to hide his amusement with my sarcasm. "That's true."

Pastel smiles. "I would prefer it if you waited until we reached Rallem. That way, the city guards could at least be on the lookout and help you. Jameson and I would feel better knowing that you were not fully alone. Regardless of that, it seems you've decided already, so I won't object."

"I will." Jameson didn't like Pastel's comments on the matter. "I don't want you alone with him, period. That would just be stupid." He takes a deep breath, calming himself when he sees what must look like me, contemplating if I'm going to kill him for speaking to me that way. "I see that your request is a courtesy, not an actual request. I'll accept your decision, but know this much, Pastel, and I won't be resting. We'll remain on high alert; in case you need us."

I give him a wide smile. It is my turn to fail at hiding my amusement. He seemed so determined not to let this happen and he just gives up because of the look I gave him. Goddesses, I love being terrifying. "You are such a prince, barking orders like that. Remember, I, too, am of royal blood, and do not answer to the likes of you. Here though, I agree. It would be reassuring to know that you were looking out for me from a distance, Jameson. Thank you."

Rath interrupts with a fake gag directed towards our interaction. Jameson's focus changed when Rath comment. "Quit flirting. You two sound like dogs in heat and it's making me want to kill the angel. It's as if you forgot I can hear you all. Like it or not, Josie is my niece, regardless of how many generations removed the bond is. If she wishes to spend time alone with me, that's her prerogative. I also remind you of the last time I started a war. I act when fools threaten my family's well-being by carelessly taking the relationship beyond what is appropriate for a human and angel to have."

Jameson, fed up, flares his angelic power as if to show he intends to be the dominant one of the three of them. The sheer light of it blinds us all for a moment. It's impressive. It's the first instance in which he instinctively reached for his angelic power. Without even realizing it, he fuels this enormous power further. With his impressive mastery of runic magic, he fused angelic power and water runes, this time with intention and prominent control. It amazes me. A minor dispute helps him master more of his angelic power. As opposed to the training he's had that did... nothing? Simple-minded, I remind myself. Men are simple-minded. Rath, meaning to shield me, jumps in front of me. It's instantaneous. He flares his power to counter the force coming from Jamesons. He is much more controlled because of his years of experience and obvious mastery. Pastel, not having any natural magic or power, turned to his enchanted blade to shield himself from the impact. Though he used a weapon unlike the rest of us, I knew he had yet to show the blade's full strength. The force of his sword as he thrust it into the ground threw us all off balance. The action caused Jameson and Rath to release even more power. None of them are backing down. I have no choice but to step in.

I move myself to the center of all three powerful energies. "Settle yourselves, now!" My voice thunders, intensified by my power. The men tremble at the sound. Even Rath backs down. Though he is stronger than me, I'm more fierce. Seeing me get annoyed this way must have shocked him a bit. Each of them calm their powers and swallow their egos. They seem to let the subject die after that. Though it was at my expense. For the next hour, they joke together, calling me 'mother.' It amazes me how simplistic they can be. They went from being ready to brawl to laughing and joking together as if it were a natural transition. I quite admire the forgiveness in their hearts. I'm not sure that I could forgive those who have wronged me with such ease. Then again, I might. After all, I've yet to retaliate against those responsible for the death of Cal, and by extension, Kai. I think back to the idea of family that I had been pondering on. Kai and Cal are my family. Yet they are a type of family much different from the one I was born into, as are Malachi, Johanna, and their son. Lilly, too, of course. Family is not as my parents brought me up to believe. Instead, it became defined by those who move as one. Bonded people with the singular purpose of caring for one another.

When Kai and I first met, before we even knew each other, he cared for me enough to find and defend me. It was when those thugs attacked me in Nollent, the Island of Rock and Mountain. It was as if we immediately swore ourselves to one another the moment our eyes first met. He knew I would be important to him. On second thought, though, Cal needed a bit more persuading. He taunted and evaluated me for a good bit when Kai first introduced us. He may have been slow to trust, but once he came to see me as trustworthy, it became obvious how loving a partner he was. To both Kai and me, he held plenty of affection. They were both amazing men. Neither of them intimidated by my power, status, or by my will. Both of them were so willing to let me fight for what I believed in. They charged into danger at my side with reckless abandon. They protected me with their own lives if things went wrong.

There wasn't one I cared for more than the other. I loved them both. It's why I know now that I must risk it all to bring them both back to me. I spent so long concerned with the fate of nations that my own needs became blurred to me. To secure the future of others, I lost the only people who made my own future feel secure. That girl Malachi met in Loft prioritized the well-being of the masses. Even over myself and those I loved. I must thank Malachi for that someday. He saw in me what no other had and gave me the opportunity to become the hero this world knows me as. In fact, he is the authentic hero. It was his ambitions that led us, his persistence that bound us, and his throne that made this all possible. Now though, just this once, I have to choose my heart over my duty. It's what I must do to see that when the bells toll, I leave this world without regret.

***

Laughter fills the air as I spar with Jameson. "Jameson!" I exclaim. "You soaked me, jerk."

The mischievous look on his face is contrary to his apologetic words. "I'm so sorry. I thought it was a water war."

"No, there's not even supposed to be any water. You're supposed to be using angelic power. You know, the one you aren't good at yet."

"Oh, yes. I remember now. My bad for not letting myself get obliterated by reaching for a power I can barely use while having light spears chucked at me like throwing knives."

I smirk. "Smart ass."

He raises an eyebrow. "Overpowered lunatic."

I faint feeling of irritation pokes at me during the verbal sparring part of the match. I suddenly feel this urge to play with him, to coax him, to envelop him in the desire he tries so hard to hide. "Too bad. I thought you were more fond of my power. I had the impression some part of you longed to be trapped beneath it."

He looks like a puppy desperate for affection when he replies. "Not some part... Every part. I won't lie, not when you bring up the subject in such a way. I want to be subservient to you. Hell, I'd say that I am. I want you to own me from my body and power to my heart and mind. Even my soul is yours. I don't care if I can never live in your heart. I care for nothing but knowing that I, my existence, am yours."

Amusement overcomes me. Damn, that is so hot. I can't deny that I feel something for him. It's just not what I felt for them. He's antagonistic and adorable, a dangerous combination. I almost want to take him up on that offer, but I know I shouldn't. There's a plethora of ways that would backfire and I don't put it past Lady Fate to implement every one of them if I give in to this. "Jameson, you know we can never be. There are so many reasons that we can't. Among them is the fact that no matter what I feel towards you, I will always love them."

"So?" He replies. "That changes nothing, Josie. I'm not asking for your heart. I'm aware such an invaluable gift could never grace someone like me. All I am doing is giving you mine. There is no expectation that you return the gesture or even appreciate it. You don't even have to respect it. You can trample and destroy it. Whatever you do or don't do, it's your choice. I have no say. There is but one choice that is mine to make. It's that I will give you my all, regardless."

I smile, then softly guide him to his knees so I can reach his forehead. I place a gentle kiss on it. "My property is not unworthy, nor shall it ever be. You deserve every invaluable gift this world can muster. I only wish I could give you the one you desire." I wrap a hand around his throat and squeeze just enough to make him quake for me. "Speak of yourself that way again, and you will not like the consequences. You are *mine*, sweet angel."

I release him and he bows his head to me. "As you wish."

The act of submission makes a growing sense of ownership within me triple. He looks so mesmerizing when he's being such a good boy. I giggle, then we continue on about our night, eating and relaxing. With Malachi gone, it takes quite some time to make a fire to cook over. As I feel the inconvenience of his absence, I wonder how he and Lilly are doing. I find it best not to think about that too much, though. It wouldn't take much for the worry to turn into a panic attack. By the time we finish eating, we're all tired. Each of us returns to our individual tents and rest for the night.

After several hours of restless sleep on the cold, hard ground of my tent, I'm awoken fully by a sense of an unfamiliar power. I leap up without hesitation and dart from my tent. I unleash some spiritual energy to alert the others without alerting the potential enemy. They all rush out and stand with me within mere moments. Rath and Jameson both seethe with irritation at the unexpected turn of events. Meanwhile, Pastel draws his sword without making a sound.

We observe our surroundings for several moments. We can all sense the threat now, of that I'm sure, but we can't find it on the ground, nor in the surrounding trees, nor even in the air. Finally, I grow tired of the games. "Whoever you are, show yourself."

A shrieking sound echoed around us before a large swine launches toward us. Recognizing the creature, Rath, Jameson, and I all hold our ground, but don't attack. Pastel, however, acts on instinct and raises his sword for a strike. I grab his wrist and flip him, pinning him between me and the ground. I snarl. "Kill that boar and we will all die today."

He just grunts, struggling against me. I hold him there for a few minutes until the boar finally passes. When I release him, he stands up and stretches his arm. "What the hell was that?"

I sigh. "Sorry, I didn't mean to hurt you. It's just... that wasn't just some pig. I couldn't let you kill it."

He sighs. "I didn't ask what it wasn't. I asked what it was."

Rath explains. "It's called Hildisvíni, the battle swine."

Jameson continues. "It's a Goddess' war animal. It appears to those to whom she is considering offering favor. If they respect the creature and let it pass, she blesses them. If they try to harm it, she'll appear and kill them."

Pastel rolls his eyes. "Sounds like superstition."

Jameson snaps, not liking Pastel's tone. "Says the man traveling with a descendent of angels. What did you think Rettferd meant when he referred to his 'Master?' Angels serve no one but the gods and goddesses who contract them, fool. Keep your feeble mortal opinions to your damn self."

I speak up before things escalate further. "Anyway, the point is, no matter what your beliefs are, Pastel, we would appreciate it if you respected ours."

He nods. "That... is a fair point, Josie. I won't discount your beliefs off hand. That was wrong. I suppose exploring cultural differences like that is good, anyway. It may help our kingdoms to get along."

With that, we agree. Each of us returns to our tents and continues our rest.

***

After more than a week of travel, we've all grown weary, and with that came irritability. Arguments continue to break out among the four of us every few hours until we can barely tolerate looking at one another. As usual, I feel trapped by the duty of the Peacemaker, which increases my irritability. It isn't long before we stop speaking to one another altogether.

In the silence, my thoughts boom in my head like taunting spirits that sought to destroy me. I linger near Jameson, using his presence to offset my overwhelming desire to explode. He seems content with the closeness as well. Although it was silent, he accepts it because it gives him what he wants. As he said, his lone wish is to be useful to me, and that much I can give him.

***

Food grows more and more scarce as the wooded areas around us fade into a dry plain filled with nothing but brown grass. It looks as if there had been wildfires. The herds must have abandoned it. No creature could have thrived here after such destruction. It's through Jameson that we stay hydrated enough to survive, but I can see the toll giving us water is taking on him. Between the exhaustion and the hunger, he couldn't sustain this much longer.

To preserve his magic reserves for as long as possible, we stop training at night after we finish our daily travel stint. Still, we need a proper solution, not just a temporary measure that allows us to put off the problem. With five days left until we reach Jubilee, our fates are looking rather bleak.

***

After another long day of starvation and travel, relief finally came. A doe who must have lost her herd wandered into our camp. "It's the Goddess' favor." My tone is relieved, but quiet, so as not to startle the creature away. Though, I doubt it would run far if I did. I imagine it's just as tired and hungry as we are.

Jameson stands. "I'll kill it."

I shudder a bit at the thought. "You should not speak of taking life so coldly. I know we must do it, but do it respectfully, or the doe will not be the one I feast on."

I can sense his arousal upon hearing the threat in my tone. It filled that sweet voice of his with more nectar than ever. "That doesn't sound unenticing. But... I'll do as you order, Milady. He takes my hand and kisses my fingers. "I'll make it as painless as possible. You have my word."

He makes sure I turn away before he kills the doe. Then, he skins and prepares it prior to bringing it to me for cooking. Not too long after, we have a meal. Majority of it gets devoured. What remains when we finish, Jameson summons water at an extremely low temperature to freeze. We store it in the food wraps that we keep in our supply bags. It isn't much, but it should be enough to get us through another day or two if we have small portions.

JAMESON

She and I are growing closer with each passing day. I'll never understand why, but she's tolerating me loving her. Sometimes, there's even moments when it seems like she's enjoying having me near. I'm sure she's just using me, as I told her she could, to help curb the pain of their absence until she gets them back. Still, I'm so grateful that she chose me as her emotional pain reliever. It means everything to me, especially since she could have any man she chooses.

Infuriatingly, the closer she gets to me, the more irate Rath becomes. He's rushing now, urging us to move faster even though he knows Pastel can't. It's like he's worried that if we don't get Kai and Cal back soon, that it'll be too late. That gives me hope, though. If he's this worried, I wonder if that means her heart feels for me more than I realize. If not, why is he suddenly so eager to speed this mission along?

When night comes, the temperatures drop much lower than they have in recent days. I worry about Josie sleeping alone. I'd hate to seem like I'm taking advantage of the circumstances, but I should at least offer, shouldn't I? At least then, it'd be her choice. Besides, Josie has never been the type that hesitates to vocalize a 'no.'

I approach her from across the campsite as a gust of wind blows her beautiful hair into her even more beautiful face. She groans as she works it into a messy updo by using one long strand to wrap the rest and tucking it. She's stunning, and yet so ignorant of it. It confounds me. I notice her almost imperceptible shiver as she looks my way. I smile. "Hey, Josie. Are you okay? I know it's pretty cold out and I was wondering if you might want to..."

"No way in the nine realms is that happening, Rettferd spawn. Stay away from my niece. I won't warn you again." Rath's interruption seems to imply that my proposal was rather obvious. "I'll make sure my niece is warm. She can take my overcoat. Now, leave her side. Before I murder you, please."

I glare up at him. "Would you shut up? Josie can decide whether she wants to share her tent for warmth."

"I'll do no such thing, angel twat. Josella is unaware of the effect your kind has on humans. Any consent she may or may not give you is uninformed. I've seen the destruction of angelic love, and I won't allow it to touch her."

Josie loses it before I have any chance of replying to his absurd opinion. "By undermining my given consent, it is you who endangers me, Rath. I will not hear any more of this, dammit. It is I who decides what I will and will not do with a man, not you. And that applies to what I need to know before I consent as well. I will ask any question I feel I need to. All you do by stepping in is imply to men that my consent holds no value because clearly a man can give or not give it on my behalf. You're lucky that neither Jameson nor Pastel would ever allow your lunacy to alter their perception of what I am capable."

Rath looks at her. I can tell that he's enraged, but some part of him also understands her point. "Will you? There are questions to ask that you don't even know exist."

Josie's hostile expression is unwavering. "That is for me to be concerned with. You do not get to question me whatsoever. Stand down."

His jaws tenses just before he storms off; he won't stand against her, for whatever reason. He has the power and certainly the desire as well. What is holding him back? I don't like this man, not one bit. He's untrustworthy. It's hard to say why or when, but there's no doubt that he will betray her.

Putting him from my mind, I look back to her, but I in no way do I lessen my guard. I will continue to watch him. "You look like you're freezing. Would you like me to lie with you tonight? It would, of course, be for warmth only. I won't do anything you do not ask me to do."

Her eyes shine as she looks up at me. "I know you'd never hurt me, Jameson. Not just because you physically can't, but also because it's not your style."

All I can do is tilt my head, unsure of whether that was a yes or a no. Slowly, she walks towards her tent. Her hips sway in a melodic rhythm that hypnotizes me instantaneously. She glances over her shoulder, looking back at me. "You coming?"

I gulp as nervousness stealing my voice as I try to force words out. "Oh, uh... I-I-I..."

I give up, sigh, then follow her without answering. Josie giggles at that as we enter her tent. She lies down first, raising her arms to open and close her palms a few times. It's a silent invitation for me to join her. For a moment, I just stare, taking her in with my eyes. I berate myself for a moment, knowing I'll regret asking what I'm about to do. "I need to hear you say it, goddess."

Her amusement is apparent as she speaks. "Come lie with me, Jameson. I'm cold. And don't call me a goddess. I'm not a Goddess."

The moment she orders me, I move to her like a magnet, wrapping my arms around her petite frame. "Yes, you are. You're the owner of an angel. By definition, that makes you a goddess."

Josella doesn't argue as she curls into me. I rub her back as I hold her, driving the cold from her bones. Before I know it, she's sound asleep, and it isn't long before I am as well. I'm just so comfortable with her in my arms like this that I can't help it.

***

I wake in the morning to the sound of Rath calling from outside the tent for us to get a move on. My attention drifts from the sound of his voice, though. Suddenly, my attention locks on Josie, who is still asleep beside me. I realize how we are laying. I'm not holding her. She is holding me. As in, I'm the little spoon. I can feel her body pressed to the backside of mine and it is as if I'm in the great hall of the God's realm sitting upon a throne. She's the closest thing to heaven I've ever known.

Rath interrupts my joy again, this time hollering like a madman. "If you two don't come out of that tent in the next thirty seconds, I'm killing the angel."

Josie wakes from her tranquil rest. For a moment, she looks as if she'll slaughter Rath on the spot. "Rath, if you don't get away from my tent, it is you who will die on this fine morning." She looks at me. "And for fuck's sake,

Jameson. When are you going to stop letting him speak to you like that? You belong to me. You have no right to allow another to belittle my property."

I nod, feeling an erection pulsing beneath my chiton. I try to cover it, but Josie is using my himation as a blanket, so I can't pull it. "Um, yes. It won't happen again. I promise."

Rath butts in. "Ten. Nine. Eight. Seven."

Josie stops him. "We're coming. Stop counting like we're incompetent children."

"I would, if only you would stop acting like incompetent children. Besides, aren't you trying to get Kai and Cal back? Isn't this cheating? Not to mention, the angel is married, isn't he?"

I'm not letting him get away with that one. I dislike his implication. "No, the angel isn't." I emerge from the tent angrily. "I got divorced because my wife actually cheated. Besides, my marriage formed from politics, not from love. As for Josie, you couldn't be further from the truth. She remains loyal to Kai and Cal. We slept next to each other; not with each other. Do not speak of as if she's whoring herself."

He and I spend the entire day of our travel at each other's necks because of that one. Pastel and Josie stayed several paces ahead, trying to block us out of whatever pleasant conversation they were having. Naturally, that made me want to pick a fight with him, too. Though, I refrained from doing so. Pastel was an annoying existence, but I'm more concerned with the predator than the pest right now.

***

With this being the last day of travel before we reach Jubilee, the growing animosity between me and Rath gets put on hold as we both lean into the excitement of reaching the halfway point of our journey. He and I still don't speak. Rather, he gravitates towards Josie. I can see that she's looking forward to getting to know him more. As much as she likes to deny it, she craves attention from a biological relative, and out of all her living ones, he's the one she relates to best. She can't hate him as much as she wants to. In a way, she needs him, so I couldn't blame her for feeling that way, but I don't like it either. I know in my heart that he can't be worthy of her trust. If they grow close, she'll end up hurt. I want to put a stop to it, but don't know how to without hurting her. Who am I to insert myself into her dysfunctional familial dynamics, anyway? It's not my business, and she would get pissed off at me if I did. Perhaps I should wait and see how this plays out? Even if it goes poorly, as I'm sure it will, I can be there for her when it blows to shit. It's certainly better than butting in where I'm not welcome. Unlike Rath, I don't care to make her hate me by trying to override her decisions.

Instead of making a fuss, I stay quiet, watching her. She seems more lively today than she has been in recent days. Maybe having Rath near, even for a short time, is lightening the grief some. At least, I hope it is. I hate to think that she's gotten so good at covering up her pain that I can't even see past it anymore.

The day rolls on and eventually; we complete our thirteenth day stint. Pastel, addressing the group, asks, "I was thinking, and I wanted to run something by you guys. Tomorrow, we'll still have one hundred and seven miles before we reach town. It'll be late when we get there. How long do you all actually want to stay before we move on?"

My eyes turn to Josie, as does Rath's. It takes but a moment before she realizes that the decision is, primarily, hers to make. "Well, a night, a day, and a second night. It would leave us all enough time to rest, eat, and bathe properly. As well as enough time for Rath and me to gather what supplies we need to continue on our trip."

We all agree with that assessment. It made sense the way she broke it down. After we make camp, we rest. We're out of food again, but we all bear it under the certainty that we'll have plenty tomorrow night. Coin will be no issue, thanks to mine and Josie's wealth. Pastel has plenty too, but I suspect there isn't much left on him after being away from his home for so long, so she and I will make it work between the two of us. If she's doing supply shopping, I'll pay for the rooms and the meals. I don't want her spending too much trying to make sure the three of us are okay.

Tonight isn't as cold as the night prior. It's warm enough that Josie won't need me to warm her. So, I pitch my tent, not wanting to assume that she will want me by her side when it isn't necessary for her comfort. It's disappointing to go back to sleeping alone, but I'll live, so long as she's well.

"Jameson," she approaches me with a raised eyebrow as I pitch my tent. "What are you doing?"

I stutter. "I-I... I'm pitching my tent."

She chuckles. "Do you not want to sleep beside me?"

"No! No, I definitely do. I just thought..."

"That I wouldn't let you? Obviously. Stop being ridiculous and come lie down."

I nod, then put away my tent. With my head down, I follow her to hers. We take a few moments to lie down and get comfortable. "Sorry. I didn't mean to come across as pitiable."

"It's fine, Jameson." She cuddles up to me. "Just stay with me. You're the only thing that makes the feeling of loss tolerable."

"Oh, Josie." Kissing the top of her head, I re-assure her. "I'll always be with you. It's loathsome that you're suffering at all."

Tearing up, she replies. "I miss them so much, Jameson. It's too much for me to carry without you."

I wipe a tear from her cheek. "I'll do everything in my power to get them back for you. That's a promise. It doesn't matter what price I must pay. I will sacrifice my life and anyone else's if it means your joy will return to you, my goddess."

Her quiet sobs soak my chest with her tears. She doesn't reply, but her grip on me lets me know everything I need to. If I let her go right now, she'll break. I just need to hold her, to quell her demons the best way I know how. Silently, I hold her to my left side. I use my right hand to activate my runic magic, drawing her tears off my chest to store them. Directing them into my empty canteen without her noticing. I have an idea, but it might take me a while to complete it.

JOSIE

We run through the wilderness playing and goofing off, all four of us fully engaged with each other. The need for rest and food, alongside my emotional turmoil, has led to a long overdue break from sanity and I've opted to drag Pastel, Rath, and Jameson into the unhinged playtime with me. The best thing we can do for ourselves right now is disassociate. Reality sucks right now and we've earned a break. Besides, we are still making progress, so what's the harm?

I levitate above Pastel and shoot down a playful burst of energy. "Hey!" It comes out as a half-yell, half-laugh. "Josie, cut it out." He chases after me from the ground, but gets halted by Jameson, who sloshes some water onto the ground to make it muddy. Pastel slips and slides about four yards.

"Do not chase after my goddess, mortal." The threat is playful, but I roll my eyes, knowing it's not entirely empty. Jameson spreads his fluffy, angelic wings and hovers next to me in the air. I can feel the gentle flapping of them as they stretch out behind me. I turn to look at him. He's so majestic looking when he's in this state. With a massive size and long, white feathers that never seem to have a single speck of dirt on them, they emanate a glowing energy as the sun reflects off of them.

Rath levitates up and tackles Jameson from behind. "Stop hypnotizing my niece, brat." Even he is playful right now. He and Jameson crack up when they both crash to the ground.

Pastel comments. "This is getting unfair. Everyone here can fly but me."

I smile. "Rath and I don't fly. We levitate. There's a difference."

"Yeah, I'm sure there is." He replies. Then his mouth falls open as he looks ahead of us. "Guys! Look! I can see it. That's Jubilee up head."

I hadn't realized that we were so close to the village already. For a small village, unclaimed by any kingdom, it seems to be a rather lively one. We ran towards it, desperate for the food and sleep we would find there. As we approach, we come across a young woman at the river just outside of the town. She greets us. She's quite a unique lady, around my age, it would seem, but far more voluptuous. In fact, Rath seems quite taken with her figure. Pastel, too. He scanned her perfect body in awe. Seeming to get stuck on her enormous chest and hips. I could almost hear his mind praying that she would turn around. Jameson averts his gaze altogether. A smile came over me after seeing the awkwardness on his face. It's adorable.

Rath had a different approach to the situation. He flirts without reservation. He's giving no thought to whether that is appropriate under the circumstances. Rath may be older in years, but he still appears young. The young woman seems as attracted to him as he is to her. He addresses her. "How can the men here allow a gorgeous young lady to carry pales of water from the river? Here, let my companions and I help you with that." He glances over at Jameson and Pastel with an intimidating snarl. The girl gave a lingering and flirtatious smile.

Jameson and Pastel sigh as they pick up two of the pales and begin walking. They murmur along the way about how they deserve to rest after such a journey. They wonder why Rath thought he could order them around. I find it hilarious how two royals act like a couple of children. It's as if they haven't learned to behave like a gentleman. Admittedly, I did sort of enjoy their boyish behavior. After dropping off the water, the girl introduces herself. "Nice to meet you all. I'm Nubella." It turns out she's the local innkeeper. In a show of gratitude, she offers us a free meal to go along with our rooms that night. Rath accepts her invitation without consulting us, not that we have any inclination to complain. He sounds eager and definitely hopes to get to know her a bit better.

We follow her inside, where she shows us around. "Down here is where the tavern and reception are. Just up the stairs are the rooms. How many will you all be needing?"

I take a moment to consider her question. "Three sounds good."

Rath shot a glare at me, not liking that Jameson and I are sleeping together regularly now. He refrains from commenting though, thankfully. We all head up to our rooms, desperate to bathe at last. Food and sleep will all be the better if we're clean first. When Jameson and I get to ours, we look around briefly before he shifts his gaze to the ground. The realization that the tub and room have no separation dawns on him. "You can bathe first. I'll just fill it up and go wait downstairs."

I shake my head. "No, that's alright. There's no need to displace yourself. The tub looks plenty big enough for two. Why don't we bathe together?"

His face lights up as if I just offered to fulfill his greatest fantasy. His voice comes out smooth like honey and deep as the oceans he commands. For the first time, I get a glimpse of the confident, glowing angel he will be if I continue to reaffirm his self-worth. I'm mesmerized by it. From the faint spike of angelic power that leaks from him when he has my attention to the way he seems taller now because he stands with more pride than ever before, the way I effect this man consumes me. He fills the tub with warm water and watches me in awe as I slowly strip away my dress, then my undergarments, and stand completely nude before him. His Adam's apple bobs in his throat before he removes his himation and tosses it aside. He steps towards me a bit and removes his chiton, too. "May I?"

I nod. He doesn't hesitate to scoop me up into his muscular arms and carry me to the bath. He's careful as he places me inside. "Is the temperature good for you?"

"Yes." It comes out as a whisper. Slowly, he submerges himself into the opposite end of the tub. Turning so my back is facing him, I bring my round backend to his length as he wraps his arms around my waist. I can't resist the urges to tease him when I feel his arousal pressed against me. I squirm in a not-so-accidental fashion just to highlight his longing for me further.

"As one would expect from a goddess, you're a total sadist."

"Oh, perhaps I should cease my torture, then?" I threaten with a knowing smirk.

He squeaks a little before he answers. It's adorable. "You should not. Being tortured by you is an honor, not a burden."

He's so damn sweet. Some part of me feels like this is a betrayal to Kai and Cal, but there's something about him I can't shake...

I pull his face closer and kiss him. Without warning, without thinking, and without restraint. I kiss him like I own him. His whimpers and moans taste so sweet as I consume each one of them through the taste of his lips and tongue. He sounds like a puppy, but it's so sexy hearing those whining noises from him. He makes me feel alive and in control, two things I haven't felt in so long. Two things drive my need for him as I kiss him deeper and deeper, making sure that I'm the only thing he can think or feel. I want to be this angel's weakness, this prince's ruler, this puppy's owner, and this man's heart. *I want to be his everything.*

A knock on the door pulls our mouths apart, leaving us both panting. It's Pastel's voice that rings through. "Guys, Rath is getting to be incorrigible again. He's going to bust in here if you two don't hurry it up. Besides, I'm hungry. We should all get downstairs and eat."

Jameson's stomach growls as we suddenly recall that we are half-starved. I call out. "We'll be out momentarily. We'll meet you and Rath downstairs."

I hear Pastel's giant boots thumping against the creaky wooden floor as he walks off. We smile at each other for a few moments before finding the willpower to remove ourselves from the bath and get dressed. I know we should talk about what happened, but I also know we'll both avoid doing so. As we scarf down our food, an underlying awkwardness tinged the lively atmosphere of the inn's tavern.

Nubella comes to check on us after a while, though her kindness seems to be directed at Rath. She looks right at him as she asks, "Is everything to your liking?"

He raves about how much he loves the local cuisine and how grateful he is for her efforts. We all get a sense of where this conversation is heading and excuse ourselves so they can have some time alone. I feel jealous that this random woman is getting to know my uncle before I do, but I take consolation that I need to wait no longer than tomorrow's arrival. Then I'll finally have him alone.

Jameson and I fell asleep pretty fast when we got back to our rooms. It was a great sleep. This inn felt like a luxury after two weeks of camping, even though it didn't hold a candle to our palaces and estates back on the islands.

***

The next morning, Rath and I wander about town searching for supplies. As we enter the next leg of our rather eventful voyage to Rallem, things are going to get more intense. According to Pastel, this would be the most perilous part of the journey. Unlike our previous encounters, he said the beasts beyond this village are lordless. I can't even imagine what a lordless beast would be like. Our connections would be of little help to us. He also mentioned that there are scarce resources.

Lack of water and food is something even the most powerful are susceptible to in the wilderness. He thought we should be well-prepared. Thus, I sought to gather as much as possible. We need to be sure we have enough medical supplies and food. As for water, we don't have the means to transport much. Aside from our canteens, which had a rather limited capacity. It's rather risky. Jameson can create water, but that's limited by his own access to it. As we saw in the wilds prior, he struggles in dry climates. It won't be easy if this leg is even worse than that.

As we looked around in the different shops, Rath and I talk. We familiarize ourselves with one another. We discuss our interests. I learn that we have a few things in common. He also enjoys cooking and is a lover of animals. He loves to read as well. Learning those things helps to humanize him a bit in my eyes. He talks about a pet he used to have named Mili, a dog, who was his most loyal companion. I told him about Kimble, the fox spirit I used to keep as a familiar. He seemed to be sympathetic when hearing about how I lost the bond with her. He asks, "You have experienced some real trauma, haven't you? How much has that changed you? You must see how challenging it is for one not to change when faced with such experiences?"

"Of course, I do, Rath. I'm changing more by the day. It's worrisome. What if I become like you were or are? I don't want to be that kind of person, but I fear I may not have much of a say in who I am to become anymore. By trying to control my life, I seem to have lost control of it altogether."

"Oh, my dear niece, you could never become like me. The love in your heart differs from what I felt. That loyalty you all have will be your salvation. I was not loyal to my sister, but to the vision I had of her, to the future I wished for her, and to the feelings I had toward her. Never to the person she was, though; it is hard to admit, but I never even got to know that person."

Rath's words linger in my mind as we continue shopping and chatting. It sounds like he regrets the way things happened between him and Linola. Some part of me wants to believe him, especially since it explains some of his actions. Calling me to the spirit realm to free him relieved her spirit from its duty and offered her peace. It also gave him a second chance of sorts, to truly bond with a younger female family member and perhaps, through understanding me, he thinks he can understand Linola. That worries me too, though. He knows I'm not Linola, right? He makes that distinction; I hope. Who knows? The man is a total enigma. Trying to figure out what he's thinking or feeling is about as productive as slamming my head into a brick. For now, though, I'll give him the benefit of the doubt. After our time together, I still have so many questions, but I know enough to feel confident that he is not intending to betray us.

That night, he spends even more time with Nubella. I can't help but wonder what he will do after we finish our mission. Could he be considering returning to Jubilee to be with her, or perhaps inviting her to stay on the islands with us? That way, he and I can actively be involved in each other's lives. It's a nice thought. Kai, Cal, and I, together again. Lilly having her father's back. My uncle living nearby where we can visit him and his bride. Johanna and Malachi would be back together, their son, growing up alongside Lilly.

The beautiful dream ends there as I'm yanked back to reality by one distressing thought. *What becomes of Jameson and me?* Is that it for us? Does he just go back to being some guy I hang out with once in a while after I get Kai and Cal back? The thought is disturbing. We've grown so close. I don't like the idea that we wouldn't remain close, but... Kai and Cal. I love them and I've always loved them. It isn't possible for me to choose any-one over them. Whatever Jameson and I do, it's noth-ing more than a pain reliever. He is nothing more than a pain reliever; I don't love him. I'll never love him.

A liar. I think to myself as I lay beside him tonight. *Such a liar.* His scent hypnotizes me, making all my guards fall away. Like a freshwater spring on a warm summer's day, surrounded by lovely red maples and blueberry bushes. *I love him too.* I haven't stopped loving them, but I've started loving him. But asking them to let that go isn't an option. It's too selfish, asking them to take on a third male. The two of them were together before they met me, so that was different. This would be me bringing them back to life just to tell them they had to share me with a guy they barely even knew. It's wrong. I can never tell Jameson how I feel about him. I'll let him believe he's a pain reliever. Hopefully, by the time I get them back and leave him, he'll hate me enough to move on and be happy without me. He can never know the truth.

I continue lying there, on this lumpy mattress, between these thin sheets, holding him as he sleeps. I try so hard to sleep too, but my mind denies me that as it continues to wrestle with these feelings. We'll be back on the road tomorrow. I really need the sleep, but as the hours pass, I know in my heart that it will not come. Monsters don't deserve to rest peacefully.

LILLY

_____

As I trudge through the mucky waters, my soaking wet dress weighs me down. This is disgusting and there's no end in sight. I hate to sound like a bratty child, but the urge to complain overtakes my still developing a sense of maturity. "Ugh! Uncle Malachi, this terrain is a nightmare. Are you sure we had to go through this swamp?"

Malachi sighs. "Of course I'm not, Lillianna. I've never been to Alacrium before either; I've no clue where we should be."

A groan with a mix of impatience, exhaustion, and frustration makes its way from my gut out into the air surrounding us. "I wish Mom were here..."

"Me too, Lil. Me too."

He lost himself in the thought of how the other team was holding up. The thought of them being without him makes him nervous, and it's visible. Even if he did trust Rath completely, which he doesn't, he knows there are still other threats. We both do. His concern for us and the others is palpable. What if someone attacks them or if they get injured? What about food? Without him and Johanna, they are down their best survivalists. These are the questions I imagine rampage in his mind, the same way they do mine.

"For Valhalla's sake! Where the hell did Rettferd disappear to?"

Rettferd appears in a flash of light. It no longer startles us. We are becoming used to his antics. "I'm right here, my boy. How silly? You mean you could not see or sense me all this time? You've yet to master that demonic power of yours as well as you think. An average three-year-old demon can sense angels from miles away."

"Well, if you've been here the whole time, why aren't you helping us?"

"Simple. You didn't ask me for my help."

Malachi rolled his eyes. "I'm asking now."

"Fine then. I will inform you that you are not in a swamp. In fact, you are sitting on solid ground and have been for the past hour. It's illusionary magic. Presumably, set forth by one of the guard demons of Alacrium. It's to prevent idiot strangers from wandering into their territory. If you activate your runes and shoot a small burst of fire, it should free you both."

Malachi clears his mind, and the runes that run from his wrist to his neck glow. With a quick burst of flames, Malachi scatters the illusionary magic. It also took out a sizable part of the forest surrounding the base of the majestic mountain. It's safe to say the illusion, by numbing our senses, also numbed his sense of his own power. I worry though. According to the stories, the mountain that the Alacrians call their home is sacred ground among the demons. His overwhelming hellfire consumed far too much of our surroundings and I doubt they'll take kindly to it.

Rettferd shakes his head in utter disappointment. Then shouts, "You idiot demon! Now the Alacrians will never help or trust you! You have destroyed a good five acres of their beloved Freewood. It's one of the few places on this planet safe for demons to roam in their natural state. You know, without having to hide from those who loathe them!"

"Get off my back!" Malachi hollers. "I'll figure out how to make it work, okay?"

"You can't make it work, stupid. I can, though, but I must warn you that this is not something I do often. It will tire me and, most likely, my angelic power will be inaccessible for a few hours. If you're attacked, you will be on your own."

I interject. "No, he'll be with me. Now fix it, jackass."

Malachi attempts to hide his amusement under a scornful face as he corrects me. "Watch your mouth, Lilly, you know better. Although, in this case, you're correct. It's not appropriate still. A noble lady shouldn't say such things."

My eyes widen, and I nod, but with an air of defiance. I don't know why my family still insists on treating me like a child. I haven't been one for such a long time. That privilege got wrenched away from me, forced from my body along with any sense of safety I thought I knew. Mom adopting me went a long way to help me move forward, but in truth, it was never the same again. I had to grow up after that. I knew she would protect me, but we were still at war and in war. There are no guarantees of safety. I have to be stronger than our enemies. After all that training that I poured my blood, sweat, and tears into, I must be. I may not be at Mom's level yet, but that doesn't make me weak. I'm still more powerful than ninety-eight percent of humanity.

Rettferd sighs. "I'll go ahead now."

He recites an angelic spell. "The chains of death knock upon your door. The flames march forth to ruin you more. As I see your light fade away, it is with my angelic ties that I pray. Revive yourself on this day. Let freedom once again turn your way. This soul of yours it must stay. Rebirth is what I grant you this day."

With the powerful flash of white light passing over the land, life returns to it. Trees that were once scorched by the hellfire of Malachi's runes once again grew colored leaves. It holds more vibrance than ever before. Grass sprouts as if spring has come in a mere instant. The flowers bloom with a vivaciousness I would never believe if I wasn't witness to it. It is a beautiful sight to see something that had been lifeless, now teeming with life once more. When Rettferd saw the results of his fine work take hold, he felt relief. The drop in stress allows him to collapse from the exhaustion. Malachi catches him when he falls. He doesn't like Rettferd much, but he knows he owes him in this instance. He tells me, "Set up camp. We will lose a bit of time, but we should care for him. By morning, he should be back on his feet, so it's not too bad."

I do as Malachi says. There, we settle in for the night. I attempt to use my spiritual power to restore some of Rettferd's energy. Transferring it the way me and Jameson did when Rath dragged Josie into the spirit realm. It's a gentle, but steady, flow of a similar energy meant to empower an ally. It seems to work well. Within minutes, Rettferd regains consciousness. Though he can't stand or move around much. I'm proud of my work. Malachi, having made some broth, went to Rettferd's side. He feeds it to him in the hopes it would help him recover further. Rettferd flashes a weak smile. "You are kind. Most demons that I have encountered would have abandoned me the moment I ceased to be of use to them. I suppose you are more like Myrkr than most of your species. Then again, a half-demon like yourself, this may well be the influence of your human blood."

Malachi scoffs. "You're such an arrogant ass, Rettferd. Are you and Myrkr not brothers? If so, why do you hate me? If I am of his blood, does that not mean I'm of yours as well?"

"I don't hate you, child. Calm yourself. I do not trust you. There is a difference. We may have distant blood ties, but you are not my family. Jameson, I relate more to him. He is one I can accept as my own."

"Of course, because he's an ass as well."

I smile, knowing how much Malachi loves Jameson. I doubt Malachi could understand this if I said it, but I believe that he and Rettferd might act like family.

Without reason, Malachi tackles me. Or I thought it was without reason. He forces me to the ground just before we hear a deep and ominous laughter. We can't identify the source, or even the direction from which it came. It sounds as if it is surrounding us in totality. Rettferd, still weak, whispers to Malachi. "This laugh is my brothers. I am sorry."

Malachi snarls as he helps me back to my feet. "Back me up, Lil."

I shake my head as I rise with a confidence Malachi had never seen from me before. The look of shock on his face as I speak boosts my surety even more. "I am the daughter of Lady Josella Spade, the great priestess and equalizer of our land. I will not hide away like some frightened child backing anyone up. Today, I will stand and fight alongside my uncle as my mother and fathers once did. This is my destiny, and it is time that I live it out."

Malachi smiles with pride as he speaks in a hushed tone. I suspect more to himself than to me, "She is your daughter, huh, Josie? Seems she's growing up to be much like you. I remember, before we even met her, you said something quite like that. During the battle of the dragon brothers, wasn't it? I trusted you then; this time I trust her."

He took a deep breath, then says to me, "It is my honor to have you fight alongside me."

With that, we stand at the ready as Myrkr reveals himself. He emerges from the shadows as one would expect of the king of all demons. His appearance is frightening and impossible to read. His attacks are relentless and unpredictable from the start. Malachi hadn't a moment to think, let alone launch a counterattack. In this state of battle, Malachi couldn't even release his runes, let alone any demonic energy. He fears he and I will die here, and I don't blame him. I remember something from my training with Josie. We were standing in a field. Josie was attacking at a speed so unbelievable that it left me defenseless. I remember crying out. "*Mom! I cannot keep up with these insane attacks. Take it easy. You forget I am not yet as strong as you are!*"

The memory replayed in my mind. Josie replies, "*Oh, so that is your plan, is it? You think you can ask an enemy to take it easy on you because you lack the training to meet your full potential. No, child. You must learn to counter those stronger than you. Like me, you are a priestess. If your offensive power is not enough to counter, turn to your defensive power. Our abilities of defense are, in reality, much stronger than our offensive talents. This is because, unlike the runic magic carried by the others, the primary purpose of our spiritual energy is to protect. Whilst theirs is offensive by nature, our offensive abilities extend from our defensive power. Now, defend, Lilly! Show me your strength!"*

I nodded at her. Josie once again began her overwhelming onslaught of ruthless attacks. I attempted a barrier, one that no one but I could summon. Later on, Josie dubbed it "Living Barrier." What this specific power did was create a sort of conscious, living sphere of my spiritual power. It expands until it engulfs an entire battlefield, rejecting those I see as having malicious intent. It does this by emanating light meant to purify them. I remember Josie saying that the reason she survived the attack was because she was already pure in my eyes. That barrier would kill those who had allowed themselves to become tainted. Its attempt to purify them would destroy most. She urged me to never use the attack again unless it was against a true enemy. Now, facing Myrkr, I knew the time had come.

Reluctance flows through me as I extend my arms. I try to focus on who I want this barrier to see as an enemy so it wouldn't also harm Malachi and Rettferd. As I cast it, Myrkr senses its immense power, causing even him to shutter for a moment. This finally allows

Malachi to fight back. As the barrier engulfs us all, my nervousness about the power corrupts it. Its intentions and mine are no longer aligned. This leads it to attack Malachi as well. It senses the darkness of his demonic power and confuses it with Myrkr's because of their ancient blood ties.

Malachi tries to conceal his demonic energy from the barrier. His attempt proves useless. Having already released some amount of it in his own free-will, it's too late to take it back. Together, he and Myrkr scream in agony whilst I search for a way to regain control of the barrier. Myrkr, though, seems to have a better solution. Rather than hoping I could fix it before he and Malachi both died, he implements his own solution. He begs Malachi, "I know how you feel about me, but please. In this moment, the best way to survive this is if you trust me when I say that I do not wish to die here. It doesn't serve me if you die, either. Take my hand, please."

MALACHI

I snarl, realizing I don't have time to think. I extend my hand to Myrkr. In a flash, Myrkr teleports us both to safety. We land well beyond Lilly's range. It takes a few minutes to catch our breaths, but when we do, we address one another. I beat him to the punch there. "Want to explain why you tried to kill me if my death did not serve you?"

He quirks an eyebrow. He's not playing dumb here. His confusion is genuine. "I knew you would survive my attacks. Whereas that barrier, without a doubt, would have killed us both."

"I see. So, what do you want from me?"

"You already know the answer to that. If you remained unaware, you would still be at Josella's side."

I clench my teeth. As expected, Myrkr will not be an easy foe. "Take me back to the camp, now."

Myrkr chuckles. "You know, I would, except if we teleport again this soon, our limbs won't be accompanying us. Flying would be a better option if you ask me."

I sigh, exasperated from both the battle and the teleportation. Still, I let my black, demonic wings sprout from my back, tear my shirt, and leave my upper body exposed. Myrkr does the same. We both take a moment to observe the other one's wings, as we know one's wings can tell you a lot about them. To my surprise, our wings appear much more alike than I had expected. Regardless of our blood relation, there are differences in our personality. Differences that should have made our wings look like opposites. To me, this means that Myrkr and I are much more alike than I ever dreamed. There are a few differences of note, though. We both have massive, pitch-black wings, and hellfire red tips that resemble daggers. Mine have fewer feathers, though. They are also smaller by comparison to his, although reasonably larger than the average demons would be. I assume this is because I'm a half-demon, unlike Myrkr, and so I carry a fraction of his regality. Myrkr put an end to that thought right away. He speaks as if he's in my mind. "There is no such thing as a half-demon, child. One born of both demon and human lineage can never be less than a full-fledged demon. In the womb, as the 'half-demon' forms, the demonic DNA eats away at the human DNA. By the end of the second trimester, none remains.

Meaning that, since three months before you were born, you were nothing less than a demon. The same applies to Rettferd's spawn, though he would refrain from saying so openly. All that it means is that you are weak-minded. To have still not accepted the fact that you are, without a doubt, a full-fledged demon is pathetic."

Without taking the time to observe the devastation on my face, Myrkr takes flight. The devastation turns to shock as I struggle to keep up. His speed is incredible, and the beating of his wings alters the flow of the wind. It's amazing to think of the "butterfly effect" on the scale of him but also terrifying as I can hardly imagine the tragedy of being him, knowing that his mere existence is more than likely wrecking some poor, unknown village far from here.

I contemplate trying to speak with him as we fly. That's not a good idea, though. I opt to enjoy the silence. Somehow, it feels like we communicate our innermost thoughts and feelings without speaking. I can't help but notice the similarities between us. It's like looking into a mirror in some ways. In others, it feels more like that mirror is showing me an idealized version of myself that I will forever fail at living up to. Suddenly, I understand how I must make Jameson feel. It's horrifying to see how brilliantly you have failed your bloodline. If I endured this for as long as he has been, I might hate myself, too. Of course, that's not to say that I'm giving up. It's true, after all. Without a doubt, Myrkr and I are the same, and that means I could one day be as powerful as he is.

It feels like Josie is at my side as we fly together. This is what family feels like. Now, the last question standing is if that means Myrkr was a good guy, or if I'm not one. Or, more likely, that I'm overthinking this whole generational mirror concept that was posed days ago, and that there is no correlation between our moral compasses whatsoever.

Contemplating it is useless, though. Instead, I focus the energy my thoughts would have consumed towards seeing this new place and taking the time to enjoy the outstanding scenery. The wilderness surrounding the base of Mt. Alacrium is worth more attention than thoughts that seem to lead nowhere but my peril. It would have been a waste. Alacrium is beautiful and I should enjoy it. With its vast beauty, full of evergreens, this place inspires a sense of awe. I use my demonic energy to enhance my eyesight. By doing so, the radiant colors become even more perceptible. By doing the same with my ears, I take in the serenity of the sounds. From the wind's gentle whispers to the songs of the wildlife living in this blessed land, I hear it all. I wonder how something meant for demons can be so gorgeous. Then I wonder if evil has to be gorgeous, because if it appears to be ugly, it would then be recognizable. That would make it unable to thrive in the shadows.

Myrkr seems to enjoy watching me lean into my demonic energy to find more beauty. "It's unlike anything in the world, isn't it? Seeing Alacrium from this point of view is an unforgettable experience."

I nod. "Yeah. For once, it's like I'm resonating with my surroundings. That's not even the case in my kingdom. There, I am watched by all those that surround it. They lurk, waiting for me to screw up so they can call me a monster and drag me through the mud, using my heritage as a chain. I hate it."

The look in his eyes appears almost empathetic, but he doesn't convey that out loud. Rather, he just beats his wings again, as if challenging me to keep up with him. After flying for about thirty minutes, Myrkr and I spot Lilly and Rettferd. An immediate sense of relief overcame me when I saw her unharmed. Even with her nearly killing us both, she's Josie's kid, and like I worry for my overpowered sister, I worry for her overpowered daughter. That will never change, no matter how many years come to pass.

We swoop downward to land; Lilly is in distress, and she isn't bothering to hide it at all. I realize she thought her barrier obliterated me. She hadn't seen us escape. I call out, mere moments before my feet touch the ground. "Lilly, it is okay. We teleported, otherwise there was no way we would have survived that barrier of yours. It is impressive. Once you learn to control it better, it will be an amazing asset to our team."

LILLY

Tears burst from me like lava from the depths of Tendu's volcanoes, feeling an indescribable relief at the sight of Malachi. "I'm so sorry," I sob. "I am so, so sorry. In my attempt to prove myself, I almost killed you."

He smiles with grace and mercy in his eyes. "No, that's not at all what happened. In the intensity of a battle that we were losing, you made a decisive judgement call. In the end, that allowed us to draw with an opponent beyond our level. You should be proud. I have had many more years to hone my abilities and master them. Yet, I still have a long way to go. It's most unreasonable of you to expect yourself to have mastered yours."

I think back to my time on Mallishrine, the island of my blood, where weaker versions of priests and priestesses like me and Mom are everywhere. There, I struggled because of the brutal and barbaric training methods of my people. I wonder how that trauma still affects me for a moment. Are my expectations still so skewed? Will I still accept nothing less than perfection from myself? It hurt me to think that after all I have been through with Josie and the others that I'm still terrified by my past. Am I still a little girl they found lying on the beach in Oceanica? I know that now was not the time for fear and insecurity, so I push those questions aside. I rejoice in knowing that Malachi survived the attack. Soon though, I come to realize that me and Rettferd are missing some major parts of the story. I let out a low growl as I glare at Myrkr as I ask Malachi, "What is he doing here, and why did he bother to save you?"

Malachi sighs. "I am not sure. He saved me, though, so we at least owe him the courtesy of hearing him out."

Together with Rettferd and me, he fixes his intense gaze on Myrkr. Myrkr laughs. I can taste my fury in the air when I hear the intentional slight in it. "You're not wrong to place suspicion on me. I'll tell you that my motivation for coming here isn't 'good' or 'pure.' I do, in fact, want something and it's rather self-serving, but you'll need me. My daughter, Alexandria, who rules the Kingdom of Alacrium, won't give heed to anyone besides me. She won't allow you on the mountain unless I'm here to escort you. Knowing my daughter, the moment you touch the mountain, she'll treat it as an invasion. It will be an act of war in her eyes. She'll attack you with everything she has. So, self-serving, or otherwise, you need me."

Malachi rolls his eyes. "I suspected as much." He changes the subject to something more productive. "I would use my wings to get up, but this mountain is so high. It's ridiculous. Alone, I'd be fine, but carrying Lilly? She can't do this herself; levitating is still difficult for her. Not to mention, Rettferd can't either, at least not in his current state."

Myrkr glances over at Rettferd. "Yes, of course. How could I forget? My dearest younger brother, Rettferd, how did you end up in this pathetic state? Have you become so complacent that restoring a forest can now render you useless? A burden to your newfound friends?"

Rettferd tries to summon the strength to stand. As he struggles to lift himself, his shaky joints buckle. This left him to fall back to the ground, groaning from the pain. Myrkr barks a sinister laugh. "Oh, brother, worry not. I won't kill you now. That's a pleasure I intend to save for after I get what I want. For now, we are on the same side."

Rettferd replies, "I could say the same to you, elder brother. Believe me, your life will be mine when the time is right."

Myrkr looks as if he wants to retort, but Malachi speaks before he can. "So be it, then. We will travel together for now and after we have done what we came to do, the three of us can kill each other. Jameson and Rath can join in as well, for all I care. What's important now is that I deliver to Josie that which she most desires; the return of the men she loves."

Everyone has an understanding that any alliance between us is temporary. It would last only until the point at which our goals diverge. In a way, it serves to further motivate each of us. The prospect of obliterating one another is exciting. Although, it's exciting in the most twisted and corrupt sense of the word. This sort of sadistic excitement could rise nowhere else but in a group of warriors. Malachi, although a decent person, can't deny that some part of him longs to battle. Even more so, against those who pose a genuine threat to him, offering a level of intensity where no one holds back. In fact, some part of him even feels disappointed, I'm sure, at the idea that he and Mom may never clash in an all-out battle. Myrkr sees this darkness which lingers deep within his descendant's soul. He knows it's something that might play to his advantage, given time. I see it, too, and find myself concerned with the fates of those I care for. Is there no way for this journey of ours to end besides in violence and death? I wonder why it must always be so.

I can't understand how anyone longs for carnage. The feelings of grief and depression that come as a result aren't worth the cost. From experience, I know this. I remember feeling angry at Kai for choosing to follow Cal to the grave after he died in the war. His actions were selfish and wrong. Although I've never admitted it aloud, it stirs a rage in me I seldom feel. I feel abandoned all the time. Even worse is the pain of knowing I may never see them again if we aren't successful. There was a time when I thought that neither Mom nor I would survive the pain of their absence. Here, I have no such qualms about facing death. If Malachi persists down this path of defiling the heroic man that I know him to be, I will have no other choice. I would have to voice my thoughts on the matter and even stop him by force if it came to that. It's no longer a surprise to me that my barrier attacked him. The Living Barrier must have recognized the same polluted soul in him as it did in Myrkr. It sought to exterminate the source of the evil before it took form and brought harm to me or those I love.

Ten

JOSIE

We prepare to leave Jubilee early in the morning, just as the sun peeks over the horizon for the first time in hours. We pack our things, say our goodbyes, and move on. As the hours pass, the town fades further and further. The grass turns to sand, and the warmth turns to blistering heat. It's a desert, and from the energy seeping from the ground, I'd say it's a cursed one. I've seen a lot of cursed things in my time. Cursed caves. Cursed realms. Cursed objects. Cursed people, even. A cursed desert is new, though. How do I always end up in these situations? Can't any of my problems be normal? I could deal with everyday issues. I was prepared for those my entire life. Guests show up at the dinner without an RSVP. I can handle it. The education of a duchess accounts for that. Want to know what it didn't cover? Cursed deserts.

I feel I've been relatively tolerant of the changes I've encountered since discovering that I'm a great priestess meant to protect the alliance of the islands, but I really stepped into it this time. And I mean that literally because there is camel crap on my shoe. "Yuck!"

Jameson tries to hide his amusement with my clumsiness. "Here, lift your foot. I got you."

I do as he asks, and he uses his water magic to rinse it from my shoe, then places a gentle kiss on my ankle before releasing it for me to lower. Rath scoffs. "Cut that shit out and move! Both of you!"

Jameson and I look at each other, beginning to notice that our closeness is becoming increasingly agitating for Rath. It's concerning, to say the least.

***

Another long day walking through this vast desert passes. With each step, I feel the cursed energy growing more potent. It's taking its toll. The hope is draining from me. Everything seems so bleak. I groan. "Pastel, how the hell did you make it through this the first time?"

"It wasn't as prominent, last I passed through. It's grown much more severe. I don't know if we can make it."

Rath adds, "We can. We just have to find the source of the curse and put a stop to it."

He and Jameson seem less affected than Pastel and me. It makes sense. Jameson is an angel; he probably has a biological immunity to shield him. Rath doesn't, but he's light years stronger than I am. He's probably developing one. "It has to be you and Jameson." I state matter-of-factly. "You two are least affected by the curse. High levels of immunity and all. Go, please." I look at Pastel. He'll collapse any minute, and I won't be far behind if I don't conserve what little energy I can muster. "We'll wait here."

Rath and Jameson both look uncomfortable with the proposal. For several reasons, I'd imagine. Not wanting to leave me alone, not wanting to be together without me as a buffer, and so on. Rath responds first. "No. Only one of us is necessary. You go. I'll stay here with my niece."

"No." Drenched with underlying possessiveness, Jameson's sarcasm is booming. "It will be the other way around."

I interject before they can descend into an all-out quarrel. "The longer you two spend arguing, the more at-risk Pastel and I become. I don't care who goes, but one of you needs to. Now."

Jameson looks at me as if I just ripped his heart from his chest and crushed it in my bare hands. "You... don't care?"

My heart sinks. "No, Jameson. I-I-I..."

"No," He stops me. "It's okay. I understand. I'll go."

He sprouts his wings and flies off before I can answer. I hadn't meant for it to sound that way. Damn. What have I done?

Rath pats my head. "It's okay, Josie. It's for the best. This way, it'll hurt him less. You shouldn't wait until Kai and Cal have returned to your side."

I tear up, but I know Rath is right. Whatever is happening between me and Jameson must stop. I don't want to break his heart. I don't want to be a source of pain to him. This was never what I wanted.

***

The next morning has come. Why isn't he back? What if something has happened to him? "Rath,"

He cuts me off before I finish the thought. "I know. I'm going. Wait here."

He leaves, heading to figure out what is holding Jameson up. Meanwhile, I wait with Pastel. He's not even conscious anymore. I barely am, so I can't blame him. I'm conserving all the energy I can, but this curse is strong. Combined with the dry, desert heat, it's wretched. If they don't hurry, we're dead.

The hours pass like seasons. It's as if I can feel myself growing decrepit. My attention snaps away from my weakened state when Rath and Jameson come charging towards me, screaming. "There's too many! We have to fight!"

Behind them there's a massive hoard of... No. Shit. Those are Sleipnir, eight-legged battle horses prone to trample anything that disturbs them. They must be the source of the cursed energy. This is bad.

I leap to my feet, ready to fight. My body is still struggling, and my mind feels feeble, but I have to help. One, two, or even fifty would have been nothing to Jameson and Rath, but they're upwards of five hundred. I have my doubts that we can fend them off, even with all three of us. I wish Malachi and Johanna were here. Now isn't the time for that, though. I run towards Jameson and Rath, meeting them a little less than halfway so we could make our stand. They turn to face the creatures alongside me.

They hurl themselves toward us and we brawl. I launch as many light spears as I can manifest, all shooting in different directions. It's my attempt to take out as many as I can before what little energy I have left dries up like everything else in this hellhole of a desert. It's not enough though. I hit about one hundred of them before I fell to my knees, panting. Jameson follows up. Surprisingly, he reached for his angelic energy rather than his rune-based water magic. Large, glowing orbs disperse, obliterating roughly two-thirds of the remaining Sleipnir. Rath leaps in front of us after that, taking out most of what remained with... bolts? Are those thunderbolts made up of spiritual energy? He really is a magnificent warrior. I knew he was strong, but I never imagined that.

Less than a handful of Sleipnir remain after that. The cursed energy disperses to a reasonable level that Pastel and I could sustain. I feel my energy flow back into me like a river. I imagine Pastel did as well, because he was on his feet within thirty seconds. Jameson rounds up the rest of the Sleipnir. "Guys, I have an idea."

We knew exactly what he was thinking. It was insane, but why not? Rath answers. "Not a bad idea. It would get us there much faster, which is nice because we've lost a fair amount of time."

Pastel and I agree. So, we did it.

***

"Whoo-hoo!" A free-spirited laugh rings through the desert as we ride side-by-side on our Sleipnir. "This is amazing!" Jameson finishes.

"Yeah!" Pastel follows up. "I wish I had one of these things the first time I made this trip."

We rode furiously, making our one hundred seven-mile stint in what I assume was about six hours. This is far more efficient than walking, and it leaves way more time for training after our daily stint.

***

We decide to ride further, making up for lost time. At this rate, we'll make it to Rallem in eight days. It'll still fit into our original timeline, which is relieving because once we get there, we'll be able to communicate with Malachi and Lilly. I hope they're holding up okay. I can't wait to check-in on them.

***

We ride and ride and ride, stopping for nothing but necessity. To hydrate, feed, and rest ourselves and our beasts. I worry though. Jameson and I still haven't spoken about what happened before he left to find them. He's stopped sleeping with me. He's barely spoken to me at all. I can't bear it. It hurts. I love Kai and Cal, but I love him too. I hate that I have to choose, but Rath is right. It's better for Jameson if I just leave it be.

Emerging from the desert, Rallem comes into view, albeit faintly. The city looks huge, and we are eager to get to it. I can't wait to see Pastel's home. I look forward to getting to know my friend's culture. More important to me, though, I look forward to making another stride towards bringing Kai and Cal back to me. It relieves a bit of my stress about Jameson. Maybe after they are back at my side, things will return to normal, and Jameson and I can just be good friends again? That sounds nice. Although, I know it's nothing more than a naïve dream. I don't think he could bear just being friends again. Besides, that would feel like too big a window for me to cheat on Kai and Cal.

CHAPTER
Eleven

JOSIE

———————

A las, we arrive at the gates of Rallem. The guards at the gate greet us with startled expressions when we rode up on the Sleipnir. "Uh, Prince Pastel." One of the duo starts, "You're home. Welcome."

Pastel's demeanor shifts to that of a prince, rather than a guy hanging out with his friends. He sits strong and proud upon the back of his beast, not even bothering to meet the eye of the guards. "Well then, open the gates. And do not be disrespectful. You are to greet my guests, for they are guests of the crown."

The guard's bow. "Of course, my apologies, your highness. And welcome to Rallem, guests of Prince Pastel. We hope you enjoy your time in our kingdom."

It seemed the last leg of our journey had taken an eternity. We spent most of it trudging through the terrible landscape that tried to consume us with more than a few sink holes. Luckily, we found these Sleipnir to aid us. I stand alongside Uncle Rath, Jameson, and Pastel when we dismount and hand off the Sleipnir to the guards to be taken care of. By now, we've broken them enough that they are easy to handle. We take in the sights of the kingdom as we walk through the gates. Pastel's culture is marvelous. It differs much from the cultures of the islands. Uncle Rath seems familiar with it; I suppose he must have visited here before he got sealed by Linola. As the locals sing music in the streets, he sings along. It's as if he's one of them. I smile at the sight of his happiness and immersion in a culture that is so foreign to the rest of us.

It seems they had a heads up to let them know we were near. My guess is that the watchtowers allowed them to see us coming from a distance. The welcome issued to us is far grander than one would expect. Even considering that we are a group of royals and nobles visiting as ambassadors. Or that their own crowned prince is escorting us. It's obvious this festival and greeting from the entire of royal family is a display of wealth, as well as one of power and unity. From the moment we stepped into this kingdom, negotiations had begun. Regardless of our shock and adoration, Jameson and I reserve ourselves. We refuse to express the fact that we are both completely enamored by what we're seeing. Along with the king and queen, it seems our restraint also impresses Uncle Rath.

The king clears his throat. "Greetings, heroes of the islands and heads of the grand alliance. You're now known throughout the world as the most powerful to have ever existed. We welcome you to our humble kingdom of Rallem. To my right stands my stunning wife, Gloria. To my left, my brother, who serves as Prime Minister of this land. His name is Jaden, cousin of the great Julius of Alacrium, suitor of their queen, Alexandria. I'm the king, but you all can call me Hubert."

We all give a light bow, out of respect for their positions. None deep enough to warrant anyone believing we are submitting. Then, the king continues, "You must be Lady Josella, or do you prefer Josie?"

I reply, "I much prefer Josie. In truth, my position as a lady no longer exists. My parents disinherited me for running from the engagement so planned by them."

Queen Gloria nods. "I can understand that; it makes some sense. I suppose I was lucky that my unarranged lover was also the king of our lands. Otherwise, my parents would have forced me to marry Lord Somell. He is much elder than I and rather decrepit. Fortunately, my parents couldn't exactly say no when the King of Rallem asked for my hand."

Pastel glances over at me, flushed in the face. I suppose he feels embarrassed as his mother discusses her love life. Jameson gets a bit riled. He must have mistaken the interaction for flirtation. I don't see Pastel that way, though. Honestly, we aren't particularly close. I just found his change in demeanor to be interesting. We're friends and it's nice to see him for the first time interacting with his family. It bothers me that Jameson thinks I'd flirt with Pastel. I'd never say this out loud, not in such an upfront way, but he should know that if I were to choose any man besides Kai or Cal, it would be him without even a second thought.

As we venture inside the palace, Jameson bickers with Pastel. It's like I'm watching two toddlers fussing over their favorite toy. Pastel's parents seem to find their child-like charm entertaining. As I watch them giggle, seeing Pastel and Jameson fussing with one another, I become curious. It's odd to me. I find it so endearing to see Jameson get jealous. I recall feeling a certain since of joy when seeing the antics of Cal. He shares a similar nature of being boy-like. I also recall an attraction to Kai's stoic and more masculine nature. In truth, I have no clue what I find attractive outside of someone actually being Kai or Cal. I don't think I have ever noticed particular traits that draw me in. It's more individualized. Kindness is the sole trait that seems consistent. I doubt I can make a lifelong commitment to someone for no other reason than because they are not a terrible person. If that were the case, I would have likely felt an attraction to Malachi. He is the most kind and fair man I have ever known. Even more so than Kai or Cal; he was pure, regardless of his demonic lineage.

Cal's nature is more selfish, anyway. He was open to self-sacrifice when it was also self-serving. For example, when he followed me into battle and sacrificed his life for mine. The decision, no matter how selfless it may seem to others, was one he made with his own self-interest in mind. The alternative, for him, was guilt, pain, loneliness, and grief. To him, death was by far more preferable to experiencing extreme emotions such as these. He made that choice for one reason. He made the choice that spared him the most pain. With a past such as his, he knew the impact that profound emotional suffering can cause. His death was painless; he knew it would be over in mere moments. A life of suffering compared to a few moments. That was his decision on that day. I suppose it was also Kai's after the fact. Oddly enough, I think that's why I loved them so much. That in-depth understanding of emotion led them to a place where they could love more thoroughly than any other. They loved me and each other with such intensity. It made every weight on my shoulders and every burden I've born for the benefit of others feel like it was worth it.

I don't feel that with Jameson, though. It's different when I'm with him. More... in those moments when I look into his eyes, the world just feels so much less cruel. It doesn't make the burdens feel worth it; it makes the idea of abandoning them feel worth it if it meant I could have him with me always. To possess him in the way I hate to desire. It feels like such a betrayal to Kai and Cal. Yet it's such an undeniable, unquenchable, infuriating need that I cannot shake.

As we make our way through the palace halls, we look well at our surroundings. No one was sure why, but something seems off. Jameson, Rath, and I all take notice of it. Most important, though, is that Pastel does as well. This is his home, so the fact he seemed alarmed by the movements of the palace guard and royal family is odd. It makes it seem that something isn't right. The question that remains is who he would betray now that he knows we're under attack. Us, or his own family. At the moment, none of us feel confident that he's still on our side. We steel ourselves, ensuring that we can defend against him if he attacks. With no magic in Rallem, he's the only one here that can pose an actual threat to us, but if Rallem had fought magic before, it is possible they learned to defend against it. Even without harnessing it themselves. Maybe they have advanced enough technology to do so. Or they sought help in planning their attack. Otherwise, why would they ever think of doing something so reckless?

They attack. I'm completely in the dark about what strategy or power they used. They overwhelm us right away. I awake presumably hours later next to an unconscious Jameson in a cell. It's dark, damp, and cold. As I look around, I see Rath isn't with us. I wonder if it was him. If he had turned his back on us, it would explain how they gained such effective methods to counter us. It's the most probable reason I can think of that he would be out there while we were here. I wonder about Pastel as well; had he also betrayed us? My anger grows deep. I can't yet say that I understand what's happening here, but I know I need to find out. Even if it met that, I would have to bust out of this godforsaken dungeon and demand the answers myself. My determination to get them was undeniable.

I hear footsteps coming down the dark hall of the dungeons. Someone is approaching. I call out, "Who is it? What do you want from us?"

A deep, monotone voice replies, "Oh, Josella, who says we want anything from you? Our attack on you is not personal. It's your connection to the half-demon and this precious little angel of yours that we wish to exploit, not you yourself.

I strain my eyes, attempting to discern whose voice it is. A figure emerges from the shadows in the most ominous of ways. It's Rath. He lets out a vicious laughter before he continues. "You must understand, I will never allow my line to feel the threat of these creatures again. You'll never be safe this way, contained until he's dead. Jameson, angel though he may be, is a creature of darkness, just like the demon. Whether intentional or otherwise, Malachi cannot exist without being a threat and nor can he. I may not have seen eye-to-eye with the angels, but do not be mistaken. This is not prejudice. I just see clearly now. You will never abandon this foolish attachment you have to them, even if your loves return to you. When you look past all the noise, it's not I who sealed Linola's fate. It was the angels and demons that did this to her, and to me, and I will not allow them to do it to you."

Tears rise to my eyes as I hear the hate in his speech. I try to suppress them, but in the end, they fall anyway. I cry out, "Uncle Rath, how could you betray us? How could you betray me? After everything, I expected more."

He shakes his head. "No, Josella, I did." The disappointed and stern tone he uses makes me more repulsed by the venom he spews. "After discovering the blood bond that you missed throughout your life, you chose this. Your decision was to betray me. You would allow harm to befall yourself at the hands of angels and demons after all I gave to protect you from them? It is treachery in its most heart-breaking form."

At that moment, Jameson wakes. He glares, seeing me on one side of the prison's bars, alongside him, and Rath on the other. He immediately realizes that a grave betrayal has taken place. Seeing that Pastel is also missing, he sighs. "Was Pastel with you all along?"

Rath smirks. "No, the young prince lacks the stomach for such plans. His parents were, though. They are pretty sick. You know, they're doing this for petty reasons, unlike me. They disliked the idea of the islands growing stronger through your alliance. They hate magic users and want to be the most powerful kingdom. Thus, they sided with me, hoping they may preserve their pride. They hope to restore what honor they believe themselves to have had. Vengeance is a corrupt idea that I've yet to understand. It's Nubella who helped us plan this. That faked attraction was but a ploy to help me get alone with her. She's from my old sect. I knew it right away when I spotted her. That magic of hers is impressive. She hasn't aged a day. Anyway, she facilitated this for me, not Pastel."

Jameson scowls. "What have you all done with him?" He attempts to summon his strength through the magic of his runic markings. He finds that both his angelic and runic powers somehow are inaccessible. It has to be Rath's doing as well. I assume that my spiritual power was also gone. I hope it's temporary. Whatever he did, I doubt he would leave me unable to defend myself for too long. Besides, Rath is strong, but this has got to be taking a toll on him. The only way he could seal angelic and spiritual power off at the same time is to use his own life force as collateral. Much like what Linola once did to him, but with a different application. He'll die if he holds this for too long. He's too self-involved to offer his own life to reach his goals. Instead, his intentions are to stall for time. What they intend to use that time to do, I can't say. I doubt he would tell us either, provoking us to anger would make his role in this more difficult. Too bad for him, though, his plans will still fail. I am far past the point of anger. The best thing to do is try to break his hold by force. It's a gamble, though. If we manage, it will mean draining his life force completely or bringing it so low that he breaks the seal himself. If we do not, though, we may well waste our own life force and kill ourselves.

I look back at Jameson, hoping he realizes the risks as well. Without his help, I have no chance of pulling this off. The decision is his to make, though. I will never take that from him.

Jameson's eyes gleam with adoration and pride as he nods. "If I'm to die, I will die alongside the woman I love in battle, as Cal once did."

I smile and take his hand. Fear takes a back seat as the joy of feeling his touch once more took over. Whispering to one another, we finally admit the emotions that had been brewing between us. "For all the love I carried for them, I cannot deny that since they passed, you have come the closest to filling the void. It's through your efforts to see my heart restored that you became the love I never expected. I wish for you to know this: That love has not diminished the love I felt for Kai and Cal. It hasn't been less than that which I felt for them either, though. It is equal, in every way imaginable. I love you, too, Jameson."

He looks completely at peace, hearing my words. Opposite to Jameson, Rath seems much angrier after hearing them. All three of us push. The overwhelming force of our deadlock colliding causes the entire palace to tremble. We each understand that such a force may well bring down this historic building. It could kill all that walk through the halls. In that moment, we all chose ourselves and our own desires over the other people.

Once upon a time, I found myself willing to sacrifice my own well-being for the safety of those around us. Now, though, I am not the same pure-hearted girl whose sole desire is to change the world. The pain brought by love has forever tainted my soul; a pain I refuse to let go of for as long as I can breathe.

As the surrounding walls crumble under the pressure, my gaze remains fixed on Jameson. In the back of my mind, a subconscious thought arises, one that I had pushed down for quite some time. In that moment, the words seem to slip from my tongue as if it were the only natural thing to say. "I should have died with them, as Kai did for Cal. I should have joined them in the spirit realm."

Both Jameson and Rath freeze. Their respective powers come to a screeching halt as they realize how I felt. It's not what either of them wanted to hear. Jameson speaks with softness, taking great care to say the right thing. "You spoke to them, didn't you? In the Spirit Realm. I remember it was before we left for Rallem. You knew them best, right? Then, you tell me, how could you believe that either of those men wanted you to die alongside them? You, my love, are the part of them still free to walk this realm. You are to live the life that the three of you should have shared. It is selfish to believe that you should abandon that to ease your own pain."

Rath growls. "Hate to say it, but the angel has a point there. Niece, we may not agree on much, but have you even stopped to contemplate the pain you would leave behind? Do you wish to put Jameson, me, Lilly, Johanna, and Malachi through what you are going through? How is that fair?"

I snarl, the sound of Rath's voice destroying my moment of sadness and replacing it with rage. "Whatever, Jameson, let us finish this. We can talk later."

As I reach once more for Jameson's hand, and he reaches for mine. When our hands meet, we push once more. This time it felt different, though. My power, along with Rath's, is being dwarfed by Jameson's. It's humongous. Hearing me say what I did must have pushed him in ways I didn't think it would. I shudder at the mere sight of the pure energy that surrounds me as I nestle myself deeper into his embrace. Then it all ends. The palace walls finally reach their limit, as did Rath. I watch him collapse as the building crumbles down around us. I look at Jameson for a moment, hoping that he would allow me time to save Rath. He nods, though I knew it was little more than half-hearted.

I use my power to levitate Raths unconscious body behind us as we flee the building. I notice something quite off. Jameson isn't behaving as his usual self. His movements are distinct, more fluid and gracious. There's no sign of hesitation or insecurity. In that moment, he's not the young prince I had met so long ago whose jealousy of Malachi had overtaken his heart. Instead, he's the angel some part of me had been yearning to meet. The elegance, confidence, and purity visible in him are radiant. Even more radiant than all the light of the universe. If it all collided, the brilliant flash in the moments before the world met its end would seem dim. Dim compared to his light, at least. The sight of it is so entrancing that I can no longer deny I long for his touch. It's as if both his physical and spiritual presence have consumed me. It forces yet another truth that I had choked down to the surface once more. I have craved him ever since the time we spent together in Loft. Yet I had denied myself the pleasure of knowing him in such an intimate manner. Out of loyalty to the long-departed Kai and Cal, yes. Also, out of fear of what those around me might think and how it would affect the alliance of the islands.

As we run, crumbling chunks of brick fall all around us. I reach out to cling to him. Without ever looking, he reaches back, grabbing my wrist on instinct. He must have sensed my desire to feel him. Once clear of the palace, we stand as if we're attached to each other, waiting to see if any others emerge. For several minutes, there's nothing but silence. As we are about to give in and assume there were no other survivors, we see a shadow emerge from the smoke and dust. We wait for the dark silhouette to become clear to us, our breath stolen from our chests. We prayed to our gods for Pastel's survival. One can imagine our relief as the dust settles once more. We see Pastel, along with his parents, emerging from the ashes. They're like phoenixes rising as if it's a most natural thing to do. The gasps of air, of relief, fill our lungs as we run to him, overwhelmed with joy. As we approach, he laughs, calling out, "Jeez, guys.

You couldn't have waited for me to talk to my parents; you had to go blow the whole place down?"

We laugh in return. Then, we offer sincere apologies to him for the lives lost, though it didn't seem to bother him much. He understands that killing wasn't our goal, but an unfortunate side-effect of the circumstances. After all that, we got settled; we knew it was time to talk. We need to figure out what comes next. Unfortunately, we wouldn't have much time to plan. Rath awakes sooner than expected, unphased by what insignificant damage he took. He launches an immediate counter-attack on us. Of course, his allies, Pastels parents, join him. Until he made a mistake. As the purple aura of his spiritual power continues to expand, his attacks become fiercer. It's clear he won't hesitate to destroy Rallem in his quest. He'll pay any price to destroy the angels, demons, and all who descend from them. I realize that the king and queen are growing scared. They sought to make their kingdom more powerful for its protection, not to light the fuse that would lead to its ruin. Rath is crossing a line, and they don't intend to allow him to do it. Knowing we would need more help to defeat him, I resort to provoking him. If I could make him say that he would destroy this kingdom, they would switch sides.

I called out as I dodge another immense blast of his energy. I look over at Jameson and realize that we were both completely exhausted. "Rath, please, stop. You will destroy this entire land if you continue. We should settle this elsewhere!"

He chuckles. "Oh, dear niece. Do you believe me to care about such a thing as this kingdom? We will settle this here and now; those who die are too weak, undeserving of life anyway."

The eyes of the king and queen are wide as fear strikes the deepest crevices of their hearts. Though that fear develops into determination in mere moments. They turn to the remaining forces and guards, saying, "I want every fighter in this kingdom. We are, as of now, on a war-footing. Your orders are to assist my son and his friends in any way they ask. Your end-goal is bringing us that madman's head on a platter. Now, move!"

CHAPTER

Twelve

JAMESON

I have to protect her. That is my only thought as the moments pass and a massive attack force gathers. We have the numbers, but I'm not sure that it will do us any good. First, it is the guards following the orders passed down by their rulers. Then it's the people; drawn by the fall of the palace. Untrained commoners who still seek to defend their rulers and their land. There's honor in their actions, but honor doesn't spare lives in battle. Tears come to Pastels eyes as he hears their words, "Don't worry, Prince, we've got your back!" and "We won't let this freak destroy us!" It brings boundless joy to Pastel's heart to know that his people have grown to love him. They feel assured that he will be a suitable ruler, as well as a leader, to follow into battle. It's the realization that the crown belongs to his parents, but the people are following him. His parents see this too. They await the battle with anxious hearts. As they do, it settles into their feeble minds that many of their decisions as of late have hurt their people. In this new day, they thought, a new leader could better understand the plight of the common man and woman. The traditional ways have expired, having long outlived their usefulness. In this new generation, a more global outlook is necessary, and it's their son that has the vision to bring this about. He has pursued peace and alliance. Meanwhile, they have led their people into danger. By aligning themselves with a war criminal, they have led their people to the brink. I hope that one day, when I sit upon my father's throne, I'll receive the same admiration from my people as he is by his. Like my cousin, too, 'king' wasn't just a title he has. It's a state of being.

This field of beauty that will soon be a field of bloodshed floods with philosophical thought. It seems the moments before the battle are more like decades, or even centuries. Everyone knows that the consequences of this fight will affect generations. They hold an unimaginable determination to succeed in their conquest. If for no other reason, to ensure the futures of their children, grandchildren, and so on. In this suffocating, unfathomable intensity, the first moves in the battle took place. It's at that moment that I finally come to understand the warnings given to me by Rettferd. I wonder if Josie and I will bring about another great war. I can't say it matters if we do. Come Niflheim or Ragnarök, I'll follow this woman 'til the end. The probability of this being that end seems to rise with each passing second. Yet I remain unable, or unwilling, to alter my course.

Rath reveals the true extent of his unparalleled strength during his first attack. He hurls a mass of energy so large that it devastates our forces. Seventy-five percent exterminated in a matter of seconds. Our best hope is to force him into a retreat, for victory wouldn't be possible on this day. Only at our full strength would we stand even the slightest of chances. We don't even have a full team. The smug look, now plastered across Rath's face, made obvious he wouldn't hold back in the slightest. He intends to kill all that are present. I can't tell if Josie is even an exception anymore.

Knowing that his next attack may well kill the rest of our allies, it's up to the three of us to protect them. This battle has become one that will decide if the Rallian people would survive. We need to produce a plan without delay. That's easier said than done, though. The three of us have never been in a proper battle together before. We hardly understand each other's ability. Pastel has no magic and I'm trying to grasp his angelic power; Josie is our only hope. As I look at her, she says the one thing that ensures I won't let her carry this burden alone. "If you guys give me up, he may lose interest in attacking."

"No," It comes from a place within me I hadn't realized existed. I feel a violent thrashing within me that steals my ability to breathe. "No, Josie. Never say something that ridiculous again. We can do this; we need nothing more than to figure out how."

"But..." she begins, but Pastel interrupts, "I have a plan for a combination attack, guys. You must trust me, and we will have to move with haste. There is no time to explain, so you will do as I tell you without question."

Withholding my reply is my best course when the pulsating urge to kill him for trying to order Josie and me about rises. I wait to see her response first. I will put my faith in Pastel if she does. Thus, with her response, we agree. The three of us try our best to dodge and defend against Rath's relentless attacks. We do so while Pastel tries to relay the instructions. Once we all understand our respective roles, we make our move. I will function as our decoy, launching a head-on attack. Since Rath believes I'm the threat, his priority is killing me. I'll make for a perfect decoy; Pastel didn't have to explain that much. He won't suspect my attack to be part of a strategy because I'll make it seem emotional. Rage driven. He'll believe it to be a random attack, lacking in both wit and a strategy. Pastel follows up, attacking him from behind after I make my move. With Raths heightened instincts, he can defend against this attack with relative ease. Although it is unlikely that he predicts it. Alas, Josie attacks using her light spears formed from spiritual energy. I infuse as many as possible with angelic power as they descend upon Rath. It should render him incapable of defending himself further if we're lucky. To be sure, we release a barrage of attacks in his direction. We can't see him anymore because too much dust and debris has kicked up, but we know enough to have a general direction. I doubt we can do enough to do actual harm to him. It might be enough to make him think twice about continuing his attack on Rallem, though.

Taking a deep breath, I hurl myself into the dust cloud and towards Rath. I decide on an uncontrolled, massive attack. I *need* to kill him. First, I make sure that the ball of angelic power is large enough that his only choice will be to counter it, if he can. Dodging is out of the question. Once Rath gets preoccupied with my attack, Pastel goes in from behind. He uses the powerful energy stored within his magic sword to sharpen its blade as he lunges forward. Rath does the only thing he could. He turns one arm towards Pastel, and away from my attack. This means he's defending with a maximum of half his strength on either side. He can't possibly come out completely unscathed while doing that.

It's up to Josie now; Pastel and I have no choice but to believe in her. What seems like an eternity passes as we wait to see if she succeeds. Although it's but a few seconds. We need to see that Josie had retreated to safety before attacking Rath once more. You can imagine how our faces lit up when she gives us the signal. The three of us will now attack at full force. What I have not yet said to my allies is that I intend to attack in a way that I never have before. Rather than a blast of angelic power or controlled water, this attack is more targeted. It's a single, linear shot containing a concentrated angelic power. It mirrors Josie's light spear but is much more potent because it comes from an angel. She's engraved herself into my soul so deeply that my fighting style reflects hers to some extent. My new, most destructive attack is all about her. It's so packed full that it consumes all the energy I have left. I watch her and Pastel move in once again. Then, as they release their attacks, I point my finger, aiming it at Rath's heart, and take my shot. The collision of our three energies met in the exact spot where Rath sits. It causes an explosion that would have killed those who stand behind us if we didn't defend them.

I hurry to put up a pathetic, rushed barrier, using what remnants of power still linger in my veins. Josie assists me. As exhausted as she is, though, we can do nothing but hope that it would weaken the explosions' impact. We want to save at least some people. Though, our efforts are for naught. The explosion takes our barrier out. It obliterates over twenty percent of our remaining troops, leaving all but ten percent of our original numbers. The three of us look around to see so many of our allies dead or dying. I clench my teeth at the abhorrent sight. How could we have let this happen? If we could get him to retreat, we would have time to gather our strength. We could call in reinforcements from the islands. Alone, though, this task seems impossible. As Rath stands up, we know we are out of moves. Josie whispers to herself, "I'm coming, my loves..."

I hear it even through the sounds of battle. She intends to seal him, like Linola did. Step by step she draws closer, observing to see if we damaged him enough to cause some clear weakness for her to exploit. What she sees is something unthinkable. With all of our power, we attack this man, yet he stands strong, nearly unscathed. A few scratches to show for our efforts. We have completely failed. Knowing that I'm short on power at the moment, I resort to pleading with her to stop. I can't bear to lose her. As she sacrifices her soul as collateral to the spirits. They grant her the strength she needs to follow through on this in return. It allows her to draw on the strength necessary to rid this world of her line for good. It might ensure that this world would have a future, even if she can't be here to see it. I couldn't let it happen, though. Rushing towards her, I take off, so desperate to stop her I'd do anything. She doesn't deserve to end this way. I know her strength, her beauty, her heart, her soul. "I will not lose you!"

With one arm, she creates a barrier around Rath to ensure that he can't escape, but also to keep me out. That's when he realizes she's trying to seal him. With her free hand, she reaches deep within his chest, searching for the wretched soul that she hopes to drag with her to the spirit realm. Inch-by-inch, it comes free from the body to which it only exists when tethered to. Then, the portal appears, consuming it, and her, bit by bit. I feel the air leaving my lungs and the life draining from my body as I watch her slowly die. She struggles to tear his soul out. It's nearly imperceptible, but her resolve weakens momentarily when she hears Pastel and me screaming for her to stop. A single tear rolls down her cheek, though she doesn't turn to look at us. She's trying to maintain her focus. Even more, she probably doesn't wish for us to see the insufferable pain that she's being put through. She draws what she thinks will be her last breaths in this realm.

Then, at the last possible moment, Rath finds the strength to fight back. He recalls his soul back into its body and stuttered. "I-I won't l-let y-you die..." his consciousness is returning, "and I won't let you kill me."

Her grip weakens in her shock. She gets thrown to the ground, exasperated, as he frees himself from her grasp. He's tired too, though. I can see it. That must have taken a lot out of him because he looks weakened. Very weakened. Fortunately, she failed, but it still took all he had to stop her. He won't fight any more today. She had succeeded in that way, at least for the time being. She falls unconscious. The last thing I remember hearing before I slam through the broken barrier and rush her to get medical attention is Rath's parting words. "Take care of her," he orders, "and we will meet again soon."

LILLY

"Ah, alas, my dear Alacrium, I've come home to you!" Myrkr rejoices as we approach the fortified entrance to the kingdom.

The guards posted at the gate met our group with suspicion, as expected. Myrkr chuckles, "Has it been so long, boys? Do you not recognize me? I am the great demon king, father to Queen Alexandria Spade of Alacrium, and you will let us pass."

The guards shutter out of intimidation as they reply. "We know, sir, and apologize for any offense we may have caused. Our queen has ordered that you and your party not enter the kingdom."

Myrkr sighs, "Did she offer any reason on why that is?"

"We are not in a position to question our queens' orders, sir. She scares us."

"Ugh, fine. We will do this the hard way, then."

He clears his throat as he summons his demonic aura. His eyes turn the same red as Malachi's have on so many occasions before. Although, his aura is much larger. It's he who has the power to destroy the entirety of not this kingdom alone, but this region, if he so chooses. All but Rettferd tremble the moment they feel his true presence. It leaves us wondering how he hid it so well until now. One thing becomes clear though, when he attacked before, he held back more than we realized. He was being honest when he said he wasn't trying to kill us. I know that now because he wouldn't even have to try, he just would, period. His goal was to assess our strength; we had yet to see his true power.

Rettferd smirks. "I forgot how much of a brute he is. You see, our master, or... mine, anyway, made him first. He may have been a little overzealous in his creation of Myrkr. Far more than even I, the head of the angels, his power is most unthinkable. If I had to guess, he is the lone being to have ever existed that could fight master and live to tell the tale. I used to admire him so much. Now, there's nothing. Nothing but the same paralyzing fear the rest of you feel when faced with his exceptional, but terrifying, power."

It seems his daughter, the queen, felt his presence, too. Realizing that he wouldn't take no as an answer, she descends from the palace. It floats above the mountain's peak and hidden by the cloud bank, much like the islands. As she approaches the gate, the clouds drift apart so ominously that it sends a chill down my spine. It's almost as if she's descending from the heavens. She leaps downward and uses her wings to guide her towards the gate. She lands and starts throwing blades of demonic power at Myrkr to let him know she would fight him here. Her intent to kill is abundant. The rest of us move to the side, attempting to evade her vicious attacks. Myrkr doesn't seem at all phased in the slightest. He smacks the powerful blades out of the air with ease and approaches her with a stern look on his face. Once they stand face-to-face and Alexandria realizes how powerless she is. She snarls and agrees to let us enter the kingdom, saying she will hear us out. None of us quite understand the purpose of her failed attack. Or what they communicated between them during it. Whatever it is, it seems to have changed her behavior, at least for now, anyway. She becomes friendly and warm as she guides us on foot through the kingdom.

It's not at all what you would expect from a kingdom of demons. It's rather peaceful, and the citizens seem to be cheerful. Many of them greet her with smiles as she passes by, and she's careful to acknowledge them all. Her presence has the aura of a true ruler. In fact, it reminds Malachi a lot of the way he and his people interacted. He must wonder if he behaved more like a demon than he thought. I'm sure he even questions if that's such a terrible thing. The methods of ruling typical of the demons are ones that lead to joyful and pros-perous kingdoms. They are sanctuaries for the people. Meanwhile, many human rulers have historically cho-sen greed and stature over the well-being of those they lead.

Entering the halls of the palace, Alexandria takes a moment to welcome us to her home. She sighs. "Malachi, right?" as she glances over at him. He nods in reply. "We are relatives, are we not? Please take no of-fense to my desire to keep you all out. You have always been and will always be welcome here. It's Rettferd and my father that I wished to keep away from this place."

Malachi smiles. "More than you might think. I under-stand why you would wish for such a thing."

"Ah, yes, you too are a ruler. The great nation of Tendu and their revered king. Malachi, whose name echoes throughout the continent. Where is your wife, out of curiosity? I was hoping to meet the warrior queen who stood alongside you as you pursued your birthright."

"Johanna stayed at home this time around. Her wis-dom is most needed at home, by both our kingdom and our child."

Alexandria hesitates. "Yes, I suppose that even in one such as her, the instincts of a human mother supersede those of a warrior. They suppress her longing for battle and freedom."

As she finishes speaking, we enter her great hall. Here her advisors stand, prepared to greet us. She introduces them. "I am unsure how much you all know of this land and our ways, so allow me to explain as I introduce you to everyone. First, this is Julius. He is my butler and closest advisor. He knows me best and is the most influential person in Alacrium besides myself. We have been friends since childhood. He is from the noble fox demon clan."

Julius bows. "Thank you, my queen, for that marvelous introduction. As for our other guests, I must apologize for the state of the palace. We had little time to prepare for your arrival."

I'm the first to answer him. "It is no problem. We have traveled far and ended up sleeping outdoors most nights. I am quite confident that anything you have prepared will be much more comfortable."

Alexandria looks at me. Her curiosity about my power as a priestess is palpable. Then she continues. "Next, we have my general, Mari. In her combat and strategic ability, none can match her. She is the daughter of my mother, my half-sister, and likely my equal in every way except for royal lineage."

Mari bows. "You are too kind, my queen. I am hardly your equal in anything, to be truthful. I must warn our guests though, if you come to bring trouble to this land, I will destroy you all. Unfortunately, Myrkr, Rettferd, that warning applies even more so to the two of you."

Rettferd scowls. Myrkr scratches his head. A failed attempt to cope with the awkwardness. Then, mutters, "She's definitely Olivina's daughter, that's for sure."

Rettferd whispers back, "You are not kidding. That woman scared the hell out of me even before she killed her husband to follow you to Niflheim."

Myrkr recalls her and reminisces about their time together. He thinks to himself about how angry and hurt he was after losing Linola. Olivina was the one to bring him solace after that time. He may not have ever been in love with her, but he loved her, and the memory of her brought him great sadness. Towards the end of the great war, there was a massive ambush on a camp that was being led by Olivina. The purifying light of the angels left no survivors. She died fighting tooth and nail. Ever since, Alacrium has remembered her as a great hero. It's for that reason that Myrkr left the kingdom in the hands of her daughters. Although, one of whom was born of her first husband. It was a decision that he knew the people would accept.

Alexandria takes notice of his pain but continues her introductions, anyway. "Next, we have my economic advisor, Maxwell, of the shapeshifter clan. Shapeshifters are best known for their skill in intelligence work and academia."

Maxwell bows but doesn't speak. Alexandria continues once more. "Finally, we have Alathoth, from a distinct branch of the noble fox demons. He serves as both the head of foreign and domestic affairs. We isolate ourselves from other kingdoms, so it's unnecessary to have separate advisors for the two. Besides, he is capable. It is thanks to Julius and him. I have been able to turn

Alacrium into what it is today because of them. Now that the introductions are through, you must rest and recover from your journey? Or would you prefer to get straight down to business and tell us why you have come here?"

I clear my throat. "Your majesty, while we look forward to a chance to rest, as well as to better get to know Alacrium and its people. Our reason for coming here is quite urgent. This time sensitive matter is best heard as soon as possible."

Alexandria nods. "So be it then," as she sits on her throne with her advisors aligned on either side of her. "Tell me about this urgent matter you speak of."

Fourteen

JAMESON

———————

"Josie!" I cry, "Josie, please wake up!" I continue to sob. Pastel and his parents stand behind me in a quiet storm of pain, anger, and sadness. Pastel watches me as I lay beside Josie's unconscious body. His gaze turns to his parents. He becomes irate, losing control of his rage as he addresses them. He grabs his father by the collar of his shirt and berates him. "If she dies, I will kill you both. Your deaths will be public and cruel. It will be a proclamation to our people that I intend to rule with justice. Those responsible for her death will face punishment. No matter what their station or wealth amounts to."

As his parents' protest, I turn to them as well, tears still streaming down my face. "Make no mistake, if you keep running your mouths, I will kill you long before he ever gets the chance. Now leave this place so she might rest in peace!"

The king and queen walk away. Their regret radiates throughout Rallem as it becomes clear this is the end of their reign. Later that day, they made a public announcement to renounce their claim on the throne. With the people's unequivocal support, Pastel ascends to it. He wouldn't have a crown until his coronation, set to be held many months later. Still, he holds all the power of a king within minutes. With a fight on the horizon, there's no time to waste on extravagant ceremonies and formalities. What Rallem needs now is a powerful leader. Besides being the natural heir, Pastel is best prepared to fight alongside them. They have to preserve what shreds remain of their once glorious kingdom.

A few days later, she's still unconscious. Pastel and I take it upon ourselves to plan. First, I reach out to the islands via letter to Oceanica. I wrote,

Father,

Please excuse the lack of formality written in this letter. I have an urgent message that I must convey. Since the start of our journey, events have been unfolding. A great war like the one fought by our forbearers is brewing. I have spoken to the angel Rettferd, as well as our allies, and it has become clear that this fate is inevitable. I ask that you read this and help us prepare for this dim future that will soon come to pass.

The Lady Josella, as you know, descended from the great priestess who brought the first war to an end. What we did not know was that she did so by sealing away her own brother, who has now become free once more. He seeks to reignite the war and exterminate all lineages which threaten his own. Meaning both angels and demons are to come under attack. This puts both Oceanica and Tendu at considerable risk. He is no ordinary foe. He is one with enough strength and willpower to render Josie unconscious. She is fighting for her life. Even with my increased mastery of angelic power, we failed to stop him. The result is the near destruction of our friends in Rallem. I believe he will not be our sole foe in the battle to come. Reports from Malachi, who is now in Alacrium, state that Myrkr and Rettferd may seek to destroy us.

You must send word to Tendu and the other islands asking that they, too, prepare to fight. Also, I ask that the ruling class also prepare for battle. You, Johanna, and the Chief will all be important powers if we wish to defeat this foe. I pray it will be enough, father, but I hold my doubts about it. I love you and hope to hear from you soon.

Your son,

Jameson.

I send the letter via magical means. It's a little-known fact, but most magic users can pass messages to their home kingdom simply by applying the intention to their runic magic. It isn't long before I get word back. My father's reply is reassuring. He tells us that most of the allied kingdoms of the islands are already preparing for battle. He mentions, however, that Johanna is refusing to prepare Tendu. I figured she'd give us the most trouble. That stubborn woman is probably still angry about how she and Josie parted ways. The only one who can force her to cooperate is Malachi himself. Luckily, with us in Rallem, it's easy to contact him as well. I do just that. He'll redirect Johanna with relative ease.

With her cooperation, I know we'll have the full support of the alliance. This allows me to spend my time tending to Josie. I spend day and night at her bedside, pleading with her to come back to me. I hadn't realized it at first, but those pleas are a magic of sorts. The more I want it, the more my angelic power reacts to my desire. I wonder if it is trying to help me figure out how to heal her. I toy with it for a while, using great caution so as not to cause further harm to Josie. Eventually, I find the trick to help her. It's a slow process and it will still take some time, but it does something, and that's what matters right now.

If asked, I'd have to call it spirit mending. It's like sewing, but with angelic power and a soul, rather than a needle and cloth. It requires great precision and near perfect control of the energy. I can sustain doing it for around thirty minutes at my current level. It's far too tedious to do for any prolonged period without putting her at risk. So, I mend her soul in thirty-minute increments over several days.

"No matter what, I will save you, Josie." I whisper, then kiss her forehead.

"Your love for her is true, yes?" Pastel's voice rings from behind me.

I turn to look at him. "With everything I am, and everything I ever will be, is how I love this woman."

"I see that. She's lucky to have you."

I shake my head. "No, I am lucky she allows me to love her."

"Why do you think that?"

"Because loving her is my physics, biology, psychology, philosophy, and religion. What would remain of me if she didn't?"

Pastel's eyes widen. "I see. Then, yes. I suppose you are incredibly lucky. I can't think of a better woman for you to base your existence around. She's something else."

I snarl. "That something else is *mine.*"

He chuckles. "Yeah, I hear you. No worries, man. I didn't mean it like that."

I settle down some yet still position myself between her and his line of sight. "Good."

He shakes his head. "I'll leave you to it, then." He pauses and looks back. "Oh, and Jameson, you really should get out of this room. You need food, drink, a shower, and rest. You're losing weight and there are bags under your eyes. She wouldn't want you to kill yourself worrying about her."

I nod, and then he's gone. He has a point about me taking care of myself. Besides, at this rate, I'll make a mistake during the soul mending. I'll go for a while, take a brief break. The nurses can watch over her while I rest.

LILLY

M alachi, having explained the situation to Alexandria, paced. His anxiety overtakes him in a guest chamber of her palace as he awaits an answer. I pace alongside him and Rettferd sits in a corner, concerned about Myrkr's effect on these deliberations. It's unclear whether he intends to speak for or against our cause. Although his daughter rules, his people still think of him as their one true king. Not even Alexandria can oppose him. It's likely they will do whatever he orders them to do. To him, the title of king is unnecessary because he holds the unyielding power of one. We can only hope that he speaks in our favor.

Sometime later, we receive a summoning to the throne room. There, Alexandria waits for us with none but Julius at her side. "We will help you access the gate to free your friends of death in the spirit realm. We'll even help you fight Rath. Based on the readings of energy I've been picking up from the direction of Rallem, you'll need as much help as you can get. I ask that you understand one thing, though: we are not allies. We share an interest in accomplishing this. There will come a time when we are no longer on the same side. Are we clear?"

Malachi nods. "We understand. Thank you for assisting us in the meantime, though. For the warning that this is a temporary arrangement, too. Rettferd here gave us a similar warning. For now, I will await word from my friends in Rallem."

Alexandria agrees. "Yes, please explore, socialize, and get to know our kingdom in the meantime. It would be good for you, Malachi. There is a lot of history here. You can learn a lot about our family and our people."

"Sounds good," Malachi answers, "let's get to it, Lil, come on!"

Together, we wander about the unfamiliar palace. We don't seek enjoyment from it. Although, we find ourselves interested in many of the grand artworks. The unique cultural pieces that we see are interesting. When we stumble across a library, we grow even more intrigued. It's unlike any library we've ever seen. Possessed with great demonic magic, this library has enchantments. It delivers to its visitors the answers they need most, even if they don't seek such answers. To Malachi, it brings a book detailing the start of demon-kind and the events of the first great war. To me, it brings a book of future events as foretold by the great prophets of history.

Both of us read these books and learn much about ourselves. Malachi tells me later that day, "They all loved her, you know? None of them ever meant for it to go as far as it did. They wanted to protect her. It all started with Myrkr. He had fallen in love with a mysterious woman that he encountered wandering by the lake. They had spoken for a brief time, but that fleeting moment was all that he needed. He was sure of his feelings for her."

I sit and listen to the story, interested to know how they ended up in this situation. What Malachi told me was something I never expected. After meeting Linola, Myrkr rushed home to tell his master about the human woman who captured his heart. It was he who fell for her first. He needed to get permission to court the human woman. Linola had yet to gain her power as a priestess. Rath, her elder brother, already had his, though. Rejoiced by the news that Myrkr cared so much for a human, his master granted his blessing. Rettferd failed to see how such a normal human woman could have seduced Myrkr. His brother was brilliant and powerful. To him, they stood above the humans for a reason. Rather than arguing with Rettferd, Myrkr decided it was best to introduce him to Linola so that he might see her light for himself. Together, they traveled back down to the mortal realm. There, they sought a second meeting with Linola. This time, Rath joined her as well. He had concerns about her safety and wanted to make sure that Myrkr meant no harm.

For a time, everything was fine between the four of them. Rath came to trust Myrkr and Rettferd, and Rettferd became enamored with Linola, just as his brother had. Her relationship with each of them was quite different, though. With her brother, she was quiet, reserved, and usually let him take the lead in their interactions. When with Myrkr, she was more free-spirited and jovial, as if she had not a care in the world. With Rettferd, she grew bold and argumentative. They would talk forever about humanity. They explored the differences between humans and heavenly beings. The conversations were passionate and often ended in arguments, but neither of them could get enough of it. As they became closer, Myrkr came to notice that there was a tension between them. One that seemed to imply his younger brother had fallen for the same woman he did. He went to Linola, frustrated by her relationship with Rettferd, and asked that she not see him again. Surprised by her blunt refusal, he inquired about her feelings for him. Unable to lie to a man that she cared for, she told him, "I have fallen for your brother. It is neither less nor more than I have fallen for you. My heart will not choose one over the other. This is something Rettferd has noticed in recent days. It is one he believes himself capable of accepting. Do you feel the same, my dearest Myrkr?"

Myrkr became outraged, seeing how fallible humans actually were. He saw these lesser beings would fall in love with the presence of any being of his status. Thus, in his anger, he took flight. He did so without paying mind to how near Linola was. As his large and powerful wing hit her, she went flying. In a panic, Myrkr fled the scene and was missing for quite some time after that. About an hour later, Rettferd came down searching for his precious Linola and found Rath by her body. Rath was distraught at the sight of his beloved little sister bleeding from the head. Sensing Rettferd's presence, he shot him an intense glare and says, "This is your brother's doing! He will die for this! Why don't you high and mighty freaks stay away from my sister? Dammit!"

Rath's heart became poisoned by the trauma. Rettferd hesitated to approach, not wanting to send him overboard. Still, he wanted to help Linola. So, he asks in a soft voice, "Can I approach? I know it looks rather bleak right now, but I can help her if you give me the opportunity."

Rath nodded. But he watched Rettferd's actions with great focus. Rath growled in suspicion as Rettferd funneled his power into Linola's dying body. Having the divine protection of a priestess, the impact of her injuries would lessen. This allowed her body to heal much easier. A few days later, she was back on her feet and seemed as good as new. Rath tried to help her master her new power. He insisted that she not see Rettferd or Myrkr again. Linola, not wanting to defy her elder brother or give up either of the men, tried to figure a way to make this work. Rath saw this refusal as treachery... as betrayal. Thus, from that day forward, he gathered support from his followers. He was raising an army. That army tasked to rid this world of those heavenly beings. They posed such a threat to his line and any other they took an interest in.

Days later, a tracker pinned down Myrkr's location. The regret of what he had done to Linola had caused his better judgement to erode. He had fallen into depravity. Because of his overwhelming strength, no one that got assigned to retrieve him returned alive. A week after killing the last agent, he returned home of his own accord. There, he swayed some of the other lower-ranking angels to his cause. He sought to end all the angels, as well as his master, believing it would rid the world of those with the power to seduce the woman he loved and steal her away from him. Rettferd, of course, would not hear of such a thing. He tried to explain to Myrkr that Linola loved them not because they were angels, but because of who they were. She loved them because she saw how they made her a better version of herself. Myrkr refused to see this truth, though. All he felt was the sting of the betrayal conducted by both Linola and Rettferd. With that, war was brewing, and no one had the power to stop it any longer.

Soon after, the fighting began, bringing substantial loss to all sides. Months passed, there was no sign of a peace blossoming. Rath continued his relentless assault on angels and demons, and it looks as if he will win. Linola saw this and decided that her brother had gone too far. She would stop him, even if it meant she had to end her brother's life with her own hands. During battle, he held her in a nearby camp and insisted that she remain under guard. Once she resolved herself, though, those guards failed to serve their purpose. One day, overhearing her brother's plans to devastate the other two armies, she knew it was time to act. She attacked her guards that day and headed off to the field of battle. When she arrived, she stood in the center of the field, where she stands in clear view of all three commanders. Rettferd and Myrkr halted their troops so as not to hurt their beloved Linola. Rath saw this as an opportunity to attack at full force while the angels and demons held back. He came for them, but Linola was not about to let him succeed.

She gave her soul as collateral to bring her brother to justice. Her power surrounded him, bonded him, and dragged him inch-by-inch, down into the spirit realm. The other armies watched, knowing that they are powerless to stop her. It took a full hour for her seal to be complete, at which time Rettferd and Myrkr both rushed to her side. As she lay dying, they wept, apologizing to her for the pain they had caused. In her last moments, she looked into the eyes of the men she had loved. She pleaded with them to allow the peace she had given her life for to blossom and thrive. They agreed, and since that day, her peace had stood. Neither the angels nor demons sought to battle each other anymore. Instead, they turned their attentions toward rebuilding. They each ensured their respective people could thrive. Still, the resentment between them never diminished. One thing had always been clear: the war that they postponed for her sake would restart one day. No matter what that meant for any party. It was as if this peace had been an extended mourning period.

Neither angels nor demons could die from natural causes, they are almost immortal. Short of dying at the hands of each other, or a priest. Thus, from their perspective of time, her death is still recent. It remains fresh in their hearts. It seems now, though, to me and Malachi, that the war between them is brewing once more. With Rath's reappearance, both parties are on edge. We could only hope that we would succeed and put an end to this before any major losses occurred.

As the next few days passed, we continued to get to know the Alacrians and their history. Malachi had even found a sense of family among them. I focused on observing and gathering information. This allowed me to notice that Rettferd and Myrkr had both been rather quiet since their arrival. I wondered what thoughts plagued the minds of such men. I wandered to Rettferd's chamber one day to ask him. On my way, I encountered a strange-looking crystal. I felt drawn to it and no matter how hard I tried to stop myself, I could not help but touch it. At the moment my fingers grazed the crystal, I had a premonition. The details of which I thought best to keep to myself for the time being.

CHAPTER
Sixteen

JOSIE

———————

I've finally come to and seem to have regained my health. Overcome with relief, Pastel and Jameson hold a small celebratory feast in my honor. The people are more than willing to assist them with it after witnessing my actions during the fight. They think I'm heroic. During the festivities, I ask Jameson if he will join me for a walk tonight. I wish to speak with him about something that has been on my mind since before the fight. Of course, he agrees, and that night we rendezvous at the site of the fallen palace. As we walk through the rubble, looking up at the beauty of the night sky, I say to him, "Jameson, for a long time now you have cared for me. You have told me so more times than I can count. It's unfair of me to refuse to convey my feelings toward you. Even if Kai and Cal came back, I find it unlikely that these feelings would change. The reason that I haven't is that I'm not sure that my feelings for you would matter if they came back. So, I've decided it's best to leave the decision up to you. Do you want to know the truth of it, even knowing that you may end up hurt when this is all over?"

Jameson smiles and shakes his head. "You're wrong, Josie. It doesn't matter what happens with Kai and Cal, or how much I end up hurt. There is no version of this world where your feelings about anything become irrelevant to me. I want to know more than anything. Even if we could never be together, knowing that you long for me would bring me the strength to carry on. So, please, tell me."

I cry upon hearing his plea. It's as if his words reach down into my soul and drag my feelings out, transforming them into words that rush from me like waters from behind an annihilated dam. "I love you, Jameson. I've loved you for a long time. When we got closer to one another, things got more intense. But, in truth, my longing for you has gone on for much more time than that. In Oceanica, when we first met, you doted on me and treated me as a lady. I had never felt like royalty before, even growing up as a duchess. I had always felt powerless, small, and overlooked. It was you who made my nobility seem as if it could make me the most powerful and beautiful creature in any room. It was you who made me stop seeing my lineage as a plague. I must admit, I am drawn to the same qualities in you. Your heritage as a prince and an angel, it is sexy. It overwhelms my mind and sends chills through my body when I see those qualities shine through you. It is as if the sun is beaming down on my face every time you look down at me. Even now, I cannot deny that I crave you so. It may well be selfish to say it, but I want you, and I will not deny that any longer."

Jameson stands silent and shaken by my confession of love for him. So many words cross his mind and every one of them appears in his soft eyes, but he could summon none to his lips. I watch, plagued by anxiety, silently begging for him to say something. In my anxiousness, my eyes turn toward the ground, and I bite my lower lip. Although it's not my intention, Jameson finds this irresistible. With no warning, he takes my hand. The breath leaves my body the very instant I feel his touch. He falls to his knees before me and wraps his arms tightly around my waist, clinging to me like I'm the source of the breath that fills his lungs. Finally, he finds the words he wishes to say to me. "Milady..." He stops, then shakes his head. "*My Goddess,* I am at your service. I beg of you, let me be of use to you. If only you allow it, I know I can please you."

It's hard not to let the sadistic joy show in my expression. I feel intrigued by the sight of an angelic prince on his knees, submitting himself to me. It's a power I know only I can hold over this man. I reply in a teasing and playful tone as I wrap my hand around his throat and squeeze just enough to make him release a soft groan that sings of his pleasure. "Show me you can please me then, my naughty little angel."

Hearing my words, Jameson loses all sense of inhibition. He kisses me with every ounce of passion in his body. He worships me. It's with an ease so masterful; I hesitate to wonder where he learned it. He reaches around me and loosens the silk strings of my bodice, slipping it off of me. Much like his himation, my outer dress falls from my body without difficulty, leaving my shoulders exposed. He shields me from the wind, as well as the eyes of any other who may linger nearby. Pleasure courses through my veins with reckless abandon as he lifts himself to kiss me from my neck to my shoulder with such wanton lustfulness that I don't even notice my skirt has come off, too. The tension builds at a rapid pace, even while his motions remain slow and intimate. He lifts my chemise and brings it up, over my shoulders, and off of my body.

For a moment, Jameson steps back. With awe-filled eyes and a voice dripping with passion, he admires me. "Your beauty is exquisite. O' how I long to taste it. To coax the sweet juices from your bodies' most holy anatomy, I will dedicate myself to your whims and pledge myself to your yearning. O' Goddess, tis ye' I worship. May I parish in agony should I ever act against thee."

His vow makes my arousal flow all the more freely, a poetic spell meant to bind himself to me. He embraces the submission with an eagerness that floods my core and drips from my cunt. Then he lays me down atop a chunk of cement from the fallen palace. The stone is cold and hard but feels luxurious, given the heat consuming my body more with each passing moment. A gentle kiss, placed upon the bottom of my foot, calls my attention to the equally soft and sharp features of his face. "May I?"

I nod, permitting him to proceed. Working his way up my leg, he leaves a trail of intimate kisses, each eliciting a soft moan from me. The longing is too much to comprehend by the time he makes it to my inner thighs. He worships my body with such patience and tenderness, passing over my wetness for the time being and focusing his attention on my ear. He nibbles on it softly before whimpering into it. Such a sweet sound. "Your nasty little angel wants to be used by you so badly, goddess."

I can hardly believe the possessive growl that comes from me as I reply. "That's right, so filthy. You must think you're slick getting me all riled up this way. You'll come to regret that. There's no escaping me now, little one."

I guide his lips to my nipples. Like a good boy, he waits for permission before taking them into his mouth. He begins with a simple nip, running his tongue along them in such a way that it skims the peak. In the cold air, the wet saliva causes them to harden to the point of torture. *This fucking brat is teasing me.* The next time he opens his mouth; I shove it down on my tit roughly.

"When your goddess offers you her tit, you take it fully and without the bratty nonsense." I reach down and give his bottom a light tap. A cry so delicious that the sound of it becomes engraved into my mind for eternity comes from him, along with a muffled, "Yesh, God...dess."

I continue to guide his mouth. First, to my other tit and down my stomach to my navel. Then, I lift it. "Now, be a good boy and beg your goddess for a meal."

Desperation laces his words as he begs. "Please, Goddess. Please, let me eat. I promise I'll do a good job. I want to worship your pussy so bad, Goddess. Please let me."

So. Fucking. Sexy. "Yes, you may eat, little angel."

He dips his head between my legs. His oceanic blue eyes don't shift from mine as he tastes my arousal for the first time. He locks onto my clit. First with slow circles of his tongue, which escalates into sucking like he wishes he could deep throat it. What began with soft moans turns to screams as he eats, and eats, and eats. He adds one finger, and then two, teasing my G-spot as he devours my clit. My hips buck wildly, but I never even give him a chance to stop. My legs wrap themselves around his head, my thighs locking him in place. He alternates between mild and severe intensity at my behest, pleasuring me for a full hour before I decide he's earned his reward. I squirt in his face, drenching him in my juices. The orgasm is intense, each wave more so than the last. He takes it all so well.

I beckon him to me, caressing his lean muscles as he crawls up my body. The lewd expression on his face as he pants, eyes pleading for more, is simultaneously adorable and seductive. I pull him into a kiss, tasting my orgasm on his lips. The kiss is needy and desperate. We are far from done. He presses his body against mine. His thick, throbbing cock rubbing my cunt. It pulsates and convulses, begging to enter me before he could even ask permission. In that moment, regardless of how badly he wants this, his primary concern remains my comfort and pleasure. His tone is hushed as he speaks his next words, "Is this okay with you, goddess?"

I smile with affection, finding his concern for me sweet. "Yes, I'll let you fuck me now. You're too cute when you're horny, little angel. Let your Goddess feel your love, baby."

He smiles and kisses me before I wrap my hand around his throat and order him inside of me, yanking his head back by his hair as I do so. He's timid as he sinks his cock into me in one push that moves far too slow for my tastes. "Stop being a little bitch about it. I told you to fuck me."

That's effective in shoving the hesitation from his mind. He thrusts into me harder and harder until his length feels overwhelming. "Fuck, Goddess. Your pussy feels so good. Thank you. Thank you for letting my worthless cock inside your holiness." His passionate cries are like the soothing sounds of a harp harmonizing with a sexual maelstrom of passion. Each thrust better than the last as he takes me higher, lifting my proverbial throne so far above mortal reach it towers over the God's realm. His moans are loud as they fill the air alongside mine. It feels as though our souls are colliding each time our hips met. He groans into my ear as he lays into me time and time again. "Mm, shit! I love you, Goddess."

I cry out, "I love you, too, angel. You serve me so well."

Hearing those words further sucks him into the sheer bliss that he finds only within me. His eagerness to please me does *not* go to waste. I reach climax several times before he does the same, filling me with his seed. When it's over, I find myself curled into his arms. We're silent for a long time. Any words we could have spoken would be useless. There's nothing I can say. Words are meaningless compared to this serenity. After some time passes, tears fall from my eyes. Jameson continues to hold me in silence, never questioning them. He understands the tears are no reflection on him, but a mere moment of grief. After all, he's the first man I've lain with since Kai and Cal's passing. It makes sense that it's overwhelming for me. His only desire is to support me. If I need to feel this pain, who is he to deny me at this moment?

It's quite some time before my tears die down. He helps me dress, then we return to the building where we were staying.

LILLY

The next day, all await word of the war to come. In the meantime, we occupy ourselves with vain attempts to lessen our worries. In Alacrium, Malachi and I spend our time talking with Myrkr and Rettferd. Our thought is that one-on-one, we can coerce more information from them. We need to know about the plans each of our targets have for after Rath has fallen. Unfortunately for us, neither the angel nor the demon want to give such answers. They are both men of great intelligence and strength. It would take an obscene amount of trust to provoke that level of information. With such little time, the attempt is desperate and ill-considered at best. Still, we know we have to try.

I find Rettferd in the privacy of his own chamber once more. I'm relieved that he is in here. At least, he wouldn't worry about being overheard by demons if we stay isolated like this. I sit in a chair near his bedside, where he lays staring up at the ceiling. I ask, "How are you feeling, since restoring the forest? Have you been able to get enough rest here?"

He sighs, then follows it with an obvious attempt to sound pleasant, though I could tell that he doesn't want company. "Yes, I am restored. Thank you for your concern. You are a kindhearted young lady. Little Linola has taught you well."

"Indeed," I reply. "My adoptive mother is among the greatest blessings I could ever have received."

"Child, she is your mother. The matter of to whom you were born became irrelevant long ago. The moment your biological parents abandoned their duties to you; they gave up the right to call you their daughter. Josella has long been your mother in the eyes of my master. It may sound odd, given the events of the past, present, and future, but I ask you to trust me. At least when I say that this little group of yours, even the half-demon, finds great favor with him. I quite like most of you, too. It's only the half-demon that I cannot trust."

I nod. "I see. Can you trust us and our judgement of him?"

"Humans are prone to corruption by a demon, child. Your judgement is most clouded."

"As is yours..."

Rettferd chuckles. "Yes, you may well be right. I don't suppose there is much to do about that. It isn't too late for you and your friends, though. Of that much, I assure you."

"We will see, Rettferd. Thank you for your time. Now, I will be on my way."

Scurrying from the room, I feel panic set in. Not only did he see through my façade, but he gave me the information that I sought without a fight. This leads me to believe that his confidence in his plan is absolute. His target is Malachi, and Malachi alone. I will report this to Malachi later in the evening so we can discuss counter-measures. Recalling my vision, the news that he is being targeted is cause for alarm. Rettferd's plan mustn't succeed. I'll stop him at all costs.

Meanwhile, Malachi himself had found Myrkr speaking with Alexandria in the throne room. As he neared them, he realized they were arguing about something. He hid himself and listened in to hear the contents of their disagreement:

"But Father! We are blood; you cannot ask us to do such a thing!"

Myrkr scoffs. "I can, and I have! You will follow my orders as you have always done! After I exterminate those pesky little freaks that he hangs out with, you will console him. By doing so, you will grow closer to him. In time, you will seduce him, wed him, and bear his child. Together, the four of us will rule this continent in its entirety. Then, we can return to the goal of eradicating heaven, as we have always planned."

"No, father, I cannot do as you have asked this time."

"Alexandria, it is because he is our blood that it must be him. With the power held by both of you passed down to another of our line, we will have created a being of equal strength to me. Then, with training, that being can help me defeat the master of my past. We will rid the realms of his annoying angels."

"Fine, but I must have assurances he will allow me to love of my own accord after we have an heir."

Myrkr nods. "Not only will he allow it, but it is also likely that he will take lovers of his own after the fact. Unless you too actually grew to care for each other romantically. Which is not improbable if you have a child together. As you know, I was never in love with your mother, but I was loyal to her while she lived, and I cared for her. She was my best friend, in truth, and the only one to understand me. I miss her."

Alexandria nods. "I suppose that such a bond is acceptable if love isn't an option."

Having heard the conversation, Malachi fleas to the nearest bathroom. Here, he vomits, then he mumbles to himself, "I can't do this..."

It was then he realizes he has being followed. "Oh, but you will. My father does not take well to disobedience. You will regret it if you don't comply. Trust me."

Malachi turns to see Alexandria standing behind him. She continues, "You did not think we were unaware of your presence, did you? Our senses exist in a heightened state. We have honed them for centuries; we could sense you from anywhere on the continent."

Malachi sneers. "Thanks for the warning,. Let us watch and see how things play out before we write off, my friends." He walked away.

He and I met shortly after and exchanged some information. I, unable to hold back, finally tell Malachi about my vision. He declines to hear the details of it, though. He tells me that some part of him knew how this would end for him to begin with. The result won't surprise him whatsoever. He feels this path to be the right one, no matter what it costs. I nod and agreed not to relay the information to anyone else. This will be our little secret for the time being. Malachi takes some time alone after that to contemplate all we've learned. Finally, it seems he has an answer to the questions that have plagued his mind for so long. He and Myrkr are, in fact, separate beings with some striking similarities. They don't need to share a fate. Rather, Malachi has received some confirmation from me. Myrkr and he will suffer different futures, but they will both suffer.

He has always viewed Josie as being above him. She's his sister, after all. Brothers protect their sisters. He knows in his heart that her destiny is more than he can give her, but he'll always be on her side, even knowing the issues it'll cause with Johanna. To him, it makes perfect sense. He loves Johanna with all his heart, but she isn't like Josie. She'll never carry that sort of weight, and she will never need him. Josie does, and he doesn't intend to let her down. As he admits this all to himself, Johanna's insecurities came to mind. Although she loves Josie, her fear that he will always put his sibling relationship over his marriage likely stems from him doing exactly that. She isn't wrong. He worries about his wife. Hoping she'll be okay; not wanting to cause the growing resentment in her heart.

As for his demonhood, he has to embrace it more than ever before. Seeing this place and its culture, he has a desire to grow closer to those who share his lineage. Before this, he'd always seen his demonic nature as a part of him he had to manage, rather than a vital part of who he was. Unlike Jameson, others always viewed his nature as a power to be feared rather than loved. Those who adore him do so believe that his human nature is the prominent part of him. They think it's only half of him that possesses the keen sense of justice and loyalty they adore. The reality, though, is that he was never two separate halves. He's never been one good side or one evil. Instead, he's a whole person who commits themselves to doing the right thing. He spends his life protecting those he cares most for, as many of the demons seem to have done.

The truest version of the half-demon ruler of Tendu, Malachi, is finally on the horizon. He feels his power multiply tenfold as he removes the intellectual and spiritual shackles. Alexandria, who continuously observes him, smiles as she senses his power grow. She says to herself, not realizing I'm nearby, "It seems you are free from the prison of your own making, Malachi. Now, you are my equal in strength and stand among the three most powerful demons in existence. I must continue to watch you. It will be interesting to see how these events unfold."

I'm concerned about a lingering issue that has come to my attention. Why has no one actually mentioned the gate Mom needs to bring my fathers back? I broach the subject with Alexandria. Alexandria shakes her head, though. "The answers you seek are not in my grasp any more than they are yours. I have been curious about the matter as well, but my father has been hesitant to speak to me about it. I assume Rettferd has the same information my father does though, he may be open to sharing it with you."

Not having much of a choice, I accept her answer and thank her for her guidance. Returning to Rettferd, I ask him about it. The curtness of my question throws him for a loop from the looks of it. He tells me, under the condition that I not share the information with anyone else. I don't wish to hold more secrets than I already am, but I agree. I know it's the only way. So, he explains. "I know of the half in Rallem, but not in Alacrium. You see, the half that lies there was a creation from your side, the side of the living. Thus, it's a fixed location. That location is about seventy-five feet underground. It's guarded by the very throne, or I guess it was. Recent reports say the throne is gone, but the gate beneath should be fine.

The half in Alacrium is a creation of the spirit realm. It's intangible. Rather, it only exists in theory, as far as I know. According to our records, it doesn't exist all the time. It comes in and out of existence, and I cannot fathom how."

I nod. "Josie's in for a rough time then, huh?"

Rettferd agrees. I worry for a few moments, but my faith in Josie restores once I remember the expression she wore. It was one of such determination that I can't imagine her giving up. After all, Josie experienced more pain than any of us, having lost Kai, Cal, and the familiarship of Kimble. Anyone else might have folded under such a mix of pressure and pain, but Josie is special. She always has been. I smile. "Well, no matter what it takes, my mom can do it. Do not underestimate her."

Rettferd, sensing my stress, doesn't wish to worry the young girl he saw any further. So, he smiles and assures me that Mom will be successful. Although, he holds doubts, especially with Rath still on the loose. Ending this fight with him will increase our chances of succeeding exponentially. With preparations complete from a technical aspect, the only thing left to do is wait. Rettferd and Myrkr are so powerful that it's ridiculous. Still, it has been centuries since they were in a proper battle. They use this lull to prepare on a personal level.

They spar with one another. After all, Rettferd is the only person around strong enough to face Myrkr in earnest. Although Myrkr is stronger, the gap in their power is far less. Compared to the power of anyone else, to either of them, at least. Since practice battles are being held, Malachi proposes that he and Alexandria spar. Intrigued, she accepts. "As soon as they finish, I'll fight you."

With that, Rettferd and Myrkr's battle begins. To avoid destroying Alacrium, they take the fighting down the mountain. It allows them to fight at full force without worry of harming anyone. Still, the shockwaves caused by the collision of two great powers are too great. Even in the palace, which floats above the city itself, the trembling is noticeable. The battle is brief, though. It ends with Myrkr taking a clear and decisive victory over Rettferd after only a few attacks. It's more than sheer power. Those who observed the fight see that Myrkr holds a brilliant tactical mind. His decision to lead their army himself has become understandable. Myrkr sighs as he extends his hand to Rettferd. "Sorry, was that too rough, brother?"

Rettferd chuckles and accepts Myrkr's hand, using it to pull himself up. "No, more so than normal. You've always been this way."

Together, they stand, laughing and talking for a few minutes. With all the tension between them, it's easy to forget that they're brothers. Malachi had thought they hated one another. In this moment, though, they look as if they are best friends, loyal brothers even. The sight leaves him confused and conflicted. "*How is it that those who love each other so much can seek to destroy one another?*" He wonders as he approaches the designated field of battle and faces Alexandria.

She calls to him from across the field. "Show me, Malachi. I must assess your strength and decide for myself if you are worthy of our family name!"

Malachi finds himself provokes by her challenge. He resolves himself not to hold back for reasons of rank or familial tie. He puts his all into defeating Alexandria. As the battle begins, they clash. With each attack, it becomes more obvious that they're equals. For every hit one of them lands, the other returns a more devastating one. They shatter through each other's defenses and constantly switch who has the upper hand. Rettferd and Myrkr watch in awe of the new generation. They enjoy observing the passion that radiates from each of their attacks. Even they can admit it. Given time, this generation may surpass the unchallenged strength of their own. An overwhelming sense of anticipation fills their bodies. They long for the day that they might fight their own descendants as equals. As such thoughts fill their minds, so do thoughts of Rath, Josie, and Jameson. They come to realize that their wish may not be what they had imagined it to be. After all, neither of them wishes for their bloodline to hate them, reject them, and even seek to take their lives.

"I'll kill you!" Malachi screams in fury as the tide of the fight shifts in Alexandria's favor. He has never had to rely on his demonic power in such a prolonged battle against such a powerful enemy. Her stamina is greater than his because she's had all the time needed to train it. Her body can manage the drain her own power takes on her. It's obvious to Malachi, although their strength was equal, he has much more training to do. He can never be her true equal as a warrior until he can match her stamina. If her next words are anything to go by, Alexandria thinks about it quite the opposite of the way he does. She acknowledges how amazing Malachi is, as do the bystanders and onlookers. None of them expected the half-demon spawn to stand equal to the full-demon heiress in any form. Alexandria stops the battle. She sees Malachi will continue to fight until his death, out of pride, if she continues. She smiles with warmth. "Rest, you, of my father's blood. You have done well. In fact, I am convinced that what my father said is true. We need you. You are my equal in willpower, strength, and intellect."

Her servant, Julius, scoffs from the sidelines. He seems displeased with the carelessness of Alexandria's words. She is a queen; no one should be her equal. After all, if someone can match her, they might beat her. What would the people think of a queen who isn't unassailable?

Eighteen

INTERMISSION IN LOFT

As tensions are growing across the continent, the evidence that war is on the horizon mounts. Many public officials come under attack by the public for this. More notable than any is the call in Loft for the heads of the Duke and Duchess, Josie's parents. Their downfall begins when an anonymous journalist publishes an article. This article calls attention to many crimes they've committed. Majority of which are offenses against the commoners in their territory. It follows up with a series of articles published in the local newspaper. The author details the neglect shown by the king and queen for letting these people rule in the royal name. These crimes include embezzlement and the hoarding of resources. The worst crime of all was in the accusation that they've taken the life of a peasant. One who stumbled his way into uncovering their secret plot. They planned to force their men to side with the opposition in the impending war. Their goal was to aid Rath in getting rid of Josie's friends. They hoped they might once again find her under their dynasty and its tyrannical rule. To do this, they planned to commit treason and betray their own people.

Because of these discoveries, angry mobs rise within the kingdom. They call for the execution of the Duke and Duchess. They run through the streets of Loft chanting, "Death to the Duke! Death to the Duke!"

In such unstable times, the grip the King and queen hold on their kingdom is tenuous. Given that the articles attack them as well and they need their people backing them. They need them to fight for Loft's future. There's no chance of that, so long as their names are being tarnished in public. Thus, they have no choice but to concede to the demands of their people.

One evening, the King gives an address, during which he states, "It is in perilous times such as these that the support of the common people shows its deepest value. To those of us who rule over you, we have a responsibility to maintain that support. It is a bond which our ruling class has treasured for many years. We understand the great trust you place in us by allowing us our wealth and power. For one of our own to betray that bond is unacceptable. It is with a heavy heart that I acknowledge the travesties committed by my blood. To protect the bond that I hold with all the common people, I will betray my blood ties to him. It is that which leads me to stand before you today. At this very moment, my guards are storming the estate of the Duke and Duchess Spade. They will bring the traitors into custody. The Duke and Duchess will face execution for their crimes against the people within the day. We already decided on the matter of their estate and lineage. Their daughter, Lady Josella Spade, is a woman of great strength and kindness. In both the ruling and lower class, she has love and respect. We leave their land and the care of their people in her capable hands. Our hope is for you to accept this gesture as a sign that your king and queen remain on your side. We ask that you support us. We march into this war to defend ourselves, our kingdom, and our alliance. These things which have brought prosperity to us all deserve our protection."

A few moments of silence passes. The King becomes anxious that his people won't accept his gesture of good faith. Then, one man in the crowd yells, "For Loft, we fight; for our kingdom, we die!"

Others follow his lead. Soon, a new chant begins, but this one was much more reassuring to the King. He joins them in their chant, "For Loft, we fight; for our kingdom, we die! For Loft, we fight; for our kingdom, we die!"

This moment lit a fire under the Loftian people as national pride swells throughout the land. The Queen smiles upon hearing of this renewed sense of unity among their people. "Thanks to their willingness to die for this land, I am sure that not as many of them will. You did well, my husband."

The King accepts her praise with a sense of relief. "Thank you, dear. I, too, believe that the best way to protect their lives is for them to fight alongside our allies. We must destroy this evil; before it can destroy them."

Within a matter of hours after the people of Loft rallied behind their king, the heads of the duke and duchess flew. Their headless bodies get displayed in the town square as a symbol to all. A symbol that assures the people that their rulers care about their well-being. The sight is brutal but also brings peace to the minds of many. Far fewer nobles will neglect their people after seeing this. They know now there are consequences to doing so.

Nineteen

JOSIE

I receive a letter sent by the rulers of Loft. The letter reads: "*Dearest Josie,*

We write to you today to inform you of matters that will break your heart and fill it with hope for the future of our land at the same time. Out of fear that the less desirable news might ruin the good, we will tell you of the positive events first. To begin, all active member states of the alliance have heard your call. We stand prepared to fight alongside you, as per the conditions of our treaty. Although some member states took more persuasion than others did. You can rest well in these days leading up to battle. Rest knowing that you will have the full force of this alliance. You have eminent qualifications, so we leave the allied forces in your command.

Next, we wish to inform you that your dear friend, the king of Tendu, as well as your adoptive daughter, is well. They have recently written from the mountain kingdom known as Alacrium. They gave instruction to the armies of Tendu. In their letter, they asked we inform you of their health. They are sure that it would bring you comfort to know that they had done well.

As for the less favorable news, two matters are of note. The first of which was also included in the information sent by Malachi and Lilly. They say, "This cooperation is tenuous and temporary. Once Rath falls, expect a new fight to begin immediately." We are not completely sure of what this warning means or what factions wish to betray us. But we have prepared to fight beyond the original scope of your call. Please, Josella, lead us well and trust that we will follow.

The last matter which we must relay to you is one we regret. It came to our attention that your parents committed unforgivable crimes. Against the people, but also against the kingdom. As per our law, they faced execution. We are sorry for your loss and ask that you not resent us for our actions. As a consolation, we hope you will accept the title of Duchess to the land once owned by your parents. We have faith that you can cleanse the Spade family name of its now tainted legacy. It holds stains from your parents' crimes. We acknowledge this olive branch may well be as much of a curse as it is a blessing in your eyes. Yet, we think this will be the right thing to do from all sides.

We hope you are well and pray for a swift end to this war so that we can once again see your lovely face gleaming with hope and passion.

With love,

Your King and Queen."

After reading the letter, I run to Jameson as I weep. He had been chatting with some men who volunteered to fight in the upcoming war. I throw myself into his arms as I cry and his heart rate skyrockets. He becomes overwhelmed with both worry and the warmth of my embrace. He's weak to me. Right away, he wraps me up in his arms with a firmness that implies he never wants to let me go again. The men he had been speaking with gasp, startled by the sudden change in the atmosphere. To Jameson, it's as if he had completely forgotten that they were standing there. At that moment, all he sees is me. As he holds me, he caresses my cheek, sweeping away my tears as my gaze and his lock. He asks me, "Josie, what is wrong? Did something happen?"

I sob. "They're dead, Jameson. My parents faced execution for crimes against the Loftian people."

His eyes widen, though I doubt it's from shock as much as it is from worry. "Josie, I am so sorry for your loss. I wish—Is there anything that I can do to help?"

"I never even got to reconcile with them. Why does everyone that I love die? Jameson, please, do not die..."

He tightens his embrace, realizing that all he can do at the moment is comfort me the best way he knows how. In the end, nothing will help this pain. His only option is to help me cope with it. "Josie, I am sorry; so, so sorry. But I promise you... No, I swear to you an oath, I will not allow myself to die without your permission."

My tears soak his shirt as I nuzzle deeper into his chest. I smile through my tears, feeling a small glimmer of hope and happiness shine through as I hear Jameson's words. "Well then," I reply. "You must live for all eternity. Beyond, even, for there will never come a day where I will allow such a thing."

Jameson knows his oath is one that is impossible to keep. Luckily, as he's a half-angel, his natural lifespan is one that far exceeds that of a human such as me. He knows that so long as he doesn't allow someone to take his life, that he can remain by my side until my time comes. The thought of watching me die terrifies him, I'm sure. Yet, he has the willpower to endure the pain he knows it will bring him. So long as it prevents me from having to endure any more grief, he can live with it. With the war on the horizon, though, he must wonder if it was wise to promise me such a thing. Could he guarantee that his life would not end with facing Rath, Rettferd, or Myrkr? As one of the most powerful fighters, it's likely that he'll fight one of these men. Each of whom hold such strength. They can each threaten an alliance formed of seven kingdoms, even alone. If he has to fight one of them one-on-one, how can he ensure that his life doesn't end?

Out of the blue, as my voice breaks his train of thought, he realizes how simple the answer to the dilemma we're both considering. He would have to win, no matter what. He feels his soul settle in as if it's found peace in such a thought. His mind and heart fill with a sense of resoluteness. There's nothing that will stop this man from keeping the oath that he has sworn me. As he watches me press myself up and onto the tips of my toes, moving closer to his ear, he knows it's the only way. I whisper to him, "I love you, Jameson. Thank you for all that you have given me."

He freezes. All the willpower that he thought he had drained from his body before my eyes. Instead, he feels nothing but a burning and passionate love for me. He falls to his knees before me, longing for the air that my gentle breath has stolen from his lungs. He puts his arms around my waist. Those around us see plainly how deep in my grasp that he is. He pleads with me, as if to love me will never be enough.

"Josie, my Josie; do you still not see? What my heart holds for you goes far beyond mere love. In truth, you are everything. The force tugging me towards you is so strong that your whims have become my schedule. Your kindness has become my mirror. To please you, serve you, and devote myself to you is my only wish. For you, I do not even fear the optics of a crowned prince who has fallen to his knees and began begging for a woman to see him. Instead, I trust that all Oceanica, all the world, will see my gesture and smile upon it. They will know that only you could bring a man like me to heel. Only you could bring a man who was born to lead the largest and wealthiest nation in the known world to his knees. I was born with everything; yet I have nothing if I do not have you. Yes, I love you, Josie, but so much more than that, too. You are the center of my existence. To betray my oath to you would mean that my life had become meaningless, anyway."

The intensity of Jamesons' words resonates. Not only with me, but everyone around us as well. The depth of the young prince's words reminds many Rallians just how young we are. It enrages many of them. To have once been the backbone of this magnificent kingdom's fighting force. Now they find themselves to be useless. They're looking to a group of people in their early twenties for protection and leadership. This fury leads them to resolve. If they are to die, they would not die useless old men. Instead, they'd die heroes worthy of fighting alongside this new generation. One man even laughs. "Look at them. They're nothing but kids. Only now are they figuring out what love is. Yet, they have shown us veterans up in every way. Let us not forget the fire and passion we once held, men! Let us fight with pride as heroes should and assure this woman that each of us would give our lives to help this idiot keep his promise to survive a war!"

All the men laugh at that, but they agree. I couldn't help but smile as I see the fire lighting beneath them. Pastel finds himself amazed. Our mere existence has motivated his men. He never got to know Malachi, Johanna, or Lilly well. He must wonder if we were all this magnetic and charismatic. Even more so, I imagine he wonders if Kai and Cal were as well. It's odd to see a group of leaders with such distinct personalities, with each personality as overwhelming as the next, who yet stays bonded together in a way such as this. To him, we are something amazing. The likes of which he doubted this world had ever seen before or would ever see again. We reflect these worldwide ideals and still provide balances of independence. We *are* friendship. Strong, yet human. Logical, yet brimming with passion. We're everything people need to feel safe on a local and global scale. He knows he's not a poor leader but worries that he might pale when compared to us. Still, he remains committed to doing what's best for his people. His belief in this alliance is as unwavering as the mountains of the Alacrium.

Jameson stands, putting an arm around my shoulder. After, he raises a glass of the champagne that had been being passed around before I ran over. "Brothers! I appreciate your love and support for our shared cause. Please, always know this: though our time in Rallem has been short, this kingdom and its people hold a special place in the hearts of us both. You are no less our brethren than those back home. Thus, we will protect you all as well!"

For the rest of the night, the party rages on. For that one night, not one mind or heart felt plagued by the inevitable cost of war. A luxury that will soon steal away from us. Terrifying news brought by our scouts arrives in the sunlight of the next morning. The message is terse, simple, and blunt. "War has come; it is time."

Within one hour, every person with the ability to fight is ready to move out. As per the discussions, we will march northwest from Rallem. Those from the islands will march northeast, and those from Alacrium, south. The three armies would converge in the middle of this figurative triangle. Right where the scouts spotted Rath in recent days. He's there alongside those who he convinced to fight for him. Because of the position he settled in, I believe he is setting up a trap. Thus, we all agreed that all three armies would approach with extreme caution. If done well, we should have the advantage, as we will surround him with three separate armies. Yet, one wrong move could still turn the tables to his advantage.

There's a thick, lingering tension in the air the following morning. Pastel, Jameson, and I gather at the front of an army of about two-thousand fighting men. We look at one another. We pray for some miracle that would bring this to an end without the cost of lives. Too many had already died in Rath's initial attack. We couldn't bear the responsibility of seeing Rallem completely annihilated. Together, we take a deep breath as Pastel calls to the troops. "Men, we march!"

It's the first step in a long and perilous march that all know is leading many to their deaths. As I hear the thundering sound of that first footstep, I shudder. "This- it is all my fault, is it not?"

Pastel chuckles. "Josie, none of us blame you. Remember, the remnants of Linolas' soul had been weakening? It's why you had the strength to break the seal to begin with; why he even had the strength to contact you? He would have broken free in time. Regardless of what you did, the result was always going to be the same. It's his decisions that are determining our fate right now. I may hate to admit that, but I can't deny the truth of it."

Twenty

JOSIE

Three nights pass as the allied army's travel. By the time the fourth night falls, we have converged. Rath, being the warrior that he is, sensed us coming from miles away. He and his new army, which is crammed with some of the most notable priests and priestesses, await us. They meet us with pride plastered on their faces, as if they believe they are doing the right thing. Even when they become surrounded by the armies of Rallem, the islands, and Alacrium, they don't waiver. Our leaders become aware we don't have the element of surprise as we thought we would. Rather than attempting an attack off-hand, we alter our plans. We give communication and reason one last attempt, in a last-ditch attempt at sparing lives. We present a united front, standing before Rath with our most powerful in his line of sight. It's an intimidating tactic, or so we hoped. We thought that when faced with so many of the world's most powerful warriors, he might finally come to his senses. We thought he would back down, but we were wrong.

For a few minutes, we are in silence, facing each other down. We exchange glares with each other, searching for some glimmer of doubt in one another's eyes. Unfortunately, there's none there to find. Rettferd is the first to speak. "Rath, once upon a time, we had so much in common. We were friends, weren't we? I ask now that you remember that time as I and my allies attempt one last time to find common ground with you. We do not seek death, war, and destruction. We just cannot allow you to follow through on your heinous threats. Destroying all demons and angels, including our descendants. Are you serious?"

Rath sighs. "I did not seek to walk this path either, but I no longer see any other way to address the threat your lineages pose to mine. I will accept your request to at least try to find a way. Let us talk. There's a hall nearby here that I've made my headquarters. We can sit there and discuss these matters."

Malachi speaks up. "Such talks might be better to hold on neutral territory. Given your recent attack in Rallem, you're hard to trust."

Rath groans in annoyance. "Does this demon brat speak for you all? If we can't trust one another enough to believe that the other side doesn't wish for peril and devastation. How is there any hope of finding an alternative option to war?"

I look around at my peers. "He's right, guys. We must all believe that these talks are being held in good faith. I loathe this man with everything that I am. Still, I don't believe that he has any desire to take life merely for the satisfaction of doing so. If there's any chance at a peaceful resolution, I trust he would seek to find it."

The others observe, realizing that it's me that Rath has harmed more than any of them. They admire my ability to set aside that pain and speak with logic and honesty. It's true, Raths' actions don't depict a man who wants to kill. Rather, one that needs to. Skewed as his thought process may be, he believes wholeheartedly that this destruction to be necessary. This gives them some confidence to believe that he can, in fact, see reason. Thus, they agree. Albeit, that agreement is reluctant. We follow Rath to his headquarters, where we sat at a roundtable. It's likely meant for him and his generals to devise battle tactics against us, and the irony of trying to create peace at a table meant to wage war doesn't get lost on me. None of us know how to begin this conversation, not even Rath. There are no definitive demands to make on either end. Compromise isn't the path to peace right now, persuasion is.

Alas, Rath begins by asking Rettferd a question. "Rettferd, I remember you to be a reasonable man of restraint. Might I ask you, why did you abandon your better judgement upon meeting my sister all those years ago? Wasn't it you who protested Myrkr's relationship with her to begin with?"

Rettferd looks around the room. The validity of Raths' question has caught the attention of everyone. Myrkr seems more eager than the rest of us to hear the answer, though. Rettferd sighs, realizing that there's no way to evade the question Rath poses. He would answer the question. Not for Rath, but for his brother. It's Myrkr to whom he owes the answer.

"I loved her. Scratch that, still do. If transparency is the goal, then I'm better off admitting that. I'll love Linola until the day I die. Myrkr, remember, I had never met a human before. I never would have fallen for her on purpose, but she was so stubborn and high-minded. It was infuriating in a way that somehow made being angry better. Anger became the most joyous emotion on the spectrum. For every point I tried to make to her about the innate selfish, egocentric manner of humanity, she had five more. It was always impossible to follow her logic and reasoning, even if I could tell that it was there. She made sense in a way that made no sense at all. By the end of our talks, she would have me wondering if I was the egocentric one. To fill an angel's heart with doubt that he understands what 'right' and 'wrong' mean. To make me question my ethics and morality 'tis a power only Linola held, brother. So, yes, I fell in love with her with no regard for the pain that it might have caused you. At that moment, it did not feel as if I could live without her. While I apologize for the pain that I caused you. I must also say I'm not sorry for loving her."

Myrkr's face contorts in anger as he lets out a vicious growl from deep within his clenched jaws. He struggles to bite his tongue. It's impressive that he restrains himself. I'm not sure I would've done so well at it. He managed long enough for Rath to think of a response to Rettferd's answer, which was a bit more honest than any of us are hoping for, of course. From there, the conversation spirals into various parties, venting frustrations with one another. For a while, both Lilly and I sit quietly as we observe. We listen to the escalating arguments between the lot of them. Finally, Lilly grows impatient with the immaturity of the adults surrounding her. She screams, "Stop!" The room grows silent. The frustration that fills her small, yet influential, voice calls their attention. "Stop it..." She shakes her head in disappointment. "This is ridiculous. None of us came here to bicker about such petty matters. This will, in no way, contribute to our efforts to prevent this war. Sit down and shut up already, you idiots. Let's discuss something more productive. Such as a potential resolution? I would like to pose one after hearing this nonsense."

One-by-one, they all sit down. The Chief of Pallentine smiles, seeing the young girl's talent for leading others. He says to me, "She reminds me much of you. You have done well to raise her this way. Soon, she'll become our light, as you have been."

Lilly gulps. Hearing his comment brought an anxiousness to her. I've heard tell of some prophecy or another that she saw, though for reasons unbeknownst to me, Malachi seems hesitant to go into detail about. She must wonder if the Chief has had a similar vision to hers. They're the only two that she knows of who have the gift of prophetic vision. I, of course, feel a twinge of sadness. It swirls into the pride I feel for the young woman my beloved daughter has become. Yes, it's saddening to see the sweet, shy little girl fading away. The thought of Lilly carrying such a burden as the one I have saddens me. Sure, it's likely the best option available to us in terms of the politics. Would placing the fate of nations on the shoulders of Lilly be what was best for her, though? Would Lilly come to suffer like I have? I have faith in her ability to lead, but she's also endured great pain. The abuse and terror she faced as a young girl was disgusting. Not to mention that since then, Lilly had endured further trauma in losing Kai and Cal. It's not fair to pass this torch onto her, not knowing the amount of suffering that comes with it.

Johanna's smile is bright when she looks at Malachi, but it's little more than a mask. "I suppose our son will soon be to young Lilly, what you have been to Josie. Is that your goal?"

Malachi nods, sensing the anger behind Johannas's radiance. The tension in the room is growing once more. Not only between the two separate sides of this fight; but between the members of the alliance. Many of us are coming to realize that change, unwelcome as it may be, is on the horizon. It seems like the peace is disappearing before our eyes. We feel nothing more than the shame of knowing that our decisions have once again led our people to the horrors of war. It's unfair that our self-ish wants and needs brought back this animosity. More than anyone, I feel that this change will be my fault. It breaks my heart knowing that the people of the islands can never be happy, so long as I continue to insist on being happy myself. Even as far as Jameson went, if I were to marry him, I would disrupt the fragile balance of power. Although I'm from Loft, I remain neutral. Until now. I had become the middle ground, the grey area that allowed those around me to exist in harmony. This is a luxury that I wouldn't have as a queen. To rule Ocean-ica alongside Jameson would mean that I have to rank Oceanica over the other islands. What the chief said may have been accurate, regardless of how infuriating I find it. It's likely time for me to step down and let someone else take my place.

Jameson glances at me, noticing the obvious distress plastered across my face. He immediately knows that I've begun second guessing our relationship. No matter the issues that come with it, though, it won't change anything for me. I'm going to choose myself this time, consequences be damned. As persistent as he is, he must wonder if Rath has some valid points regarding the effect involvement with angels and demons has on hu-mans. He mumbles in hushed tones at Rettferd. "Things might have been better had the two of you never left the heavenly realm."

The pain in Rettferd's eyes was visible; hearing it said aloud, got to him. He realizes that if he and Myrkr had never interfered here that Linola would not have died. Rath wouldn't have become unhinged. I wouldn't be suffering. Jameson wouldn't be fearful of losing or hurting me. Malachi wouldn't be at odds with his own wife. Poor Lilly wouldn't be trying to make adults do something as simple as communicate with one another. Even Myrkr seems disturbed by the notion which he had overheard. Finally, Rettferd asks Rath, "What if we left? What if Myrkr and I left and agreed never to interfere in this realm again?"

Rath shakes his head. "It's too late for that. Your descendants are here now; they can only create the same problems that you two have. If you all left, that would be different. Myrkr, Rettferd, Alexandria, Jameson, and Malachi all need to leave. I would consider this offer and even be willing to pledge to help Josie bring back those two boys. I'd offer to protect the three of them, along with this alliance, and the Alacrium in your stead."

Acting on instinct, the younger three reject the offer off-hand. Before Rath could accept their answer, though, Myrkr asks them. "Alexandria, if it left our people safe, what would be the issue with it? It's not like we couldn't come straight back if he breaks from his word. And you, Jameson, would you not make such a small sacrifice for the woman you claim to love? Do you not feel for her what I did for Linola? Malachi, your wife, and child could come with us if need be; or I could gift them the means to travel across realms. Is it so bad? Even I see its potential, although I hate to admit it. I can no longer turn a blind eye to my role in this mess. Abiding by this is doable, so long as we demons have time to negotiate with the master of old before going back. I need to be sure of our safety and freedoms before returning."

Rath nods. He agrees to Myrkr's demand for time. The younger group takes a few moments to contemplate Myrkr's valid points. After a few moments, Alexandria takes a deep breath. Her eyes wander to Malachi, then to Jameson, and back to Malachi once again. Following that, she exhales slowly. As if she would prefer to let the oxygen drain from her lungs than to say what she is about to. "It's an acceptable offer, boys. I'll agree to it if it spares the lives of those that we have a responsibility to."

Her agreement only increases the pressure on Malachi and Jameson. Now, if they decline or object, blame will shift to them for the impending war. They both hold suspicions about what Myrkr and Alexandria's true intentions are. After all, it's not a secret. Betrayal within allied ranks will become inevitable. Trust is in even shorter supply than ever before.

Having found his courage, Jameson declines the offer. He reasons, "To put the well-being of those that we love into the hands of a man who threatens their lives would be an act of cowardice. It would also be proof that we are little more than the helpless children that the elders at this roundtable see us as. I'll not abandon my country, my friends, or the woman I love. While peace is preferable to the carnage of war, there's an acceptable price for it. One which I cannot, in good conscious, surpass. Many things may get discarded or sacrificed soon. I can assure you, though, my honor will not be one of them; nor will my cousins."

The fearlessness and honor of his words touches the hearts of all. He replaces their fear and worry with a lingering reminder of what's worth fighting for. Everyone at this table, even Rath, gathers here to fight for those that they love. It's only in Jameson's words that we find this common denominator between us. Unfortunately, the thing that we have in common is the same thing that pits us against each other. We also realize that none of those gathered can back down for this very reason. The fight has proven to be unavoidable.

Malachi, who feels paralyzed by his own thoughts, holding a newfound admiration for his cousin. He realizes Jameson is becoming more like his equal. Rather than the bratty little prince of his memories. That day, we decide that because of the failure of the negotiations, the war will resume in three days' time. The respect that we found for one another leads us to agree that there will be no ambushes or petty tactics. Instead, we will gather face-to-face in a field and the last man standing will be victorious. Word of Jamesons' awe-inspiring words travels through the camps. As the agreed-upon period of rest ends, the men of the army look to him for leadership. Finally, he stands alongside Malachi and me as an equal partner. Those around him feel as if they are watching him become the king that he was born to be. The sort of king that Oceanica deserves. He will no longer hide beneath the shadow of his father. Or feel the shame of his mother's treacherous past. He is his own man now, his own king.

The night before the battle, everyone sits around a campfire. In anticipation of battle, many feel the need to discuss things of importance. In case this will be the last time we are together in peace. Malachi and Johanna sit and talk about the growing resentment between them. In the end, they still love one another, but they can no longer deny that something has changed. It's so rare for them not to agree after all. By the end, they're getting along better though. Johanna doesn't agree with many of his recent decisions, but she also understands why he feels he needs to make them. During their talk, Malachi learns of his son's well-being. It brings him extraordinary joy to hear of the young boy's growth. Although it also brings him a sense of regret. He worries about the effect of not having his father around during these vital times. Could his absence have a negative impact on his son's development? Johanna, seeing his vulnerability, tries her best to comfort him that night. They retire to their tent early and try to enjoy one another's embrace. To lie, talk, and cuddle is enough for them right now.

There's one more thing I wish to see resolved still. I understand that Johanna and Malachi need to be together on this night. However, I want to make up with my best friend before the chaos ensues. Before setting off in the morning, I pull Johanna aside. I missed her. Truth is, I know that without Johanna's friendship; I'm not even half as strong as I once was.

As the sun pierces through the trees at dawn, Johanna joins me for a walk. We go to retrieve some water out of a nearby lake. As we walk, the issues between us surface. I'm the first to address the situation. "Jo," I begin, "I'm sorry, but you have to understand why this path was the only one that I could bring myself to choose."

Johanna sighs. "I do, Josie. My anger is not because you chose this path, it's because you dragged my husband down it with you."

"But Johanna, this was Malachi's choice as well. I didn't force his hand."

"You did. You, with a profound understanding of his loyalty to you, asked him to join you. What was he supposed to do, Josella? He looked into the eyes of his broken and grieving little sister. How could he tell you no? How could he tell you no after all you had been through together? He couldn't abandon you when you needed him the most. If he had said that his family came first, how else could you have taken it? To you, it would sound like you are no longer considered a part of his family."

"Johanna, you know if it were the other way around..."

Johanna interrupts me. "Yes, I do. I know that, Josie. You would have done the same for him. I know you would have because you already did. When his throne and dream were at risk, you put your own life, as well as the lives of those you loved most, on the line. You protected him from that grief. You must understand, I speak not as queen, nor as your best friend, but as his wife. I love him, Josie, and I cannot forgive you for putting his life in danger. Not yet anyway. If he is to die on the path you have led him down, then never."

Her words cut me deep, but I haven't any choice but to accept them. "Okay, Johanna. I may not like it, but I understand why you feel how you do. I hope that one day we can move past this, but I will not continue to push you. Know, though, that when you are ready, I'm here."

With that, we fill the pales with water and return to the camp in silence. Shortly after, the time has come. We must face our enemy across the field of battle. On a remote and empty meadow, with no city or town for miles, the armies stand facing one another. We're prepared to fight for what we believe in. If we hadn't joined here to murder one another, the view might have been beautiful. There're daisies and lilies all around us. The grass here is the most vibrant green and morning dew still lingers on its many blades. The sky is clear, and the sun beams down on us. It's warm. Lilly looks around at the wild beauty and feels the light breeze as it runs through her hair. A sadness fills her heart as she looks at me. "We will destroy anything pure or lovely about this land..."

I nod. "You are not wrong, daughter, but if we do not, then he'll see everything we care for obliterated. This way, at least there remains a chance for restoration after the fact."

Lilly recalls her prophecy once more. "I hope so, mom. I do..."

Twenty One

JOSIE

Soon, we stand in a line before a massive army. It's time. Rath and his army know it as well. Our two groups met in the center of the field to exchange respects. Rath pleads. "Josella, for all it's worth, I didn't wish for things to happen this way. I love you more than I ever thought possible. The generations between us mean nothing. You're my niece. I know it's against your wishes, as it was against Linolas, but I have an obligation to protect you."

"But Uncle... How can you not see it? Who have you actually protected by doing these things? Linola still died. I still may die in the attacks of your army."

Rath groans and then turns back towards his army of stray priests and priestesses. They all seem to have lost their way before meeting Rath. Only after, when they united under a common cause and did they become much more dangerous than if faced one-on-one. Luckily, most of our army has magic to match their own. If those of us with higher levels of power can take out Rath, it's likely the rest of the enemies will crumble. Still, with all our powerhouses standing with us, it's likely that this fight won't be an easy win. After all, none of us have fought alongside Rettferd or Myrkr before. So, there are doubts about how well we'll work together. The Chief only met them in recent days too. Then, there is the matter of improvised teamwork. I Imagine it might feel the effects of the tensions between various members of the group. Johanna's still at odds with both me and Malachi. None of us trusted Rettferd or Myrkr. Pastel is a new king, still reeling from the recent destruction of his kingdom.

The first blows of the battle land as both our side and Raths call for the fighting to begin. In an instant, the once serene field fills to the brim with the screams of the dying as their blood stains the land. I shudder in horror at the sight of it, almost as if I were reliving the moments before Cal died in the last war. Anger courses through my veins and my breathing becomes heavier as I charge at Rath. Of course, he could sense my impulsive attack with ease. It's fortunate that Jameson and Malachi came to back me up. The others aren't far behind either. I form my spiritual energy to pierce Rath. Blasts of water and fire hurl towards him from both sides. Assuming that he would move backward, Lilly launches an attack from behind. It has striking similarities to mine. Our attacks converge where Rath stands. A massive explosion of power ripples throughout the continent. Even in this remote location, we know the damage will affect people's lives.

We all jump back, clearing ourselves from the smoke caused by the explosion. None of us felt our attacks connect with him. We know he's still alive, even if we can no longer tell where he is. Using this suffocating smoke as cover, Rath launches a counterattack large enough to hit us all. It's like my light spear, but it disperses in several directions and spins. This creates an array of slashing light spears that we have no hope of evading while we are being swallowed whole by this blinding smoke. We all know, though, that this array all goes back to a single point, the point where we'll find Rath. In the nick of time, Rettferd and Myrkr come in, using their gigantic wings to fan away the smoke. It's effective. What little that's left clears when Johanna calls to the wind and, in response, it blows the smoke away. Jameson and Malachi then release their wings as well. Jameson realizes Rath is attacking from above. We all join Rettferd and Myrkr in another joint attack. One that surpasses the scale of the one we had launched prior. Rath, although he emerges unscathed, also doesn't have the time between attacks to fight back. It strikes me suddenly, as I watch him, that not attacking may be his strategy for defeating such a massive number of opponents. All this time, he's only attacked once.

I call out to my comrades, "Guys, stop! There's something not right about this!"

All at once, the group pulls back, trusting my instincts. Pastel, panting to catch his breath, asks me, "What is it, Josie?"

Johanna nods, trying to disguise the fact that she feels worn out herself. "No, you are right. How could I not have seen it?"

I smile a little at the realization that Johanna and I still read each other as if nothing had changed between us. "Yes, he's only evading, not attacking. He isn't using spiritual energy. He's waiting."

Lilly's eyes widen. "Oh, no. He wants us to tire. He wants to take us all out with one large attack that we don't have the energy to evade."

Rath cackles in condescension. "Too bad; it's too late. Most of your pathetic team is already too damn exhausted to defend themselves." He raises a spiritual blast.

It becomes glaringly obvious almost immediately that this blast will do actual damage to our ranks. Myrkr screams as Rath hurls it toward us, lunging forward on instinct. "No! It will kill us all!"

The sudden burst of adrenaline fills him. He summons the vast stores of power which he keeps reserved only for such emergencies. The rather average sized man everyone had known becomes this sort of giant. He sprouts ten feet. The energy he carries is enough to bring everyone on the field to their knees. Not even Rath can withstand the strangling feel of such immense power. His knees appear to have buckled beneath him as he watches Myrkr push back his attack alone. Myrkr knocks it into the distance as if it were a child's toy. The shock and terror on Raths' face fades as he looked up at Myrkr with a menacing look in his eye. "You're ready to get serious then, I suppose?"

Rettferd realizes Myrkr wouldn't be holding back to protect his allies any longer. He warns everyone that they should move aside and let Myrkr finish Rath. Rath finds the notion rather entertaining. "You're all fools!" He exclaims. "I know well of his strength! Let me assure you, I won't fall to this demon!"

Raths' face contorts. He lets out agonizing screams to cope with the tsunami of spiritual power. It appears to be filling him from head to toe. One can only imagine the pain he has to be suffering as his form alters. It turns him into something that can match Myrkr's unleashed form. Rath calls it, "Priesthood: Five Priest Summon."

I realize when he says that name, the attack likely draws the power of the five priests who act as his general. He must be consuming their energy somehow. All that time he traveled with us, he was preparing. He's right, I am a fool. Linolas' decision to seal him seems to have only made him a more formidable enemy. The only decision that can spare this world now is to take his life.

I understand this to be my responsibility. I know I have to be the one to end it. The thought of it makes me want to cower in a corner as I cry. It's a fear I can't afford to submit to. I called out,

"Release! Seal of the Damned! Priesthood: Deranged Priestess."

The seal breaks, allowing me to tap into a store of Malachi's demonic energy. He had allowed me to store it up for situations such as these. My stature and strength are equal to that of the unleashed Myrkr. Alexandria smirks, glancing over to Malachi. "Well, I guess we better not let her show us up."

Malachi nods. "Let's do it!"

They also release their true power, as do Rettferd and Jameson. Pastel watches as titans surrounded him, as if it has dawned on him at last that he's out of place among us. He runs off when he realizes he would be ever more useful fighting with the standard troops. He can lead them against the standard part of Raths' army. Lilly has been practicing the offensive barrier she created. With the help of Malachi and Myrkr, she has almost mastered it. She steps up and helps us, too, using the attack. She directs this living barrier to attack Rath alone. Whilst she does, we also launch our more powerful attacks. Rath seems prepared for this. This time, rather than escaping the attacks, he returns them in equal measure. He proves he can counter us in combat. He also reveals his vital weakness. His stamina is depleting at a rapid rate now. Presumably from his enhanced form. We all know, in that moment, that this is our chance. We will exploit our greatest advantage now to show Rath, as well as any other enemies who might oppose our alliance. No matter the strength of the man, no singular human can stand against the partnership we have formed. We know in our hearts that we will prevail, that our endless efforts won't be for naught. We know we could beat him.

Malachi gets overcome with a sense of freedom as he fights because he can finally use his full strength against an opponent. He steps up and takes the lead, this time around. His hellfire, infused with lethal amounts of demonic energy, set the field ablaze. As the wind from his large, dark, and powerful wings only makes the flames spread. The fire surrounds Rath on all sides, as do we, leaving him no escape from our next attack. Malachi smirks. He runs his pointed tongue across his upper lip as he tastes the blood from a wound. He hadn't noticed it dripping before. It fills him even further with a sense of freedom. His tone drenches in darkness as he speaks, taunting Rath. "You'll die for me now, won't you?"

The echo of his sinister cackle hit us all like an asteroid. None of us are so accustomed to hearing and seeing Malachi's inner demon run amuck. It particularly flusters Johanna. She has always struggled to believe that this sweet man she loved had this darkness lurking. It must be difficult for her to love his darkness and light. I've always encouraged her to love both, but she never could. She appreciates me seeing the beauty on these contradictory sides of his personality. It seems to Johanna that I trust both halves of him, and with no hesitation. She often wonders what it is I know that allows me to do such a thing. As Malachi fights Rath in hand-to-hand combat, his sharp claws tore chunks of flesh from Raths' body. He leaves them to burn in the raging flames that surround him. Johanna is more than repulsed by the sight of it, and even more so by the smell of scorched flesh, which she gags on.

As Malachi wholly distracts Rath with a barrage of brutal attacks, Lilly comes up from behind. She uses her spiritual power to form a tightening collar around Raths' neck. With each passing second, it shrinks, making it difficult for him to breathe. The toll this is taking on Raths' body is plain to all who look upon him. Still, there's not a glimmer of remorse, doubt, or even fear of death in his cold, soulless eyes. He won't stop fighting until the life drains from his body. His willpower shines as clear and brilliant as the waters connecting our islands. It almost breaks my heart as I realize that this battle is approaching its end. Rettferd, from the left, binds Rath's arm using his angelic power. Myrkr does the same from the right, using his demonic power. The chief and Johanna follow up by binding his legs, using the power of their runes. Finally, Jameson and I join Malachi in front of Rath. It's clear Malachi is still longing for battle, his blood has yet to settle. As he takes a deep breath, attempting to calm himself, he looks at me. "It's up to you. Will you do it yourself, or is that privilege going to be mine?"

MARIA A LEVATO

I sigh, taking a moment to think. Rather than replying, once I decided, I make a blade of spiritual power and
take Raths' head with it. I couldn't look at him as his
head falls to the ground. Still, I could tell that it rolled a
few feet by the blood that flew from it. Immediately after, I turn and embrace both Malachi and Jameson. My
eyes overflowing with tears. Both of them wish to comfort me, but there are more pressing matters. These matters require us to remain alert. Malachi looks up, seeing
Alexandria, who has joined Myrkr at his side. We all see
him and know the alliance has come to its end. The
same for Jameson, as he looked to Rettferd. His tone is
sorrowful as he speaks to me. "Josie, it is not over."

I compose myself, realizing to what he's referring. I
ask, "Must we do this today? There's much to settle between us, of course. Still, I must ask that you honor the
alliance this day and rejoice alongside us as we celebrate
this victory."

Rettferd sighs. "I wish I could, little Linola. I do. Unfortunately, though, it's no longer my decision to make.
Look at him. He's not prepared to back down."

I observe the intensity in Myrkr's eyes. Rettferd's
right. Myrkr needs to feel as though justice is being
served. The betrayal and grief he suffered has to have a
point and purpose. It's a feeling I understand all too well.
He's not wrong about having such desires. I only wish
there were a non-violent method of fulfilling that need.
Hatred can't wipe away with such ease, not after it has
become engrained into one's soul and left to fester there

for generations. Luckily for the remaining allies, Myrkr, unlike Rath, has some sense of self-preservation. He's not okay with dying and knows that even with Alexandria and the other Alacrians at his side, he can't face us all. He scoffs. "Boy, come with me and I won't drag your friends with me to my deathbed."

Malachi shakes his head. "I'm not opposed to the idea, but there are terms which you must discuss if that is the case."

Myrkr swoops down, bearing his large, black wings as he lands about six inches from Malachi's' face. "Tell me your terms, child."

Malachi gulps. Johanna watches, wondering if this was some sort of strategy or if Malachi intends to leave her. "No harm is to come to my wife, son, or friends; of course. You'll allow me time before my departure, unsupervised, to help Josie finish what she came here to do. You'll also guarantee my submission will, once and for all, be the end of this bad blood. And finally, you'll guarantee these terms are permanent, with no exceptions. You'll do this by making a blood contract that will take your life and return my freedom if you don't keep up your end."

Myrkr looks around himself as we await his response. He contemplates Malachi's terms, as well as how they aligned with his own goals. "So long as I have your service, those terms will still allow me to reach my end goal. Rettferd!" He glances upwards. "You're the only one here capable of binding me to such a contract. Perform the ritual for us."

Rettferd looks at me and Jameson. He speaks no words, but I know he is waiting for our approval before proceeding. He understands that such a contract may hold Myrkr liable, but it'll also bind Malachi. If it happens, Malachi will remain Myrkr's until one of them dies. Which, for demons such as themselves, is far longer than anyone could imagine. Rettferd has only known of one demon to have died from natural causes, Alexandria's mother. Her body had rejected the transition from angel to demon. It sent her on a long and painful spiral toward death. They aren't immortal, but they are closer than most beings; the same applies to angels.

Neither Jameson nor I respond immediately. Instead, we look at Malachi as I mutter in a depressed tone with a hint of rage lingering beneath my voice. "Must we always be the ones to make such sacrifices?"

Malachi smiles with enough brilliance to mask the fear and sadness he feels. "'Tis the burden of those in power to sacrifice for the good of those they rule over. No true king would focus on his own happiness and safety over that of his people. Those who have neglected this duty have left little behind. Only a legacy of suffering that endured for generations. My people will not remember me as one of them."

Jameson cries, his entire body tensing up as he hears Malachi's selfless words. "For my entire life, you've been my goal, my rival, my best friend, and my worst enemy. For that, I'm grateful to you, cousin. It saddens me to have to let that bond go, but I've heard your wishes and must give them the respect they deserve. Please know that ballads of your heroism will be the song of our people. We'll preserve your memory in our hearts for the rest of our lives and beyond."

He and I look back at Rettferd. We feel our hearts break as we cry in the most profuse way. In sync with one another, we spoke. "Do it."

Rettferd nods and descends to the ground. "And so, I will."

His face fills with sadness like that of the rest of us. "You know, little demon, I've become quite fond of you. Why don't you go say goodbye to your wife? She'll need to return to Tendu after this. We'll need to go with Josie on the last leg of this journey; you'll leave with Myrkr immediately after. It's likely the last time you will see one another."

Malachi stares into Johannas's eyes as he approaches her. Memories of the time they spent together on the ship he once sailed flooded his mind, along with every other peak and valley their love had endured. As he took her hands in his, he sighs. "I know it would be wrong to ask that you not resent me for this, but please, never forget how much I love you."

She throws her arms around him and nuzzles herself into his chest as she sobs. "Resent you? I could never do such a thing. My heart will always be yours. No matter where you might go, you will always be my husband. Even if you were to love another, or remarry later on, our bond will remain unbreakable. This is my promise to you, husband."

Malachi nods, realizing he needs to be strong for Johanna at the moment. "Thank you, my queen, my champion, my wife."

He leaves the embrace, and Johanna tries to compose herself. She watches him approach Rettferd and Myrkr. Rettferd takes both his hand and Myrkr's as he binds them. The agreed upon contract uses an ancient magic that dates back to when runes were plentiful. He prays, "O' Gods of both present and old, hear my call and lend me your power! Bind these two demons in the contract they have agreed. Seal their fates for all eternity and accept this agreement as your will! Runic magic of old, let this matter settle!"

As he does this, every rune on every person present lit in response to his call. The runes lend him the power of ultimate sealing, forever binding them to the spiritual contract. All who witnessed this moment sob as they feel the loss of Malachi, who becomes bound to Myrkr permanently.

JOSIE

A fter it's over, Myrkr smiles. "We should go. The sooner we get the little priestess her lovers from the spirit realm, the sooner the three of us can get to work."

Malachi looks at me, Jameson, Rettferd, and Lilly with a blank expression on his face. "Let's go."

Our group departs. A deafening silence gets left behind as the Chief and Johanna embrace. Those of the islands watch as the man who they hail as one of their heroes leaves them for good. Once again, he's choosing to suffer on their behalf and on mine. They leave the field in the opposite direction, abandoning the scorched land that's now covered in the stench of blood and rotting corpses. Each of them returns to their kingdoms and makes their reports on the events that have taken place. Meanwhile, our group discusses the details of our plan to open the portal. Myrkr, being the only one present who knows exactly how to summon the half in Alacrium, would go there. Rettferd, of course, would go with him to keep his power in check. Finally, Malachi and I will join them. We hope that our presence might further ensure cooperation from Myrkr and Alexandria. Jameson, Pastel, and Lilly will return to open the gate on the Rallian end.

Both teams make it to their assigned kingdoms. Several exchanges of correspondence take place to arrange the exact date and time that the door will open. Myrkr presses for us to wait until the next full moon. He explains, "The Alacrian gate will be much harder to open otherwise. So much so that doing so may kill a priestess even as formidable as Josella."

We wait for two weeks because of this. During this time, I'm consumed by a heart-wrenching loneliness. Malachi is busy trying to adjust to his new life. Jameson is in Rallem. Lilly is with him. My best friend hates me. Kai and Cal are still, for the time being, dead. Rather than wallowing in my loneliness, I turn to writing. For fourteen days and nights, I wrote. My words would document everything that has taken place, past, present, and future. Then, one day, I'll release these writings to ensure that history doesn't once again repeat itself. I didn't want to force future generations to relive the horrors that me and my friends have. Or that Linola and her generation had, or that Lilly and her generation will probably still have to. Some day in the future, once Lilly has lived, she can add to them. It'll become a chronicle that spans across generations.

When the day finally comes, preparations become the priority. The Alacrian palace is buzzing as everyone attempts to do their part to make this work. When night falls, Myrkr ignites the chant to summon the portal as soon as the sun falls from the sky. He warns me that no matter what we see, the portal won't be ready to open until midnight. Hours pass as he mumbles something incoherent, lost in a state of meditative magic. Around eleven, signs of the portal appear, trickling in like drops of water. At first, it's a small black dot that floats in the air above us. Over time, it forms into a spiraling abyss, which creates heavy winds soon after. As if trying to consume everything around it. We all brace ourselves as the portal attempts to drag us into its depths.

When midnight finally comes, Myrkr calls for me to begin the process. I take a deep breath as I step forward, trusting in Lilly and the others to do their part on the other side. I funnel my spiritual power into the portal. Malachi and Rettferd hold my shoulders to help my body remain upright and stable. Rather than getting dragged around by these winds. The connection works. It's a strange feeling. As if my own thoughts have fused with Lilly's. It allows us to communicate with one another from opposite ends of the portal. I feel overjoyed to hear that she's enduring well through this process. As the connection grows stronger, I can even feel Jameson and Pastel, who are there with her. Once it's open, the connection is complete. We can all see one another because we're no longer in different places. We aren't in the Spirit Realm, but in the thin divide which separates our realm from the Spirit Realm.

Rettferd explains it to us. "You see that door over there, Josie? You must reach through and grab them."

I tug and twist at the handle of the heavy steel door, but it wouldn't open. I turn back to Rettferd, who becomes shrouded in the colorless mist that inhabits this place. "It's locked. What do I do?"

Rettferd nods, turning to Myrkr. "I see the problem now. Did you know?"

Myrkr shakes his head. "I'm sorry, Josie. I think a sacrifice is necessary to unlock it, a life you must give if you wish to receive another."

Malachi's the first to inquire. "One life; for both Kai and Cal?"

Myrkr nods. "A second sacrifice should not be necessary if it's open already."

Malachi steps forward. "I'll do it then."

Myrkr sighs. "I can't let you do that. It would void our contract. It would set me at odds with them once again."

Pastel looks down. "Then, I suppose it must be me. Mine is the only loss that everyone here can live with. Am I wrong?"

Rettferd and Myrkr step back, not wanting to take part in such a decision. My eyes intensify as I look around at the others. Everyone is too hesitant to speak. I, myself, know that agreeing to this would be wrong, but couldn't immediately reject the idea either. It's a sign of a deeper truth, one which I have avoided facing for many months now. My soul, once pure as spring water and bright as the sun, is now tainted, torn, and tattered. As the grief I feel ate away at me, I changed. I'm no longer the revered hero I had been, rather a broken woman left pining after men who died of their own free will. It's an unbearable fact, but it was a fact. Despite my attempts, it seems the others have seen it as well.

The discomfort shows on the faces of those I love as they await my decision. My decision to allow this would only serve to further contort their already tainted view of me. Yet, I couldn't bring myself to say no, nor yes, nor anything, for that matter. Some part of me wishes that someone else would take the burden of this decision on. It isn't something I can live with either way. Lilly, finally taking notice of my discomfort, steps up. "I'll allow it, Pastel. My mother has been through quite enough. I won't deny her a chance at happiness now. Come, I'll do it."

I'm shocked, yet somehow relieved at that moment. Jameson and Malachi stand between me and them to prevent me from seeing the act carried out. Once he's been bound to the sacrificial spell, his life drains from his body. Each passing second, he's closer to death. So long as the life continues draining from him, the door will remain unlocked. I distract from my primary goal and approach the suffering Pastel. "Pastel! No, why would you do this for me? What about your kingdom? They need their king; they need you. I am sorry; I am so sorry. Please, do not do this. We still need you here."

"Don't Josie..." He struggles to reply. "I have seen you and I cannot undo the feelings that I hold in my heart. I cannot rid myself of the need to preserve you and know I am an unnecessary good in a world that almost always calls for necessary evils. This is the best way that I can protect all that is right. The world would not survive your pain. I will not allow it to end by refusing to offer what you need to continue protecting it, a sacrifice to bring them back to you. Now, go! Retrieve them!"

I sob as I turn away from him and reached through to the spirit realm. "Kai, Cal, come to me." I grasp onto Kai's hand, and he holds Cal's. With all my remaining strength, I try to drag them out of the spirit realm. The moment Kai steps back into the world of the living; there he is. Rath, the traitor, trying to use them to climb back out. Even in death, it seems he hasn't yet let go of the anger he feels. Cal knows it's too dangerous to let him get free. If we do, it could very well mean the end of the world as we know it. He loosens his grip on Kai's hand, assuring him he would accept this fate. "Kai, take care of her. Do not dare come back here until it is your natural time! You heard that man," He says, referencing Pastel, "we need you to live."

Kai nods, crying out as he releases Cal back down into the spirit realm. "I'll stay with her to the end." With that, he's free, and Pastels' life has ended, closing off our portal between realms. Kai hugs me as he continues to cry. "I'm so sorry, Josie. I promise I'll never leave your side again."

Together, we embrace as our grief over the loss of Cal. We get expelled back to the realm of the living as the portals slam shut. It rejects us all back to Rallem. Myrkr tells us later that it's because we depleted ourselves too much to survive the Alacrian portal. Even after seeing the cost, I have to ask. "Is there any way that we can open it again?"

Rettferd shakes his head. "It could only to be opened once. The portals... they no longer exist, Little Linola. I'm sorry, but there's no way."

I sob. "Okay... Okay... I can live with this."

Seeing me cry into Kai's chest, Jameson approaches. He understands what this would mean for us. He joins our hug. Kai's eyes widen as Jameson's arms wrap around us both. "Josie..." He sounds so confused. "What is this? Is he? Did you?"

"Yeah, Kai. I did. I'm so sorry, but I can't let Jameson go any more than I can with you."

Despair fills his expression as he realizes I've separated him and Cal's souls, only to betray him. It breaks my heart to see him this way. "Kai, wait! You must understand. It's not as bad as it sounds."

Kai turns, walking away without answering. It's Jameson that stops him. "Now, listen here, you coward. She has suffered so greatly. Cal's death was understandable because he died trying to protect her. You, though, you took your own life and left her and Lilly with no one. Still, she loved your selfish ass so deeply that she risked it all to get you back. I don't know what makes you think you can just turn your back on her mere moments after hearing Cal's plea for you to stay with her, but I strongly recommend that you turn your ass around and hear what she has to say. Otherwise, you won't get the chance to commit suicide again because I will kill you here and now."

Kai looks shocked. He'd always known Jameson as the insecure prince that he used to be. Now, though, he's grown. He'd come into his own and become strong, confident, and fierce. He's my angel, and I love seeing how our love has helped him become the man he is today. With that being said, I also worry that he's being a bit too harsh on Kai. Much to my surprise, it seems the opposite is true. Kai turns back towards me and looks me in my eyes. "I suppose the Oceanic bastard has a point, Jos. It's not fair of me to refuse to hear your side of the story. I won't run away with my tail between my legs, not this time. Let me hear it, in your own words. What happened and how did we end up here?"

So, I tell him. I tell him how far I fell when I was grieving, how desperate I had become. I tell him about the fight between Johanna and me, and about Malachi's sacrifice, and Pastels. The journey and how hard I fought to keep Jameson at a distance, too. Everything Jameson had done for me. I leave nothing out. I tell him every detail of what happened to us after he died. He's silent as he listens. Not a single peep. Just an unreadable expression that I'm dying to understand. The others stand around us, watching like we were some kind of tragic play. After I finish, he stares at me for a few long moments. "Jos..." He takes a deep breath. "You beautiful woman. You're so strong. I'm sorry for what I put you through. I'm sorry that you suffered." He looks up at Jameson. "Thank you for being there for her. I see now why she came to love you." His gaze drifts back to me. "I'm not saying no, but I can't say yes either. You and I are fine, and we always will be, Josie. As for him and me, how we will make this work... We will see. Either way, I need some time. Beloved, for now, just know I won't leave you again."

"Yes, of course. Take your time, Kai. Whenever you're ready, the three of us can sort this out together."

He nods. After that, we let the subject be, for the time being. Once we do, we turn to Malachi as we prepare to say our goodbyes. He looks at me as tears wet my eyes to wipe them away. "Little sister, this is the best possible outcome, I assure you."

It isn't easy to force the smile I know he needs to see before he leaves. Still, I reach up to cup his face in my hand. "I know that. I'm going to miss you, brother."

A few more moments we take to say goodbye before Myrkr speaks up. "You all must be going now."

We all tense up but understand why he feels that it's best to rip the proverbial bandage off. There's no need to stay and prolong this goodbye. After all, that would only make things harder for Malachi. Before our departure, I warn Myrkr. "Keep in mind, you two are the only ones bound to that contract. If you should mistreat him, we will come for you, and we will win."

Myrkr smirks. "I suppose it's in my best interest not to mistreat him then."

I nod as I turn to walk away. Jameson and Kai stand on opposite sides of me, both pretending the other didn't exist. Lilly dances around us, though, asking Kai question after question about his time in the Spirit Realm. He's happy to indulge her. Not just for the distraction, but because he missed our daughter. She's also sure to tell him all about herself and her growth. His expression is one of sheer bliss as he watches her. Lilly seems to find a part of the childlike sweetness she had lost in the return of one of her fathers. It's a bittersweet moment for me, as I'm going to pass the torch onto her. I feel as though her innocence will only lead her to get hurt. Still, it's time to let her step into my position. On this journey, she has shown purity, leadership, and strength. Besides, many will feel less safe under my leadership now that I've led us to war for a second time. There will be those who see me as self-interested when the stories churn out if they haven't already.

Finally, upon our return to the islands, we go to Tendu and report to Johanna of Malachi's status. The news destroys her. I can't imagine it's easy to hear that I actually let him go through with this. She weeps, yes, but more so than that, she becomes enraged and lashes out at me, insisting that the events that have taken place are my fault. It's understandable why she might feel that way. I offer her the most sincere apology. It's essentially meaningless, no matter how much I mean it, but I wanted to try once again before leaving to go to Oceanica with Kai and Jameson. I know, even at that point, that Johanna will never forgive me. When we reach Oceanica, our new home, the country greets us as heroes. Jamesons' father hails us alongside the rest of the country. Once we settle in, many discussions begin.

First, I inform the king of my intention to step down from leading the alliance in favor of Lilly. Reluctantly, he informs the other leaders, and they accept my decision, but not without conditions. We all settle back into our daily lives, slowly but surely. There's still so much apprehension between Kai and Jameson. I try my best to keep the peace, though. They both continue on about loving me as though nothing has changed, but in truth, everything has. It wasn't like with Kai and Cal. These two hated sharing me because they aren't already in love with each other.

One day, something new happens, though. Something I haven't seen before. The two of them sit outside, alone, together, without me. They're actually speaking to one another. Either the best possible sign or the worst. I want to get a look at their expressions, maybe do a bit of eavesdropping, but there just wasn't a way. They're facing the opposite direction from me, and I don't doubt that they'd both pick up on it if I got much closer.

I thought to let them have their privacy and figure out what was going on later, but before I can walk away, they both lean in. Their lips lock in a timid kiss. It's so... hesitant? Like they are testing it out. Then, it grows more hungry. They're enjoying it. Soon, it's like they can't stop. I don't know how that tension turned into passion, but it seems it did without my noticing. I can't look away. Of course, until Kai calls out, head resting on Jameson's shoulder. "We know you're there, Josie. You might as well come join us."

I make my way onto the veranda. "Oh, I'm shocked you noticed much of anything while you are devouring each other's faces."

I head for the third chair, but as I make my way past him, Kai pulls me into his lap by my waist. The sound of my giggle fills the air. "Ah! Kai, what're you doing?"

He holds me tightly and whispers into my ear. "As if we could ever not notice you."

Jameson smiles at us. "Marry me. Both of you."

My heart skips a beat as I slowly turn my head towards Kai. "You heard the man," He says. "Let's marry him."

Joy, unlike anything I'd ever felt before, fills me. "Yes! Yes! Gods, yes. Absolutely. Let's get married!"

"We can all be together!" Kai hugs me tighter.

Jameson adds, "We can rule Oceanica together, and your duchy!"

His father approaches, face filled with joy and relief in equal measure. "Alas, I can step down from this throne. It has left me weary over these last few years. I will rest well at night knowing that you three will take care of my beloved Oceanica. Thank you."

We smile as Jameson jokes. "Well, we will still need your help for the first year. To ensure that the transition of power goes smoothly. We are new and untested rulers, father. So, you can't go retiring yet."

The king nods, smiling. "I'd hardly call you kids untested, but I'll do as you ask."

That evening, we stand before all. The journalists tasked with spreading essential information gather before us. Taking a deep breath, I calm my nerves. I'm completely unsure of what will happen after I make this announcement. I wonder if it would end the alliance. Cause chaos among the people. Shake the confidence of the other leaders. Or prompt the commoners to reach for my neck. It matters not matter, though. I have to do what I believe to be right. So, I give my speech. "Hello, my beloved supporters.

I stand before you today with Crowned Prince Jameson and the Lost Hero Kai at my side. With the support of the King of Oceanica, who watches from the balcony on the center floor of the palace. To be honest, I am not sure if the news I need to tell you on this day should get defined as good or bad. I know it is what is best for this country and this alliance. Please, I ask that you hear me out.

On this day, I'd like to announce my resignation as the Peacemaker, as the placeholder for this alliance..."

I pause as the crowd filled with a mix of shocked gasps and hysteric cries, giving everyone a moment to compose themselves before continuing with my explanation. I hate that I'm worrying the citizens like this. It's time though. I hope I can reassure them of that. "I know this news may be shocking too many of you, but I have a multitude of reasons for believing that this is best. Not least of which is the fact that Kai and I will marry the Crowned Prince Jameson. Thus, I can no longer be a neutral third party, as I will be a ruling royal. Rather than a noble girl rejected by her parents. I see all the many ways my judgement has become clouded by my own emotions. Which may well be the reason so many had to face the terrorist Rath in recent times. There is another who is better suited to this position than I am. Someone considered being the darling of this alliance and has shown her strength to be equal to mine. Her soul purer. It is in favor of my daughter, Lilly, that I resign from my post. She has displayed kindness, leadership, and strength during our journey across the continent."

Many in the audience still felt anxiety over the transition of power. It's a fact that's hard to miss as I look down at them. There's also hope found because most seem at least intrigued by the prospect. Lilly taking over as peacemaker is an idea they might accept. I continue once more. "I'd like it known that time will ensure Lilly is most prepared to undertake this role. Also, I'd like to remind everyone that I will still be here. My role will still be to protect the people, the country, and the alliance, if threatened. It is time that I fulfill that role differently, a way that allows me to live my heart. Besides, I have seen Lilly. This isn't what we raised her for or what she feels she must do, rather, it is who she is. She wants this life. I hope you will all allow her the opportunity to make this dream of hers come true."

The crowd feels my unwavering confidence in Lilly. The fact I believe Lilly will make a good peacemaker makes other people believe it. As word spreads, the people become split with the fear of a girl as young as Lilly leading them. The rest clinging to the knowledge that she's as competent as me. My decision shakes the alliance to its core, but all were confident that it would not crumble under this immense pressure. The leaders all know Lilly and believe in her. The fact they do convinces more and more people to accept her as a leader. Soon, everyone comes to an agreement. We'll test Lilly in every aspect of competency. To ensure that she can fulfill her the weighty duties that she'll assume with her new role. When asked, Lilly agrees to the testing without hesitation. We tell her that each of the three tests will occur at random. She wouldn't get an explanation or warning and may not even know that a test is happening at all. The prospect makes Lilly curious. She wonders if these people have underestimated her. To think that she wouldn't even realize she was being tested. It's an insult to her and her skills. Of course, it only takes a matter of moments before she realizes that this insult is also a test of sorts.

After a deep breath, she regains control of her growing irritation. With those she has taken part in saving underestimating her at every turn, it's a lot. She looks around herself, observing the hustle and bustle of the castle. She thinks out loud, "Oceanica is so lively. It used to be that this place filled with memories of the things I had endured before meeting Josie. Now, it feels like home."

The marble sparkles as if it reflects the most glistening ocean as the sunset touches it. The gold inlay that lines every corner feels so comforting. As if it were no longer a display of wealth, but instead of beauty and prosperity for this land. She knows I'll be happy here. That the wedding will be grand, the way I talked about wanting it to be when I was Lilly's age. It reassures her to know I'll find peace here. She recalls the loneliness and grief I experienced after Kai and Cal died. There were times she thought she may never see her mom happy again, and the thought of it killed her inside. This transition was the best decision for everyone. These tests aren't something she can afford to fail. Far too much is riding on her passing. She couldn't be the person to ask me to give up the joy that had finally returned to me. Although she knows someone would; the second things got rough again. They would want me, not her.

Twenty Three

JOSIE

————————————

A month has passed since Lilly began taking the tests. Finally, she passes them all. It's then that I come to her to inform her of a last trial the leadership wishes her to undergo. Frustrated, she groans. "Mom, what more could they need me to prove? For weeks now, I have undergone vigorous testing and proved myself worthy at every turn. I don't understand what satisfaction we didn't provide them with."

It isn't easy to tell her what they want. She has done so well, so I kiss her forehead. "I know, and I'm sorry. This last trial is different. In three days, you must face me in battle. We are to engage one another in combat. It will be public. They wish to ensure that you won't hold back if someone you love poses a threat to this land."

"And you agreed to this? Mom, how could you? Even without holding back, we already know that I can't beat you. You will beat me, undermine me, and leave me embarrassed in front of the entire alliance."

"I agreed to it because that isn't true. You've grown, Lilly, and you are at least my equal. The only reason you've never beat me is because you've never tried. It is your mind which prevents you. You hold a profound love and respect for me. I appreciate that, but it has prevented you from doing your best in our previous trainings. It's you, Lilly. I know you. I know that you've never used your living barrier against me, nor have you ever used a light spear or enchantments."

Lilly nods. "I see your point, but I still don't much like the way they're going about this. I'll agree with it. Three days, huh? I better get to work than. No matter what you say, I know I'm not strong enough to come to this fight ill-prepared and without a strategy."

I smile with pride. "That's my girl. I'm looking forward to seeing what you come up with."

She turns and glances at Kai, who's waiting in the doorway. He flashes her a playful grin as he approaches. "You two have changed so much. I do still see my wife and daughter, though. I'm forced to wonder if I'm needed here anymore."

Lilly chuckles. "What does that matter? Even if we end up not needing you, Dad, you're wanted. Mom was heartbroken. I've missed seeing her glow this way."

Kai tilts his head. "Yes, she is glowing, isn't she?"

He takes my hand and leads me away. "You better get to work, Lil! Your mom and I have something we need to take care of!"

Lilly sits alone, giggling as she deduces what this urgent business he and I need to attend to might be. She wonders if Jameson might join us. In the same way that I used to engage with both Kai and Cal, or if this arrangement might be different for the three of us. Of course, it isn't a mental image she needs either way. My love life has led her to wonder more about when she might get one of her own. She has long been curious about what it feels like to be in love. There isn't anyone she thought of that way, nor could she imagine anyone thinking of her that way. She's still rather young. Given a few more years, it might be possible for her to find the right person.

Kai and I have retreated to my room, where he's been staying alongside me. He throws me onto the bed in a playful seduction. Then he smiles as he tears away the layers of my dress, corset, all the way through to my skin. Kai's face lights up, overcome with excitement upon laying his eyes on my naked body. He'd missed the feeling of his body being consumed by mine. Being dead didn't end his longing for me. All it had done was add to the intensity of it. It must have been like having a scratch but no longer having a physical body capable of itching it. As he's eager to join me on the bed, Jameson opens the door. "Ah, I thought I heard the two of you rustling around in here. I'm surprised that you waited so long to get back into it. I thought you two would go at it the moment he became freed from the spirit realm."

Shocked, I hide myself beneath the blankets, unsure of what I should do or say next. Kai can't help but laugh a bit. Seeing me so nervous and vulnerable is a rare sight, after all. Jameson was more hesitant to continue his teasing. He immediately apologizes for startling me. "Sorry, I didn't wish to make you uncomfortable; I just thought that you two would enjoy the company of me as a third."

I'm surprised by what he is proposing, so I ask, "Are you even bisexual, Jameson?"

Jameson shrugs. "I'm not sure, to be honest. I lack the experience of doing anything like this to find out. All I know now is that I want to be in that bed. I have a pressing desire to feel you both close to me."

I observe the redness that covers his cheeks in such an adorable fashion, then gesture for him to join me and Kai, who seems as inviting as I am. As Jameson climbs onto the bed, he looks at Kai, hoping he might say something. To confirm that he's actually okay with this development. Kai says nothing, though. Instead, he pulls Jameson in closer and kisses him. It's a full minute before they break apart from one another, both panting to catch their breaths. I watch with intrigue as they gather their thoughts. Finally, Jameson utters words that seem to act as a catalyst for the events that follow. "Yes, I am indeed bisexual, it seems."

He leans backward, still trying to process what's happening. This exposes his hardened manhood. It lingers beneath his clothing as if trying to break free. Both Kai and I take immediate notice of it. Together, we reach forward and pull his clothing from his body. Kai caresses his length and I the plump, round toys beneath. Jamesons' moans fill the room and from there, there's little left to say. Kai takes Jameson's cock into his mouth, sucking it deep into his throat until he gags. "Fuck." Jameson grunts as I push the back of Kai's head to sink his cock even deeper. "Damn."

I move up Jameson's body, teasing his nipples with my fingers. "Look, as my nasty boys putting on this show to get my attention. So cute. You boys want to please your goddess so badly, don't you?"

A gurgled, "*Mmm*." Came from Kai as he continues using Jameson's length to suffocate himself.

"Yes, Goddess. We need you." Jameson begs, squirming frantically as I toy with his nipples, twisting and pulling at them to elicit more of those sweet sounds. He reaches one hand out to each of us, caressing us both, teasing my nipple as he grips Kai's hair. Our emotional and physical entanglement escalates into a full-blown tryst. Our self-gratifying engagement wholly consumes us with one another. It begins with Kai swallowing Jameson's shaft whilst I torment him a bit by taking my tongue to his body. Jameson squirms as he tries to keep a hold of what sanity he can. He realizes, though, that it's deteriorating, regardless.

In one swift motion, he flips Kai onto his back and places gentle kisses up his shaft. Kai pulls me in for a kiss as Jameson tastes him for the first time. I relish in the sound of his moans and gags as he takes Kai deep into his throat. I didn't hesitate to sit on Kai's face while Jameson gives him head, drowning him and my fluids and smothering him under my full weight. "Damn, I missed this mouth so much, baby."

After several minutes, I stand with Kai on his knees in front of me, lapping at my soaking wet warmth. Meanwhile, Jameson kneels behind me. He uses his tongue to provide me with quite a unique form of stimulation. The kind found between his favorite pair of cheeks. His tongue circles my asshole as his hands spread my plump ass. Then he plunges his tongue inside of it, thrusting it in and out of the tight hole. I nearly collapse from the intensity of them pleasuring me together. Yet, I'm alright with it if I do. Before either of them penetrates, three orgasms already have me reeling. Still, I can't stop myself from longing for more.

With me lying flat on the bed, Kai pushes into me. Jameson watches with a mischievous smile on his face. "One."

He presses in further. Jameson speaks again. "Two."

And again, this time with Kai calling out the number, as if playing along with Jamesons game. They're counting the inches of Kai's length as it enters my body. Each inch soliciting an incrementally escalating moan from me. Jameson seems intrigued as he watches. "Seven." Jameson's voice fills with excitement as they continue to count. I know from experience that we have four more inches to go. Kai grows impatient though and slams those four into me in one swift motion. Then he leans down over me. His intention is to offer Jameson his asshole before starting. Jameson's eyes widen. He never imagined Kai as the taker. Yet here he was, longing to feel Jameson slamming him from behind. What a beautiful, erotic sight it is.

Jameson accepts the opportunity with great enthusiasm. He wets Kai's hole using two fingers dripping with saliva and works them gently into Kai's tight ass before realizing that Kai is more than accustomed to taking something of substantial size. He's going to be filling him the way Kai had allowed Cal to. This is a privilege, an honor. Kai's way of accepting him. It turns Jameson on to think of it that way. Kai thrusts his hips into me once Jameson buries his cock deep enough. Jameson catches his rhythm almost immediately and follows suit. With each thrust Jameson takes into Kai, the force of it intensifies Kai's thrust into me. The moans between the three of us develop into full-blown screams of pleasure. We all go feral for each other. We try it in several positions. I came again, and again, and again. They did too.

Afterwards, we all lay exasperated. Yet still comfortable in the luxurious bed covered in silk sheets. We embrace one another with a profound affection as we drift off into a serene state of rest. We remain in this heightened state of romance, passion, curiosity, and excitement for. In the days to follow, we are careful to explore each way so that we can pleasure one another.

Today's fun starts when we kick the servants out of the kitchens. Jameson bends Kai over the counter and let Kai throw that sexy little bubble butt back on his cock. I put on a strap-on and peg Jameson while he fucks Kai. It's not long before his apprehension at this being his first time getting butt fucked fades away. This filthy angel's hole loves taking a woman's cock. I ram into his prostate ruthlessly, driving him against Kai's. Kai pleads. "Josie, Josie! Goddess, you're making his cock go so deep! Fuck him harder."

I'm all too happy to oblige. My thrusting becomes downright cruel as I punish Jameson's asshole. Actual tears scream down his face and still he begs me not to stop. "Fuck, Goddess! You'll split my dirty little hole in two. I love being your disgusting fuck toy! I'm such a whore for my goddess!"

His cries in combination with the strap-on vibrating against my clit make me bust. Cum squirts down my leg. Jameson and Kai both break, too. Kai takes Jameson's cum straight into his hole. I wrap my arms around Jameson's waist as we watch it ooze out slowly. After a moment, I decide to degrade them just a little more. "You boys made quite a mess. Little sluts like you don't deserve to have the maids cleaning up after you. On your knees. I want you both to lick my squirt off the floor until it's clean again. I want my kitchen spotless."

They both get on all floors, their limp cocks dangling beneath them as they press their tongues to the ground, slurping up my cum. Jamesons gets to turned on by the humiliation that his balls get tight again. I take the toe of my shoe and press it against them. "Look at you. You're so repulsive, getting turned on by your goddess's degradation. You're lucky I even bother to humiliate you."

He whimpers, sounding so full of pleasure. It makes me want to toy with them more, but we should get some rest. Lilly and I battle tomorrow. I sigh, reluctant to end this. "Okay, that's enough. We should get the food we came in here for, eat, then get some rest."

When they stand, I kiss them both gently on the cheeks. "I love you both. You guys okay? Did you enjoy it?"

I know that our play is consensual on both ends, but I also know that it's important to check on them afterwards. I never want our games to damage our love. They both confirm their happiness and well-being, so we proceed on with our plans for the evening. It takes everything I have not to fuck them again, though.

Finally, the morning of Lilly's last trial arrives. I awake feeling refreshed and confident, which surprises me given the *lovely little distractions* that have kept me from my rest as of late. After spending the last few days entwined with Kai and Jameson, how could I not be? As I prepare to make my way to the arena, Jameson observes me. Kai giggles. "Okay, now. Don't go easy on her because she's our little girl. She's brilliant and deserves a chance to prove it against your best efforts."

I nod, turning my head to flash him an excited smile. "Wouldn't dare. I'm sure that she has become rather enthusiastic about this fight, too. It may have caught her off-guard at first, but by now she'll be raring to go."

A few hours later, after eating and preparing ourselves, I met Lilly in the champions' holding area. Its location was beneath the arena. We exchange some brief platitudes with one another. We didn't engage in more serious conversation, though. On this day, we are enemies. Our relationship, as mother and daughter, put on hold to ensure the sanctity of the test. Lilly thought it difficult to keep those walls up. She's still satisfied to see the faith I place in her. Rather than treating her like a little girl, I was making a show of respect for Lilly as a warrior and priestess. By keeping my guard up, I was showing her I took this fight seriously. Lilly knew this was a compliment of the highest sort from one as powerful as I am. It meant that I wasn't confident that I would be victorious. It is possible Lilly might outdo me in a head-to-head battle.

We entered the arena, paying no mind to the thousands that have gathered to observe our match. We look only at one another as we wait for the match to begin. The officiator approaches and walks us through things. "This sparring match is anything goes. You are to use all resources at your disposal to defeat your opponent. Without regard to destruction or endangerment. Powerful barriers are in place to ensure the safety of the audience. To win, you need only render your opponent unable to fight or make them tap out. Of course, today's match has a greater purpose. So, there are stipulations against forfeiting without good reason. Or refusing to put forth your best efforts. Now, prepare yourselves. The match is about to begin!"

Lilly and I both move into a stance, staring at one another with an intensity which shook all who saw it to their core. The officiator backed away, retreating behind the barrier before shouting out, "Fight!"

Without hesitation, we both jump backward to create a distance between us. We observe one another with caution, hoping to see the others next move. Lilly breathes to calm herself. She expels any previous knowledge she has of my fighting style. She fears that as an opponent, I may well use that knowledge against her. To lure her into making a move that she should not make. Finally, she realizes that patience was likely to be her friend in this battle. Attacking with recklessness would end her faster than she could dream. No matter what, she has to bait me into moving first. She let out a bellowing scream, feigning a charge toward me, as if she were going to attack. I had no choice but to respond by blasting spiritual power in Lilly's direction. In the last moments, though, as she had planned, Lilly lifted herself from the ground and over my head. "Now, this is a position I can attack from!" She chuckles as she threw a light spear straight down towards me. It would have pierced me through the crown of my head. Straight down through my body as if I hadn't perceived it in the last moments before it touched me.

I dodge at an unperceivable speed, meeting Lilly in the air above. "You could have killed me!" I exclaim in irritation.

Lilly nodded, releasing a light giggle. "Well, you are the enemy now, aren't you?"

The crowd goes wild, watching the two of us fight this way. Everyone present could tell how serious Lilly was in attacking. They took notice of the fact that I hold back, though. It was unintentional, but the mother in me must have overrode my conscious decision. My enormous power usually brings all who witness it to their knees. Thus far, I have hardly even attacked. Lilly had a sour taste in her mouth about this, too. It offended her, as I had assured her that this match would be all out. She realizes that if she wants to prove herself, her first task would be to provoke me. Lilly knows she needs me to attack at full force. She sighed. "Must I raise your anger, mother? You undermine me by holding back in this way!"

I think for a moment about Lilly's plea and agree. "You want my respect, the respect of everyone here. As you wish, then, I will ensure you can earn it."

I raise myself higher into the sky, calling in the entirety of my power. The glow emanating from me would have been visible from Mount Alacrium, Rallem, and even across the waters. To whatever strange lands might exist away from this continent. I had made myself into the equal of a bomb. I glared down with a fierce look, meeting Lilly's now fearful gaze. "Fight me then, daughter!"

Lilly freezes, hearing the echoing challenge I issue with my now thunderous voice. Her hesitation betrays her, allowing me to take advantage. I swoop down from above, crashing into Lilly with inexplicable force and speed. It's a devastating blow. The crowd watches as Lilly falls to the ground. Many doubt she can still fight after this. Yet, as the dust kicked up by her crash clears, it reveals to them a scuffed-up Lilly standing with pride. She coughs up a bit of blood. "And I almost killed you before? You're crazy! If I hadn't gotten that barrier up in time, such an attack would have shattered every bone in my body!" She smiles with a boldness as she wiped the blood from her mouth. "Well, at least no one can say you didn't fight me for real now. That way, when I beat you, there's no doubt about my right to be your successor!"

Lilly re-centers herself, building up power like I had. She focuses, blocking out everything around her, before launching her living barrier attack. Realizing what she's going to do, I charge forward, hoping to prevent the attack before it happened. Lilly's increased level of mastery of the barrier allows it to take form sooner, though. I rebound off of it and fly across the arena. The crowd gasps, seeing that I took around the same amount of damage that Lilly had. As the living barrier grows, reaching for me, Lilly displays amazing control over it. Unlike in previous uses, it submits to her will and obeys her command. This is further proof of her growth.

Moments before the barrier touches me again, I, unable to figure out what to do, scream, "Stop the match!"

Lilly retracts the barrier as the officiator runs out to meet us. After what he had observed, he gave me a nod. "Am I correct in believing you're hoping to give up? The only method you can use to counter that attack would likely blow us all to bits?"

I pant, relieved that he understands. "Yes, the explosion it would have caused could have sent this island to the bottom of the ocean, even taking the protective wards into consideration."

The officiator smiles. "Duchess Josella has resigned! The winner of this match is Lilly, our new peacemaker!"

The crowd cheers. It seems they understand why I had to resign from the match. They accept it as a sign that Lilly is ready to succeed me. I run over, hugging Lilly in awe. "You did great, Lil. Congratulations!"

Lilly accepts my embrace and rejoices in her newfound role as peacemaker. She has proven herself a leader that all can depend on. All are confident that she'll continue to grow as well. Soon, she'll even surpass me, rather than being only my equal.

That night, a celebration is underway in the Oceanic Royal Palace for Lilly. Me, Kai, and Jameson attend together. Many others have gathered as well. Even Johanna, who's still at odds with me, attends the gathering. During the celebration, I avoid her in an attempt not to engage in a public conflict. I don't want to ruin Lilly's celebration. Johanna, being in the state of mind that she was in, though, did not see my actions as trying to keep the peace. Rather, she sees them as an affront to the Queen Regent of Tendu. For her, this was the last straw. She storms out of the celebration. The next day, official notices come out to all the leaders. They inform us that Tendu is leaving the alliance. Most think Johannas's actions at the time to be pettiness. So, they ignore the notices, thinking she would change her mind at the last moment. Of course, she didn't. Instead, she continues to deepen the divide between Tendu and the other allies. Soon, the rift became irreparable.

The remaining allies, hoping to avoid a war with Tendu, opted to leave her be. Unless she began stirring up trouble. In the meantime, we all focused on more important things. Such as the upcoming wedding of mine and Kai's, to Jameson. Our mutual succession. The memorial meant to honor both Pastel and Malachi for their sacrifices. As one might assume, all three required immense amounts of time, energy, and planning. Luckily, there are three events. Three people are to ensure that they are meticulous in the planning. Jameson assumed the lead on the succession. It made sense because he was most familiar with the ins and outs of Oceanic tradition. Kai wanted to take the lead on the memorial. Both sacrifices made were in my attempt to save him and Cal. He felt planning a memorial was the least that he owed Malachi and Pastel. They deserved his respect. Both of their kingdoms are suffering in chaos without them. That left me to take charge of the wedding, which was preferable to me, anyway. My relief is quite obvious to Jameson and Kai. They chuckle and tease at me together. Kai asks me, "Are you that afraid that we will ruin your wedding day?"

I return their teasing with a bit of my own. "I would have hated to have wasted all that energy resurrecting you, only to end up killing you again so soon."

My gaze drifts to Jameson as the playful smile on my face grows. "It would have been most unfortunate to send you back with him as well. I'm quite glad indeed that it worked out this way."

Together, we laugh, enjoying one another's company. Finally, a long sigh fell over the three of us. We relaxed into a mutual embrace, where we stayed for a few minutes. Alas, Jameson groaned in frustration. "We have to move again, don't we?"

Kai nods, sharing in Jamesons' frustration. "As much as I'll regret it, yes."

I sigh. The reluctance in my tone is obvious. "I suppose we should do that, then?"

We all agree, but none of us bother to do it until Lilly comes barging into the door. "They're here!" She exclaims, "The King and Queen of Loft are here! They have it! Come on, already, guys!"

We all smile at one another before jumping up. Our faces shining with an enthusiastic glow as we run behind her to meet them. We tear through the palace on our way to the lounge, where they wait. Our playful run turns into a less playful race between the four of us. We leap down the staircases in rapid succession, avoiding the use of our power, though, not wanting to break the palace before we inherit it. We near the lounge soon enough. The ruckus attracts the attention of Bertrand, Jameson's father, who follows us. He's confused about where we were rushing to. That makes five of us who barge in the door to the lounge. We bicker, rambunctious over who won the race. The Loftian royals laugh at our shenanigans as they stand up to greet us. "Oh, hello! I see that we have drawn quite a crowd with our visit." The queen looks at Kai. "It's nice to see you again, Kai, alive and well, at the Duchess's side as you should be."

He pauses, scratching his head. His manner is shy and adorable. "Thanks! It's nice to be back, that's for sure."

She nods. "Indeed. Well, I suspect that you all know why we are here."

The King extends his hand, offering me a piece of paper rolled neatly and tied with a bow. "This is the deed to your estate. After you take it, you will no longer be Lady Josella, but Duchess Josella. This will make you more than qualified to wed Jameson on our behalf. It will resolidify the alliance between our kingdoms."

He turns to Jameson, giving a slight bow of his head. "I'm grateful to you for your efforts in the war and hope that our kingdoms remain the best of friends for years to come."

Jameson smiles. "I wouldn't have it any other way. The future of our kingdoms is looking brighter than ever! Please, lift your head, though. It doesn't seem proper, a king bowing to a mere prince."

The king let out a haughty laugh. "No, I guess you're right. Though, you won't be a mere prince for much longer, from what I've heard." He looked up at Bertrand. "Retirement, huh? Passing on your crown to the next generation. I hope to join you in that more serene lifestyle soon enough."

Bertrand nods. "I'll be looking forward to that."

After that, we spent some time hanging out before going our separate ways. It's nice to have that day of fun and joy because the next few weeks became hectic. With the event preparations in full throttle, it felt like we hardly saw each other. Luckily, we can get everything done on time. Our hard work ensuring that things would go smoothly when the events came.

CHAPTER

Twenty Four

JOSIE

On the day we reveal the memorials to our greatest heroes, they'll alas receive their honors. The memorial was a two-part event of sorts. In the first part, we'll acknowledge Malachi, who lost his freedom for eternity. In the second, we'll memorialize Pastel, who gave his life to ensure my happiness. The crowd gathers came from across the remaining kingdoms in the alliance. There are a handful of attendees from Alacrium, sent by Queen Alexandria. She wants to ensure that we were still on good terms after everything that happened. On a personal level, I wasn't currently the biggest fan of her or her kingdom. On a political level, though, I prefer them as a friend rather than a foe. Tendu had recently left the alliance at Johannas's behest. So, we are more vulnerable than ever. Thus, I behaved in a friendly-enough manner toward them when they arrived.

While Alacrium didn't wish to join our alliance, their queen has insisted that we call on them should we need help. Dealing with the residual fallout from Malachi's sacrifice will be complex. It makes Johanna, and Tendu, by extension, an enemy. I sigh in reply, fearing that one day soon we may need to take them up on that offer. For the time being though, I try to keep our conversation on topic with the memorial. I escort them to their seats before rejoining Jameson and Kai. There's a section dedicated to the Oceanic royal family. Of course, those engaged to the royal family are welcome, too, so Kai and Cal are here. I hold the wedding about a week after the memorial. I didn't want my first act as a royal to be memorializing two friends that sacrificed everything for me. It wouldn't have been a good look, or vice versa. Thus, I memorialized them before I became royal officially. I hate thinking of these things from a calculated and political perspective. Given my position, though, I don't see a choice. Everything I do holds a political undertone. Or not-so-under tone might be a more accurate turn of phrase.

I sit with Jameson to my right, and Kai to my left. I link my hands to them both as the memorial begins. First, with the revelation of the statue of Malachi erected in the center of the palace grounds. The inscription on the foot was beautiful. "To honor he who gave his freedom for our own. To praise the demon that became our angel."

Reading those words, I wonder about the truth behind them. Did he sacrifice for us all, or for me? Both versions are authentic in their own way. He sacrificed for me, of which I am most certain, since he ensured I had Alexandria and Myrkr's help in opening that portal. He did also protect us all from Myrkr's wrath as well, though. I could no longer tell whether he was acting as a king and ally, or my brother and friend. Not that it made much difference, the result was still the same. All I knew now was that I missed him. The pain and grief I carry will remain with me as I will always miss him, as well as Pastel, and as well as Cal. I can live with this, though, knowing that he's alive and well, at least. Not to mention, now I have Kai and Jameson by my side. So, I can at least say that I have the joy and pain in equal measure, which, I suppose, is all any of us can ask for.

Regardless of my introspection, the ceremony held for Malachi was magnificent. For many, it was an important part of moving past this and into the next phase of our shared future. As morning turned to noon, the sun reached its peak. We allow the guests an intermission for a brief picnic before the start of the second ceremony. During this time, many talk and enjoy the comfort that's found in the community. To know that we all, royal and commoner alike, feel this loss allows us to share the burden of carrying it. For this, I'm grateful. It's an incredible feeling. For the first time in a long time, I don't feel so alone. I'm not sure how, but I know, without doubt, that when we need him most, Malachi will return to us.

I sit with Lilly at the picnic. She has been rather busy after assuming her new role as peacemaker, so we hadn't spoken more than a few words in the past few weeks. We talk, and I inquire about how she's coping with the stress of her new position. Her reply is simple but rang true to me. "It isn't as stressful for me as it was for you. Unlike you, I'm not exactly doing it alone. I have your support, and everyone else's. I am the last resort. The only reason your load was so heavy was because everyone depended on you. Before you even assumed the role, I mean. Besides, you didn't exactly have a predecessor to turn to when you didn't know what to do."

Her words comfort me. I feel a sense of relief knowing that the responsibility of being a peacemaker isn't too weighty for her. I wouldn't want my little girl to have too much on her shoulders to carry. Our discussion carries on for a bit before it comes time for us to return to our seats. For Pastels' honor, we reveal a statue of him erected in Prosperity Park. It's the center of Oceanica's business community. It's a sacred place for the common people to receive the blessing of wealth. In a way, that local belief had proven true. Oceanica's commoners suffer far fewer financial difficulties. Compared to those in any other kingdom, Oceanica is thriving. In fact, they have often advised other royals on how to build their country's economy for the benefit of the people. All while still maintaining the strength necessary to keep order. This statue of Pastel would be a new hope. They thought it may help Rallem rebuild after the damage they suffered. Pastels' death had added to their suffering. After the utter annihilation that Rath brought upon them, it would be a long road. It was still undecided who would rule there now.

To honor the weight of his sacrifice, there's also a small show designed to honor him. Composed of a mixture of music, as well as traditional and ceremonial dance from his culture. A few speeches too, ones that attested the memory of him. It turns out to be lovely. Though, many, including myself, felt overwhelmed by our emotions as the ceremony unfolded. Some part of me wondered if it was the tears that we all shared that made it so beautiful.

As the memorial finally slows to an end, we retire back into the palace. For the rest of the day, we are more or less meant to be relaxing. So, we sit and talk with one another. As we did, I take notice that once more, the world around me seems saturated in colors so vibrant. They seem to reflect my inner joy and peace back at me. Even having been crying, this was a sign for me. A sign that at the root of the pain was a genuine bliss capable of carrying me through even the darkest moments. With Kai and Jameson at my side, I'm whole again. I enjoy that feeling, so I talk and laugh with them for hours. It's becoming clear to me that Kai's feelings for Jameson are growing, and vice versa. He no longer accepts Jameson's presence out of consideration for me. They're blossoming a love between them that is their own in its entirety. It's a sight unlike anything I've ever seen. Of course, Kai had loved Cal, but I wasn't there to watch them fall in love. It's different this time. It feels like a privilege to see two men that I love in such an intense way come to love each other as much as they love me.

I can't help but adore the sight. I see them lean closer, as if their bodies are moving on their own. The attraction between them has become palpable. Although Kai and I were kind of already wed, I feel a sort of excitement in remarrying him with Jameson. Luckily, our wedding wasn't far off whatsoever. In one more week, I'd be able to call myself the wife of both brilliant men. There's also a sense of nervousness. I've been feeling odd as of late. I sense a power within me that isn't mine. Although still undetectable, I believe I'm pregnant. A child which would belong to Jameson. I know it because of that power I sense. It's the power of an angel. I've yet to say anything. If word spread before our marriage, my child would forever be a bastard rather than a prince. Still, at this moment, it was only the three of us. I thought telling them now would be best. After all, neither would wish this child to suffer a fate such as that.

After some deliberation, I resolve myself to tell them. "Hey, if you two don't mind, there is something I should share with you."

Jameson rolls his eyes playfully, sighing in relief. "Oh, thank goodness. You sense it too? I thought I was going crazy because you didn't mention it."

Kai raises an eyebrow, more than a bit confused. I suppose that having a different power-type that he wouldn't have sensed it. "What? What are we supposed to be sensing?"

Jameson chuckles. "She has had angelic power emanating from her stomach for a week. If I'm not mistaken, my seed might have found its way to leaving our beloved pregnant."

A grin overcomes Kai's face in an uncharacteristically expressive turn. It shone so brightly that it caused me to fall in love with him all over again. "No. No way! Josie, are we having a baby?"

I giggle, nodding. "Yes, it seems so." Worry flashed upon my face. "I fear for the child, though. Jameson, if you sensed it, you aren't the only one. Lilly, anyone else with demonic or angelic power. Or others with spiritual power would also sense it. Our child, it may get called as a bastard rather than a prince."

Jameson shakes his head. His expression is stern but reassuring as he speaks. "I assure you, his claim to my throne will not face dispute from anyone. None would dare question the child of you and me. With Malachi gone, you, Lilly, and I hold unrivaled power. Our child will be even more powerful than any of us. Then Lilly, this baby's older sister, is a peacemaker. You and I to be king and queen. We're also all hailed as heroes. Neither in strength nor political capital can any of us face opposition."

Kai smirks. "Or at least any opposition that arises would be foolish. We could put it down without even blinking."

I nod. "I hadn't quite thought of it that way. You two are correct, though. The legitimacy of this child won't face questioning. Since the pregnancy is still undetectable by more traditional means. No one will piece it together that I fell pregnant before our wedding. Even the most skilled of healers can misjudge the date of conception by a mere week."

They agree. We moved past the topic of legitimacy and onto one of celebration. The excitement they both felt was real, and it sparked a sense of enthusiasm from me as well. After telling them, I finally felt protected and safe. Enough that this pregnancy became something to be happy about. It was as if giving me the reassurance that I wasn't alone was all I required. I unwound and lived in the moment. I appreciate having men who knew that and want to give that to me. Not all women are so lucky as I. I wasn't sure if it was my power, my title, or my beauty which drew them to me this way. I only knew that I was fortunate. I smile. "Rettferd took more of a liking to me than I thought; it seems he watches over us still." I look at Jameson. "He watches over you, my angelic man. It would put his mind at ease to know that his bloodline will continue to be yet another generation."

After that, time passes once more. By the next day, we had told Lilly of her younger sibling. Rejoiced, she approaches to touch my stomach. It seems doing so triggers some sort of prophetic vision. She stumbles back, trying to catch her balance once more. The three of us circled around her to catch her. After we do, and we know she's okay, we ask her about what she saw to cause such a reaction. She sighs. "In truth, I've been getting fragments of visions for months now. When I touched you, the meaning of them became clear. The young prince who lives within you is of Jameson's seed. He will grow to be strong, brave, and educated. Then another will face him. Johanna whispers poison into the son of Malachi as we speak. If she does not change course, then this fate will come to unfold. The fate that will pit your son and Malachi's against one another is inevitable. I suspect that the chief, Johanna's father, has been having similar visions. He seems too torn between his alliance and friendship with us and love for her."

I scowl. "No! We cannot allow her to do this! Lilly, are you saying this is that fate? Is this that fight? Are you telling me that my son and nephew are the ones who will finally live out the fate of angels and demons?"

Lilly tears up. "I understand your anger and I will do all I can to evade this fate, mother. But yes, that is what I am telling you. I'll help them though. I am peacemaker and I'll face damnation before I let my brother confront this fate alone! Please, mother! Let me do my job. I beg of you to trust me. For now, your attention is better focused on my brother. Grow and raise him well. That way, if I fail, he will be strong enough to destroy Malachi's son and an entire legion of high-ranking demons. In case that is what he finds himself faced with."

"So, I will, Lilly." I agree with a noticeable hesitation. "I will do my job, and you will do yours. We must trust you when things get hard. Now isn't the time for me to treat you like my daughter, who I wish to protect. I won't barricade you away from the evils of this world. Rather, I'll treat you like a fellow priestess who is more than capable of taking care of herself. I will not step in until you request it."

After that, we separate. Lilly leaves without delay to go speak with Johanna face-to-face. She's gone for many days. On the morning of the wedding, when she still hadn't returned, I'm both livid and worried sick. What if Lilly was suffering? That was the only reason I could fathom for Lilly not returning by now. I feel like going to Tendu and shredding that palace until I find my daughter. It's far too late to cancel this wedding and go search for her, though. I try to reassure myself as I prepare to walk down the aisle that morning.

My dress is a dream dress. Hand-crafted by the finest seamstresses in Oceanica to fit my curves, it was one-of-kind. It was ankle length with no train. Rather, it had a split in the leg that led all the way to my hip. It left my entire left leg exposed, all the way to the joint itself. Then, around my shoulders are two straps which, in width, resembled those of a tank top. The neck cuts low and deep, clinging tight to my skin. It is rather revealing in the way of cleavage. The cut came together at the bottom of my sternum, but I sort of enjoyed that fact. The thought of looking both beautiful and sexy on my wedding day made me happy. I hope it makes my two husbands happy as well.

I stand straight, staring in the mirror with my hair twisted back, leaving my long curls to fall down my spine. The silver dress looked exactly as I had imagined. The pearls that dangled from my neck and ears accented the color in the most wonderful of ways. It was the shoes that I loved more than anything, though. They are open-toed strappy heels that boosted my height by four inches. Loving the pearly white that matched my jewelry in such a flawless way, I couldn't help but adore them. Finally, the tints of dark, grey eyeshadow that flared around my lined eyes shone perfectly. These colors represented Oceanica well. They would earn me favor in this ceremony, which would make me a royal to them.

After hours of preparation, it was time for me to walk down the aisle. My escort led me to the throne room. Jameson's father sat upon his throne on the far end of the room, centered on the middle of the wall. The room lined on either end with rows of mahogany pews. Which I had brought in for this event. Each pew lined across its back with white tulle that tied into the style of roses at each end. There was a well-measured slope in the center between them. In the center lies the aisle. I walk down it as I held a bouquet of brilliant roses painted blue and black. I looked straight ahead at the white and gold altar. My two men stood on either side of it, staring in awe and adoration at me. They spoke no words as I approached, but it was as if both sets of eyes screamed 'I love you' as they met my gaze with longing. Alas, I reached the altar. Both Kai and Jameson extended their hands. I turned and offered the bouquet to the woman who sat at the inner edge of the nearest pew. I then took Kai and Jameson's hands and joined them on the altar. We stood before the priest responsible for joining us in matrimony.

Having written our own vows, the priest first prompted Kai to give his as the ceremony began. He began with his face flushed, nervous. It was unusual to see his stoic facial expression turn to something so expressive. He turned to me first, "To you, my beloved beauty, I swear to never abandon you." He chuckles a bit, trying to hide his anxiousness. "As we all know, I made that mistake once already and I will forever live with the sting of regret in my heart for it. I vow to always be there to support you through both the good and the bad. No matter the challenges we face, the surety in my heart and soul that together we can overcome it is far stronger. I remember meeting you, although it seems as if it was a lifetime ago now. The first moment I saw you, sitting with your friends. It was in that quiet, hole-in-the-wall restaurant in Nollent. I knew you would become my life. For you, I will not offer you the world because I am confident in your ability to get such a trivial thing for yourself. Instead, I will vow to make you into my world." He sighs, a huge weight lifts from his chest as he finally says the things that he had longed to say to me. "I love you, Josella. I love you more than anything or anyone, and I will for the rest of my natural life. Beyond that. I will continue to love you from my grave after I die and for all eternity. That is the vow that I owe to you."

He takes a long breath as he turns to Jameson. "And to you, Jameson, I offer my acceptance. I know that the events leading up to our union are less than ideal. I know that some part of you has long wondered if you would be here. If you would be alongside Josie and me, if Cal came back with me. To you, I swear you would be. Even if that man that we both loved was here with us today. The only difference would be that the four of us would be here. From the moment I stepped through that portal and felt the warm embrace you gave. Not only to Josie, whom you had already fallen for, but to me. A man you had hardly known; I knew from that moment on that I wanted you at my side, too. The sort of light and love you offer is so rarely found. Because of that, I swear to you I will never allow it to dim. I will never allow your kindness to weaken. If something threatens to snuff that light which I rely on, I swear to you I will put down the threat. Then, I will stoke that flame myself so that you never have to feel what it is to have it stolen from you. I swear to be your right hand and support you in all ventures. I love you, Jameson, that love for you no more or less than I ever loved Josie or Cal, and I pray every day that you know that."

Jamesons heart melted hearing Kai's vows, his confession of love, here in front of the world. In that moment, it was as if all his insecurities about our dynamic were gone. It was the greatest gift that Kai could have given to him. After all, hearing such words from my mouth would have only reflected feelings that he already knew I had. From Kai, though, those words reassured him he wasn't a second choice or consolation prize.

The priest prompted me to speak next. I addressed Jameson first; my heart flutters a bit as I do. Still, I try to remain calm as I speak. "Jameson..." I paused; nervous to say what I had to say in front of the massive crowd in attendance. "Jameson," I touch his cheek, brushing my fingertips against it. "I love you. For longer than I've cared to admit, I've loved you. You see, I thought it began for us when we began spending time together in Loft. I was wrong, though. For me, it began that first day I met you, here in this palace. All my life, people treated me like the daughter of nobility, but never like I was nobility myself. You were the first to speak to me as if I held a title all my own. Like I was the Lady Josella Spade of Loft, who would one day become Duchess in my parents' absence. I wasn't a little girl to you. You expected of me what you would expect from any high-ranking noble. You spoke to me as if I were your equal from the first moment we met.

In retrospect, I see now that you helped me see myself as a noble. As a potential royal. As someone worthy of standing here marrying a prince. I fell in love with you because of the reflection I saw of myself in your beautiful blue eyes. It made me want to know the man who formed that image. I'll admit, it scared me for a long time. I feared that if I got close to you, I would discover things about myself that I wasn't ready to know. At every turn, though, you were there in ways that I had never expected. I owe you my honesty, support, and a love that is equal to that which you have been so gracious to offer. I vow to give you those things. In fact, I vow to give you that exact thing. For the rest of my life, I will be the mirror you can see the best version of yourself in. You can always rely on me to help you become that person. In my eyes, you are nothing less than an angel, and I swear to you I will remind you of that every day."

Next, I looked at Kai. The moment I did, I could have sworn that my heart stopped. All my words of love and devotion disappearing from my mind, like smoke, they all vanished. It took me a moment, but I realized that none of those mattered. I had spent weeks crafting them. The sudden realization that they were all worthless was disappointing. I realize now what it is I need to say. "Kai, thank you. Thank you for giving me the freedom I longed for most. For opening my mind and heart to the possibility of love. For sharing the love of the someone you loved with me. Thank you both for tearing your hearts in two so that I could have half of each.

Thank you for asking me to do the same because if you hadn't, I may have never even realized that I had one. Most of all, thank you for coming back to me. When I look at you, I see half of him alive and well within your soul. So, thank you both for coming back to me. Words can't even describe what I owe you for doing so, so I'll make this simple. I vow to never stop loving either of you, Kai, and Cal."

Kai's eyes watered as he heard my words. He felt a sense of relief upon hearing them. The grief that drove him to jump from that cliff faded into the background before my very eyes. I knew some part of it would always remain. The same was true of my grief. I knew now that it would never have power over him again, though. A genuine smile formed on his face, peace becoming visible through his teary eyes. "Thank you, Josie." His voice cracked as he spoke.

We took a moment, giving him some time to compose himself once more. With that, it was finally Jamesons' turn to speak. He fixed his eyes on Kai first. There was an intensity in them which I had only seen rarely. His eyes are usually bright, like stars. In this moment, though, they appeared so deep and powerful. As if the sight of the sea and sky had collided in the harshest of ways. Until the two morphed into one shimmering blue abyss. An abyss that consumed everything in its path. The look of them sent a cold stiffness over the entire room, a shiver down the spine of all who are present. He has

such stunning eyes. The words '*my prince, my angel...
Look at him...*' passed through my mind as he speaks.

"Kai, I won't tell you it has been easy for me to find
the words to say to you. It felt as though everything that
came to mind failed to meet the standards that I had
created in my mind. I searched for something appropriate to describe such a unique situation. Something like
the one that we find ourselves in. I once believed that
things that are different are lesser by nature. That belief
stemmed from the same outdated beliefs perpetuated
through the generations. Ones that once led my people and me to see the tribes of Pallentine as savage. To
see angels as more worthy and honorable than demons,
too. Those beliefs isolated us. That isolation kept us all
from reaching our full potential. Things changed one
day when a ship captained by my cousin and manned
by a crew of misfits arrived on our shores. Among that
crew of misfits was a beautiful, noblewoman and the two
men who loved her as much as they loved one another.
I thought at first that she was an enchantress. She was
toying with the low-ranking aristocrat and his rebellious
secret lover. I thought for sure that she was using you
both to keep herself entertained until a prince caught
her eye. I was mistaken in this belief. As I soon learned,
I was the misguided one. I never told you, but it was you
who first opened my eyes to the fact. I watched, observing the way the three of you interacted, noting the ways
each person's needs were best met completely by having two partners. Partners who differed in the ways most

mattered: man, woman. Noble, peasant. Stoic, playful. Logical, emotional. Wealthy, poor. It was all so conflicting, and I struggled to understand the depths of it. All I could figure out was that it worked. It was the 'how' that escaped me. Then, something that you did showed me how. You showed me one thing that you all had in common besides your love for one another. The one thing that mattered more than that love. It happened when Loft got attacked. It happened when you watched Cal and Josie sail away without you to go help while you looked after Lilly."

Jameson chuckles a bit, then he continues.

"Although, I'm not sure that she needed much 'looking out for' even then. That little girl was among the strongest women I've met in my lifetime from the moment that I met her. Point being though, the situation wasn't ideal for you. Yet, when you saw it was best for everyone that you loved, you immediately choked down the pain it caused you. You let it happen. You did so because Lilly didn't deserve to be lonely. Josie didn't deserve to shoulder the burden of ending a war by herself. Cal didn't deserve to feel plagued by the all-consuming thought that someone he loved was in danger. While he wasn't there to protect them. You put them first because you loved them, and their comfort was more important to you than your own. That's when it clicked to me. It was the similarity between the three of you; it was your bond and the thread which linked you all in such a solid way. Each of you cared for the others so much that your own needs became an afterthought. I don't suppose that jealousy could thrive in the hearts of people so pure, so self-sacrificing. Then, when I saw Josies' suffering after you and Cal died, the only thought that crossed my mind was 'What would Kai do? How would he ease this woman's unbearable pain if he were here now?"

So, my promise to you is exactly that. I will always do what is best for you and think of your needs first in all things. You taught me what it was to love another. For that I will use the love you taught me to have to love you in that exact way. To ensure that the rest of your life is one that you can live in only the happiest of ways. I want you to know that your needs are to be met without question. If anyone deserves that type of love, it is the man who had nothing to give his name to give. Yet still gave the people around him everything they ever needed."

Jamesons' understanding of Kai lit a fire in the hearts of all who heard his words that day. From that moment forward, all in attendance would strive to give those they care for that type of love. The inspiration sparked by such a sincere gesture. Caring for another more than you do yourself is not an effortless task. You must believe you needn't worry about yourself. You must believe they'll do that for you. It was a sentiment that touched the hearts of many, mine included. It was awe-inspiring to me, seeing such pure emotion and love between them after all they had gone through. They both deserved it. Although, my heart stopped as Jameson turned to me at last. This would be the final vow given among us. After what he had sworn to Kai, I knew that what he said next would be the thing to send me overboard. The wedding had already been so emotional, and it was causing me to melt. While I couldn't wait to start my life with both of my husbands, some part of me wished that this moment would never end, too. I felt as if it could continue on a loop until the end of time. That I would never stop being weak to it than I was at this moment.

His gaze met mine, and our eyes locked. The power and intensity in his eyes dissipated. He became shy, as if the mere sight of me turned him into an anxious boy asking a girl on a date for the first time. I wondered how someone like him could be so vulnerable to me. I wondered what sort of power I held over him. When the priest prompted him to begin his vow to me, I knew I was about to find out. He began, "Josie," then shook his head, "No, Princess Josella Spade, soon to be queen. You are my life. Where others saw a boy and a prince; you saw an angel and a king and never treated me as if my privileged life had made me incapable. You knew I held an understanding of the suffering of those less fortunate and had faith that if I only opened my eyes that I could see. It was your faith that gave me the courage to look. It was you who gave me the courage to actually do something about what I saw when I did. Somehow, I never doubted our ability to do the things we set out to do, or I never doubted yours, anyway. I figured that when the rest of us screwed things up that you'd be there to help us course correct. Then I realized how pathetic I was for expecting you to carry us all. I came to view you as a goddess, a queen, and a priestess. As a result, I forgot that beneath that power you are still a woman, a human woman who had feelings and felt pain. I saw your heart torn from your chest in a matter of days. That image I had clung so tight to went up in flames as the pedestal I had placed you on in my mind came crashing to the ground.

It was only then that I realized I had misunderstood it all. I was right that you belonged above us all, but I never realized that my role was to ensure that you stayed up there. I had failed by letting you crash that way." Jamesons' emotions got the better of him. Tears flow unrestrained from his eyes as he squeezes my hand. "I know my cousin felt that the failure was his, and I know you did as well. We all did, but I never apologized for the role I played in it. Josie, I could have been there! I could have saved Cal that day on the field of battle! I should have... but I spent my time placating people who do not matter and never have. Being political when what was actually called for was a warrior. That failure, my failure, belongs to all but you and Cal. We all should have been there together. That way, we could have all made it home alive.

Still, I don't regret my failure. Although, I admit my mistake. That mistake set off a domino effect that now allows me to stand here alongside you and Kai. Sorry if that's too dark a thing for an angel to admit, but it is the very thing I wish to vow to you. I vow to always be your angel, to never make the mistake of expecting you to face trouble alone again. I vow to keep you on that pedestal by protecting your mind and body, heart, and soul from every threat. For you, I will be an angel of vengeance. If it means your life, and your happiness, I will drown this world in water and oil. Then, toss a match at it. I'll escort you to the heavenly realm myself. There, I will place you on the throne which Rettferd's father sits upon. I love you, my goddess, and will forever be your archangel; he who carries out your will."

With that, we wed. Jamesons' words had moved us all to tears. He was still blubbering, too. We exchanged kisses between the three of us before meeting in the middle to share a kiss nearly as intimate as our threesomes. Admittedly, we might have been wiser if we saved that bit for after the wedding, but we couldn't help ourselves. Then we took an hour to ourselves before returning for the reception party. Most could deduce that we did not spend that full hour on changing our outfits. A little quickie was called for after that kiss.

JOSIE

S everal months later, things had changed. Jameson, Kai, and I are now kings and queen of Oceanica. My stomach had grown large and the child within it was readying itself for birth. Along with Lilly and the leaders of the other allied kingdoms, we sat around a table. The atmosphere was intense and cold. Although surrounded by luxury and grandeur, none in the room is comfortable. Lilly lets out a loaded breath before she begins. "Johanna is gone. She can no longer see reason. Her son will grow to hold strength beyond that which we can imagine. He has inherited power from both her and Malachi, and she poisons him against us. The day will come when he becomes grown. He will seek to destroy us all."

She looks to my stomach, then up at me. "You hold the only hope we have of stopping him. You must raise my little brother to become a warrior. Harden your heart against Johanna and the young prince of Tendu. It is only by doing so that we have a chance of preserving our way of life."

The Chief clenches his jaw. "I love my daughter, but this cannot be. She cannot poison my grandson into fighting against his own blood!"

He turns to Lilly. "You must promise me that when the time comes, you will do everything in your power to reason with him. Try, please try to give him the opportunity to end this without losing his life. He is innocent in all this."

Lilly nods. "I make no promise that I will succeed. Given the prophecies that we've both had, that may not be a promise I can keep. The promise to try is one I can make. No matter how complicated the dynamic has become, the boy is one of us. He deserves the opportunity the know us."

I ask, "When? How long do we have?"

Lilly looks away. "It will begin the night when my baby brothers turn eighteen. Johanna will die and the Prince of Tendu will then commit himself to her cause in his grief."

My eyes grow wide. "Johanna will- "

"Yes, by her own guard's hand." The chief adds.

"I see." I reply. "That is unpleasant news indeed. I apologize, Chief, for any part I played in the road that led us here."

Once again, the room falls silent, and soon the meeting ends. Six days later, I gave birth to a healthy baby boy. His name was Prince Callian, named for the third father that he would never have the privilege of knowing, and on the day of his birth, he became the crowned prince of Oceanica. The young prince was born with water runes and a radiating angelic power. It had a distinct amplification from the spiritual power he inherited from me. It was only six months before the boy had sprouted wings and took flight for the first time. Although he hadn't yet the physical strength and stamina necessary to do so for more than a minute. Of course, raising such a child would not prove to be a simple task, but it proves to be an enjoyable one. His big sister, Lilly, loves to dote on him.

As time went on and we came to love him more by the day, it broke our hearts to know the things he would one day face. Rather than wallowing in that pain, set it aside. We all focused on raising him to become everything we knew he could be. Each of us poured the entirety of our souls into this child. We spent our time enjoying the honor that was raising him. Of course, for Kai, Jameson, and me, there was one thing that rivaled our love for him, and that it was our love for one another. We would often find ourselves hidden away, relishing in the wildfire that was our love. Often, we even hear stories of how our passionate screams filled the halls of the palace. They echoed, nay, thundered for all to hear. Yet, we still never even attempt to quiet down. It was the opposite, in fact. Every time we found ourselves together, our unparalleled enjoyment grew more intense. With them, it was like every time I got laid was the best time I've ever had. We kept finding new ways to pleasure one another.

Still, there was a third and final thing that kept our attention, besides each other and the new baby. That was our beautiful daughter. Lilly seemed to be closer to becoming a woman with each passing day. Her power, strategic mind, and influence all grew at an astonishing rate. She captivated us.

It was my hope one day our family would reunite in full. Until that day, I would always remember those who aren't with us now as they had been. Johanna was the warrior princess. The one who sought nothing more than justice and acceptance for her people. The woman I called my best friend, who married my brother, Malachi, whose heart is the only one I know as noble as her own. Cal, as one half of my heart. Things had changed. Some of us are dead, and some are... gone. None of it changed the fact that we remain bonded, though. In fact, it only seemed to prove how unbreakable the bond is. The strings of destiny have tied our fates together are. For the time being, all those of us that remained could do was hope. Hope that as the world came crashing down around us, we could somehow find happiness in the emptiness. Grateful for what I have now, I knew it was possible. Some part of me would always long for things to be as they were. Still, I know now that sometimes an attempt to alter one's fate can be counterproductive.

I knew now that it was better to have faith that fate's beautiful tapestry is one worth trusting. I would not falter again as events unfolded. Now, I am not only a priestess, but a Loftian Duchess, and the queen of Oceanica. Faltering was no longer a luxury I could afford. Hesitation and fear would only breed more issue. That's all they ever did. The destiny of leaders is not to give into such emotions. We are still human, but we must have the strength of character to set those feelings aside. We must strive for a goal great enough to outweigh such emotions. This was something Malachi knew well. Likely the reason that even when dethroned, it was hard for anyone to see him as anything other than the king.

Although my story had reached its end, I found myself rather happy with how it ended. I took solace that this also meant another's story would have room to blossom. Stories that would now belong to the next generation. That would belong to my children, Lilly, and Callian, as well as Malachi's child, Prince Michael of Tendu.

Maria Levato is a BIPOC writer and disabled veteran. She has an A.S. in Business Administration and serves on the RWA's PRO Advisory Committee. She has three cats and a snake.